**OTHER
PEOPLE**

ALSO BY CELIA DALE

A Helping Hand
Sheep's Clothing
A Spring of Love

OTHER PEOPLE

CELIA DALE

DAUNT BOOKS

This book was originally published in 1964. It is a historical text and for this reason we have not made any changes to its use of language.

This edition first published in the United Kingdom in 2025 by
Daunt Books
83 Marylebone High Street
London W1U 4QW
publishing@dauntbooks.co.uk

1

Copyright © Celia Dale, 1964

First published in the United States in 1970 by the
Walker Publishing Company, Inc

The right of Celia Dale to be identified as the author
of the work has been asserted by her in accordance
with the Copyright, Designs and Patents Act 1988.

All rights reserved. No part of this publication may
be reproduced, stored in a retrieval system, copied or
transmitted, in any form or by any means without the
prior written permission from Daunt Books, nor be
otherwise circulated in any form of binding or cover other
than that in which it is published and without a similar
condition being imposed on the subsequent purchaser.

A CIP catalogue record for this title is
available from the British Library.

ISBN 978-1-917092-16-6

Typeset by Marsha Swan
Printed and bound in Great Britain by Bell & Bain Ltd, Glasgow

www.dauntbookspublishing.co.uk

In memory of
GUY
and for
SIMON

ONE

THE SCHOOL VERSION ended at a gallop. They had cut Malvolio's last scene (too cruel) and most of Fabian, so that the play ended with the general joining of hands and the cast lining up behind Frances, stocky in her cap and bells, for 'The rain it raineth every day'. To June this was always almost more than she could bear. Frances was a creep but her voice really was pretty and the plaintive tune, the strange half-mad words closing the rich, scented hysteria of the end-of-term play, made June want to cry – but honestly, tears brimmed her blue-rimmed lids and if she'd had to utter one of her speeches again she couldn't have done it for the lump in her throat, not even if Sir Larry himself had asked her.

Then the curtains swished together and all the audience clapped like mad, for even if their own ewe lambs weren't in it a lot of the parents seemed to have more team spirit, more sense of unity ('Jervis's is a Unity, girls; we are all members one of another', see Miss Chatham's end-of-term speech this year, last year, amen) than the pupils. If Jervis's High School for Girls didn't rank quite with Roedean it was only because at Jervis's you didn't pay fees – at least, that was how a lot of the parents seemed to feel, and there they all were out in the hall beyond the footlights, clapping away and showing team spirit and some of them, like Mum, making the palms of their hands sting with genuine pride because up there on the stage, encased in archaic and awkward costumes, masked in greasepaint on which sweat beads were standing, were in fact their own daughters, their ewe lambs.

As the curtains ebbed and flowed a smell of canvas, cloth and the cloying perspiration of girls came mildly over the footlights as far as the first row or two of seats. Miss Chatham and her staff had long ceased to notice it, fathers and the few brothers who had been coerced into coming wrinkled their inward noses, mothers ignored it. The girls themselves, squeezing hands as they curtsied (or bowed, if playing male roles – preserve the reality, preserve the reality!) staring outward now through the light to find the parents, the clan, the buttressing personal applause, grew slightly drunk on their own bouquet. Bubbles of hysteria, checked only by the astringent notes of *God save the Queen*, rose within the unnatural bottles of heavy gowns, tights, wimples, burst and foamed backstage after the final curtain. Their voices rose to parrot-house strength, they hugged each other, breathing each other's smell, someone fell against a piece of scenery and it fell on somebody's head, someone was in tears, the stage manager and stage hands pushed about crying 'Clear the stage, please – oh, do get off!' and gradually, still entwined, still chattering or in tears, still half out of their own bodies and blossoming in the maturity of men and women, wombs and tosspots, horns and cuckolds (bowdlerised but not excised) and in the heady beauty of language never at other times heard, not even now totally comprehended, they dispersed to the three dressing rooms and reluctantly, as slowly as possible, put off their costumes and came back into the world.

Parents were still dotted about the hall among chairs now pushed awry, talking to other parents or to members of the staff, when June came through the passdoor, and she saw with the little thump of the heart she could never control at contact with authority that Miss Chatham was in conversation with Mum down at the far end of the front row. Miss Chatham was tall and regal, Mum was short and unremarkable, yet they were alike in their composure as they stood together. Miss Chatham was talking and Mum was listening and on both their faces was respect and friendliness, which perhaps might not remain if they noticed June had left some make-up on her eyelids and mouth. Still, she would risk it; the pain of relinquishing her other, glamorous self with the tights and tunic of Sebastian had been lessened by keeping the blue eyelids that gave her fledgling face a mystery and depth one could not normally display when one was fifteen and at Jervis's – although of course it was all right to use a little lipstick (natural colour only, one of the awful girls in 6B had come to school with pale mauve lips and been sent home).

'Ah, here's June.' Miss Chatham smiled permission to advance.

'Good evening, Miss Chatham. Hullo, Mum.'

'Hullo, dear. What a lovely show it was.'

'And as far as I could see,' said Miss Chatham, 'there were no mishaps.'

'I couldn't get my sword back in the scabbard.'

'I didn't notice, dear. You've left some blue on your eyelids, if you've got a hankie.'

'I was just telling your mother how pleased we have been with your progress this term. I think, Mrs Baxter, she's almost certain of O-Level passes in every subject next year if she's able to keep on working steadily – except perhaps Geography. For some reason Geography,' she smiled at the girl, 'fails to strike a chord in June's bosom.'

Geography! Wiping some of the make-up off her eyelids with a handkerchief, June sneered at Geography. Rainfalls and crops and mountains – who cared about that? She smiled diffidently, lowering her head so that the two flat wings of fair hair concealed the corners of her mouth, where the smile would not have deceived Miss Chatham.

Miss Chatham was not deceived. 'Still, the shores of Illyria are all that interest us tonight, aren't they?' she said, and without change of voice or expression conveyed, with no diminution of regard, an intimation of dismissal. At her back were gathering a clump of parents, like sheep seeking courage to bolt through a gateway. 'You spoke your lines splendidly, June. I hope you're not too excited to sleep. There will be a lot of heavy eyes at Dismissal tomorrow, I'm afraid.'

Turning slightly, she enabled the new group to advance (they belonged to a Second Former who hung back, unwilling to support her parents' obstinate bravado in seeking speech with the Headmistress) and June and her mother to withdraw. The hall was fairly empty now and there was no one whom Mrs Baxter knew more than to smile to, while the girls, absorbed into their family groups, ignored each other.

June and her mother went out onto the main steps. Twilight had only just gone and the distant chill of the sea was beginning to creep up on the summer air.

'Do your blazer up, dear, the wind's cold.'

On the dark tarmac drive between the rose bushes June clasped her hands round her mother's arm. They were almost the same height, the girl slight with a swansdown fairness, the woman thickset, quiet.

'Was I good, Mum? Did you like me?'

'I thought you were lovely.'

'Could you hear me? Miss Garth always keeps on about speaking up, speaking out, throw your voice to the back of the hall . . .' She imitated the English mistress, drawing herself up, jutting her chin and her small breasts in a mimicry that made her mother laugh. 'What did you think of Maureen? She was Malvolio. Did you think she was good? Her hair kept coming out under her wig, did you notice? I hate wigs, I'm glad I didn't have to wear one.' She tossed her hair and gave a skip.

'Don't drag on my arm, dear. I thought you all took your parts splendidly.'

'They gave Malvolio to Maureen because of her accent. She's ever such a good actress but she's got a real Hampshire accent, did you notice? They try and do that with all the accents, you know, give them the clowns or the common parts. I'd hate to have an accent and be tied to always playing that sort of part. Think of never being able to play Juliet!' It was a serious thought and they walked to the bus stop in silence. How did you know if you had an accent? Did Maureen know or did she think she was given Malvolio simply because she was good at it? Had June herself got an accent without knowing it? She could imitate Julie Andrews doing *The rain in Spain falls mainly on the plain* on the *My Fair Lady* record so that she couldn't tell the difference. But perhaps someone else could? Had Mum got an accent, because if Mum had, then probably June had too?

'What's for supper, Mum?' she asked, in order to hear her mother speak.

'I could make you an omelette. Or there's baked beans. Or I could open a tin of ravioli.'

'Ravioli.' Mum had no accent that June could discern, just a quiet ordinary sort of voice, not quite like Miss Chatham's but ordinary. So June's must be ordinary too, so that was all right. Of course it was all right or she wouldn't have been given the part of Sebastian.

The bus did not go through the centre of the town but round the streets where people actually lived, away from the holidaymakers, hotels and fairy lights of the Marine Gardens and the Hippodrome. Here behind hedges and rose trees grown lush in the moist mild air were houses and villas and bungalows which were suburban rather than seaside, and clustered shops that sold food and hardware rather than souvenirs, sunglasses, beach shoes, plastic spades. The people who lived here did not let rooms except perhaps to single men and women who also worked in the town. These roads were inhabited by those who kept the town functioning, who worked at the Town Hall, in the banks, supplied the gas and electricity, managed the cinemas, the garages, the shops, taught in the schools and in the Technical College. Often they went from week to week without a glimpse of the sea, would have forgotten it was there save that the saltiness of it tasted sometimes on their lips if the wind were blowing in towards the land, and everything kept very clean. Those who were able to went out of town during the summer weekends, or stayed behind their hedges.

June and her mother lived over the corner shop of half a dozen that served such an area. The shop was painted cream, with E BAXTER in black and gold lettering along the top. The door faced the corner at an angle, and the window on one side displayed stationery, magazines and paperback books, that on the other small toys and china animals, greeting cards of many kinds and a board of advertisements. When the shop was open a rack of newspapers hung at one side, with a tin for the money underneath. Most of Mrs Baxter's customers were regulars and all of them were honest.

Beyond the shop was a dark hall with a door out into the garden, and stairs leading to the flat above: three rooms, kitchen and bathroom. Here they had lived as long as June could remember, since she was three. Mrs Baxter ran the shop alone, save for the part-time aid of a series of youths between training, girls between jobs and housewives wanting to help out with their HP payments. Weekends and holidays June helped; indeed, when she was ten and eleven she had done a paper round, but when she had moved up to the High School her mother had stopped that. June had homework, dancing and drama and swimming and the film club after school, she grew taller, her periods started early, and Mrs Baxter said she needed her sleep and not to wear herself out when there was no need. June slept so soundly she never heard her mother go down into the shop at half past five every morning to receive the morning newspapers and get the orders ready for the first customers at eight o'clock (she had discontinued house deliveries, it was too much for one person to cope with as well as the shop. In any case most of her regulars passed on their way to the bus stop, and liked her well enough to continue their custom).

For June, her mother in the morning was simply a hand smoothing away hair and sleep, a voice warning of passing time, cereal, the smell of frying, milky tea already sweetened, an aide-memoire for what June's day would need. School was the real day, although June liked the shop. It was pretty and sold pretty things, she could look at all the magazines and choose cards for her friends' birthdays and Christmas. She liked dressing the windows, examining and pricing the toys with which, nostalgically but without regret she would play a little, bouncing rubber balls, moving the stiff joints of the dolls, arranging the miniature cars and railway furnishings into streets and towns. So many mothers worked nowadays, for fun or because for some reason they had no husband, but to have a mother who actually owned a shop where some of one's friends came to buy and consult about cards and presents, distinguished one from all the others, gave one something the others didn't have. Perhaps it would have been nice to have a father who was home at least some of the time, but then she and Mum wouldn't have been so snug together. She couldn't imagine a man fitting into their lives, even into the flat.

She sat at the kitchen table eating the ravioli, talking about school and the play, while her mother moved about, tidying up, and watching the milk heat for their two cups of Nesquik. Mum never said very much but she was the background to everything; what she did say was always to the point and it was no use arguing. June always did argue but only for the exercise. Mrs Baxter was not like some mothers June knew of, always exclaiming and carrying on, forbidding this and urging that. Mum let you use your own intelligence and didn't treat you like a child of two years old and when you asked her something she would tell you and you could be sure that it was true, just as you could be sure that if she decided something was to be so, then it truly was. You knew where you were.

Where June had always been was in the world of her own skull, curtained by soft straight hair, windowed by the dark hazel eyes of her mother set in a pointed face, full-mouthed. She knew this face better than that of anyone else; she could not have given details of what her mother looked like (darkish going grey, short, pleasant, quiet – what else? She was Mum) but there was not an enlarged pore, a recalcitrant eyebrow hair that she was unaware of in her own face, nor a feature of it that she had not at some time wished were different or considered rather nice. Her eyes, for instance: their darkness with her fair hair was really striking; but why could she not have inherited the blue eyes of her father? Her nose was awful, just a nothing and it had blackheads where the nostrils met the cheeks; yet these did not show under a little powder and Mum said she would grow out of them, and was not the nose really rather delicate, aristocratic? Hair now: oh to have strong dark hair like Sophia Loren that would take and keep a real big bouffant! And yet there was Bardot with fair flat hair – only at school one was not allowed long hair unless it was in pigtails or one was old enough to put it up, and then nothing extreme, only perhaps a small French pleat, rather insecure. If she were to be an actress like her grandmother, who had died when Mum was a little girl, or her great-grandmother who had brought Mum up and whom June could just, very faintly, remember, a tiny old woman huddled up in an armchair (where? It must have been London before they came to Havenport, for she knew they had moved here when Great Grandma had died), if she were to be an actress . . . Her thoughts lost their way, dispersed, meandered. She would be on television with her own programme, The Moon and June, A Night in June; or at the Old Vic or Stratford playing Cleopatra. Or she would be a hairdresser and create her own styles and open a place in London where all the smart people like Princess Alexandra would come, try the June Dew Rinse. Or be a fashion designer, wear the Baxter Line. Or marry a Society photographer who'd been to Eton and played the guitar . . .

This skull, this world was inviolate. There had never been any occasion for its bubble thinness to be breached, for all her life she had been loved and guarded as though she were still in the womb. Calmly, confidently, day succeeded day. Way back in history things may have happened: Daddy going to Australia, Great Grandma dying and Mum bringing baby June here and starting the shop; but these were all before June was conscious of them and therefore hardly existed. Perhaps things had happened here at Havenport too, but not of importance to the child and then the girl; she could remember Mum being ill and Auntie Norah, Mum's friend who was a nurse, coming from London to look after them both. She could remember Mum telling her Daddy was ill, would be ill for a long time out in a sanatorium in Australia, but his letters had gone on coming once a month with Mum's and June had continued to write him the half-dozen lines that Mum had helped her with when she had first learned how to write. June could not remember him. Ill or well, it was impossible to visualise this man on the other side of the world whose short letters could not bring to life the hackneyed words: 'My own precious little June'; but she was not his, she was herself, her own. 'You are always in my thoughts': how could she be, she did not know him. 'You and your mum are all the world to me': but all the world lay between the man who wrote this and the schoolgirl who received it. Her answers were as unreal as school essays: Write two hundred words to your ideal father.

When she was younger she used to ask about him, what he looked like, when was he coming home? To the last her mother could give no answer except, 'One day, dear, when the doctors say he can,' and to the first she would describe him, thus and so, and bring out the photograph taken of them on their wedding day.

'Can I have it, Mum? Can I put it up to show?'

'You don't need photos to remember those you love,' and Mrs Baxter had put the picture back in the japanned deed box with the other things she treasured: the picture of her own mother holding a tambourine in the chorus of *The Gondoliers*, a pair of glass earrings that had belonged to Great Grandma, a baby tooth of her own with a big hole in it and one of June's, enamelled and pure as that of a doll, a lock of Great Grandad's hair like a coil of wire and a curl of June's like silk, letters and documents. About these June was never curious for they belonged solely to her mother, whereas the pictures and mementoes were part of June too, all that was left of people who now had no significance save that through them she herself was here.

She could remember when Mum had been ill seeing her lying in bed, with tears running out of the corners of her eyes and soaking into the brown hair and the convolutions of her ears, too weak or too indifferent to wipe them away. She had dreamed about it sometimes afterwards, but not for long, for even then, with the tears coming down, her mother had smiled at her and said something loving and reassuring, so that the child had not been frightened, only surprised and curious. The absolute security of her mother's presence, that fed, clothed, provided, loved, had made it unnecessary for June ever to fear anything, even to concern herself with anything outside the absorbing world of her own interests. Nothing filled the foreground but herself, for the background was always tranquil: the fresh light of seaside skies, the shop, school, Easter, birthday, Christmas; Auntie Norah for two weeks in June, a holiday with Mum in August, in Wales perhaps or the Lake District, never the sea, but only a week because the shop had to be closed while they were away. Twice June had been to Clacton with Allison, her great friend at school, but Allison's family had moved to the north of England now. She did not know where she and her mother were going this year, although it was the end of term and breaking up tomorrow.

'Mum,' she said, 'where are we going on holiday?'

Mrs Baxter took away the empty plate. 'I don't know that I'll be able to get one this year, dear. Would you like some fruit?'

'We must have one, Mum! We can't just stay here.'

'Will you finish up this banana, it's going black?'

'I don't like them black.'

'It's perfectly good inside. We always have the same argument, don't we? There.' She peeled the banana and put it on June's plate, pushing forward sugar and milk.

June picked up her spoon, 'I hate the smell. Why can't we go away?'

'I never said anything about you not going, did I? All I said was I didn't think I could.'

'Then where am I going?'

Mrs Baxter went over to the stove and took the saucepan off the flame, pouring the milk into two mugs. 'Would you like to go to Auntie Norah in London?'

'London!' She was dismayed.

'Yes, London. You were born there, you know.'

'What would I do in London?'

Mrs Baxter stirred the Nesquik briskly, with a jingle of spoon. 'I should have thought there were plenty of things to do in London. Museums, Buckingham Palace, the Zoo – theatres, shops . . .'

June softened slightly. 'But Auntie Norah'll be working. I'll be all alone.'

'No you won't, she's having some time off.'

'How long?'

'Ten days.'

'Can't you come too?'

'Not this time, dear.'

'When did you fix it up? You might have told me.'

Mrs Baxter brought the mugs to the table and sat down, cupping her hands round the warm pottery. A waft of night air, scented with dew and grass from the garden, stirred the curtains and sent the steam from the milk misting into her face. The overhead light set her eyes in sockets of darkness.

'I only heard from her yesterday, about her time off. She'll love to have you, she says. It's time you got to know her on your own, your godmother and all, without me.'

'But why didn't you tell me?'

'I was going to tomorrow.'

'Why tomorrow? Why not discuss it with me like you always do instead of fixing it all up behind my back as if I was a child of two?'

'I know, dear. I know. Only it's all been so uncertain. I didn't know definitely, not until last week. And I didn't want to unsettle your last days at school.'

'Oh honestly, Mum! It's only end of term and exams were over weeks ago.'

'It's not just that.' She was silent a moment, then raised her head so that the shadows left her eyes, showing them steady. 'Listen to me, Junie. Something we've thought about for a long time is going to happen. Daddy's coming home.'

June's hand with the spoon in it sank to the table; she sat staring at her mother, her mouth open. Mrs Baxter went on: 'I haven't known very long and then it wasn't definite. They couldn't give him a definite date.

I didn't want to get you all excited and then find it was going to be longer than they said. I had to think what was best to do.'

'When's he coming?'

'The end of August. The 28th.'

'That's over a month.'

'Yes. But there's a lot to do.'

June looked round the kitchen. It was a small room with everything in it arranged as the two of them found most convenient: the airer hung with their underclothes, the hair-dryer on its stand next to the small radio, the miniature oak tree grown from an acorn standing in its pot on the window-sill over the sink with a zoo of china animals disposed about its trunk, the two chairs, hers and Mum's, with their check cushions tied on with tape, their two big cups, hers and Mum's, one pink, one blue . . .

'There isn't room for him,' she said.

'Well no, there isn't,' Mrs Baxter agreed, sitting back from the table and rubbing her finger-tips over her brow. 'That was another thing I had to think about. We're going to move, Junie.'

'Where?'

'Somewhere quite different. Somewhere where we can start off as a proper family again, right from the start. We're going to Bristol.'

'Bristol!'

'It's a lovely city. There's the river and ships, and the country round's lovely. It's a real city with lots of things going on all the time, shops and theatres and the University. You might go to the University, you never know, you heard what Miss Chatham said about your GCE chances . . .'

'Miss Chatham . . .!' Her eyes filled with tears and suddenly she was crying, resting her head on her hands so that the hair swung forward and the tears dropped down into the plate of half-finished banana.

'June. Junie. Ah don't – don't, dear!' Mrs Baxter rose and came round the table, putting her arms about her, smoothing and kissing the soft hair. 'I know it's a shock, dear, but you'll like it there, I know you will. It's a lovely city and ever such a nice school, just as nice as Jervis's. And we've got a little house, dear, up near the Downs, you can go and look over the Gorge to the suspension bridge down below, and all the grass and trees, it's like being in the country. And we're near the buses, you can get the bus to school just like you do here, and a little bit of front garden and a bigger bit at the back with an apple tree in it – think of that, we'll be eating our own apples. They're on the tree now, you can see them, they'll be ready for eating before we've been there long. And if you liked you could have a cat – or a dog. With all that lovely grass and trees round there's no reason why you shouldn't have a dog . . .'

'Why didn't you tell me?' Her voice was muffled in hands and hair and running nose.

'I was going to – after tomorrow. I wanted you to have the end of term happy and settled. I didn't want you all upset for the play and everything.'

June pushed away, wiping her eyes on the table napkin. 'You ought to have told me. I'm not a child.'

'Here.' From an open box of Kleenex on the shelf Mrs Baxter took a couple and gave them to her. 'I told you as soon as you asked me.'

'And if I'd never asked?'

'Then I'd have told you tomorrow, after school was over. Junie darling . . .' She stood looking down at her daughter, her arms hanging at her sides. 'I did what seemed the best way. I had to decide what was best.'

'You've been planning and scheming, you've got the house and everything . . .'

'I thought it was best. I wrote to some house agents and then went there for the day. Remember? I said I was going to see to some business? It was your late day at school, I don't expect you even noticed, and you went back with Shirley for supper. It was a bit of a scramble to fit it all into one day, but luckily I found what was needed and then it all went straight through without a hitch. We'll go there next week for a day, dear, and you shall see it. Nothing's been done, no decorations or anything. You can help me with wallpapers and paint and things. You're so much better at that than I am.'

'Why do we have to move away?'

'This is too small.'

'We could move to a different house. Why do we have to leave Havenport and the shop and school?' She began to cry again but more quietly.

Mrs Baxter lifted a lock of her daughter's hair and laid it gently back. Her arm went around the girl's shoulders again, drawing her close. Leaning sideways in the chair, her cheek against her mother's body, June could hear the gastric juices chasing each other about inside and despite herself she was lulled by this intimacy, by the comfort of Mum's voice saying sensible things.

'We need to be somewhere new,' she was saying, 'somewhere where the three of us can start off again together. If Daddy came here he'd feel – he might feel an outsider, that he didn't belong. This is where you and I came, Junie, when we had to be on our own, make our own way as if Daddy was dead almost. We're known here on our own, if Daddy joined us he'd feel like a stranger trying to fit into someone else's life. We have to start out, all three of us together, as if we'd never been apart. In Bristol no one need know we haven't always been together.'

'Is he still ill, Mum? Is it catching?'

She smiled, pressing the fair head close. 'No, it's not catching, you silly. And he's not ill anymore. He wouldn't be coming home if he was, would he?'

'Was it his lungs, Mum?'

'You know it was. His lungs – and complications. We must feed him up – take care of him. It's not going to be easy for him, after all this time.'

'When are we leaving?'

'In just a month.'

She thrust herself free. 'So soon? We'll never be ready. What about the shop?'

'I've sold that. I'm giving it up at the end of next week but the new people will be taking it over so it won't be closed.'

'Mum! You did all that without telling me? How could you!'

Mrs Baxter turned away and began to clear the crockery, stacking it and taking it to the sink, brushing away the crumbs, replacing the used utensils with clean ones ready for breakfast next morning. As she worked she spoke quietly. 'How else could I do it? Where would have been the sense of getting you all worked up before you need, before I was even certain it was going to happen? You had the school play to think about and the exams. I didn't want you flying around not knowing where you were, perhaps not even bothering with the exams if you knew you weren't staying on at school. And that would have been silly, wouldn't it, because your marks are what matter, they carry on wherever you go, so if you'd lost interest this term it might have held you back in the future. I decided that getting your schoolwork done well was your job and dealing with all the other was mine. It's not right that children should have to share their parents' worries and problems. Time enough when they're grown up and have them of their own. Till then it's their parents' job to keep them happy and safe.'

'You could have prepared me. You could have warned me we wouldn't always be here . . .'

'How? How could I know?' Mrs Baxter stood still, staring out of the dark window. 'How could I know whether he'd ever come back? You can plan and dream but you can't ever know how things will really be. You can only go on as best you can, trying to do what's best.' She turned away, drawing her fingers over her brow and cheek again as though her skull ached. 'Don't let's go on about it, dear, there's a good girl. We're both tired and you ought to get to bed. Perhaps I was wrong. Perhaps I ought to have told you earlier, even though there was nothing definite to tell. I don't know. I did what I thought was best for you.'

'Do the girls at school know?'

'Of course not. I told Miss Chatham, naturally, because of giving notice. She thought I did right, in the middle of term and all.'

'Perhaps I won't tell them either. And next term they'll look round and say Where's June and no one will know. They'll talk about it for a time, it'll be a nine days' wonder, and then they'll forget. It will be as if I'd never been.'

'You haven't drunk your Nesquik and now it's cold. Get along to bed, dear, and I'll heat it up for you.'

'When am I going to Auntie Norah's?'

'August 23rd. Then while you're away I'll see to the move and everything and when you get there Daddy and I will be all settled in ready to welcome you.'

They looked at each other for a moment in silence, then Mrs Baxter repeated gently. 'Go to bed, dear.'

She slept, as usual, instantly and deeply and in the morning found her thoughts had arranged themselves into a more pleasing shape. She did not broach the subject with her mother; time was short in the mornings, Mrs Baxter busy in and out of the shop, and June did not want her mood of delicate euphoria unbalanced by discussion. Given a little time and no interference she would be able to transform the shock of uprooting into the excitement of adventure. Already, as she dressed and had her breakfast, she realised that Havenport was really only a dull seaside town. And how had she never before realised that the flat was much too small? Now she knew that really she had always wanted to live in a house; and really most of the girls at Jervis's were pretty dim. Bristol would be entirely different — a city of ships and steeples, masts nodding at the bottom of each street, wine merchants and the Old Vic training company where Dorothy Tutin had her first chance and *Salad Days* began, and great big aeroplane factories if you wanted to do Science, which she didn't although most of her friends did, and the University ... English, French, maybe History there, the best student of her year, and then not quite the lead but a lovely little part at the Theatre Royal which led to the Old Vic wanting her in London ...

How had she endured Havenport for so long?

She told Marilyn and Joyce and Shirley in the locker room under a promise of secrecy as they got themselves ready for Dismissal. Why the secrecy she was not quite sure save that it fitted her mood and, 'I don't want everyone in 5D coming up asking questions.' She described the new house and the parkland round it, told them of selling the shop. 'We don't want a shop now my father's coming home. He was in the Air Force before he was ill, so he'll probably work for one of the big firms in Bristol — you know, de Havillands or something.'

'Gosh, a test pilot?' Shirley marvelled.

'Perhaps. Or something in Research. His health may not be good enough for a test pilot. He's been ill for *years*.'

The bell began to sound and the shuffle of feet turned to a thunder as the school pushed out of its cloakroom down the corridors into the Assembly Hall. Voices echoing above the screech of chairs and benches shifting, the sibilance of feet on parquet, the hush and rustle as they all stood for Miss Chatham and the staff, the piano striking the opening chord of the school song, somebody dropping something at the back of the hall (they always did), and all their voices, beautiful by reason of their quantity and vigour, swinging through the words they all derided but which now – or perhaps it was just the sound, like fanfares or bagpipes – brought tears to June's eyes so that she stood up straight, singing full out to Miss Chatham and the staff without blinking, for a blink would spill the balanced tears. Goodbye, goodbye – goodbye my childhood, goodbye my youth, tomorrow to fresh woods, it sinks and I am ready to depart, the moving finger writes and having writ, the end of a chapter. Book One: The Awakening; Book Two, what? Daddy. Daddy had been in the Air Force and had blue eyes. He had gone to Australia when June was a baby as sales representative for his firm and had been going to send for Mum and her as soon as he had a house and everything ready for them. Then he had got ill and nearly died and his savings had dwindled and he'd had to stay in the sanatorium for years and years, with his lungs getting better and then worse again, and now at last his will to live had pulled him through and he was coming home . . .

He had been in the Air Force and had blue eyes. He had fair hair like her own, but in the wedding picture with Mum it had waves in it, while her own was straight. In the picture he had his arm through Mum's and their hands were clasped together so that it looked like a double fist, welded together. He had a flower in his buttonhole with a big bit of fern on it, and he looked serious. Mum was smiling; her hair was longer then and she was slimmer but she was still just like Mum, and the hand that wasn't welded into Daddy's held a small bouquet with more of the same fern and she wore a fur cape. She hadn't got one now, perhaps the moths had got it . . .

'. . . Jervis's, Jervis's,

Throughout the years we'll be your WIT-nesses!'

With a triumphant thunder and rustle the three hundred and fifty girls reseated themselves to listen to the speeches and watch the giving of awards.

Miss Chatham interviewed all the girls who were leaving. They waited in the corridor outside her study, where a light over the door burned red if she were engaged, leaning against the wall and whispering together, longing to be gone yet conscious of importance. Apart from one moron from 5B who was leaving at fifteen, the others were Sixth Form girls, women really with their busts and dignified voices, one of them with her long hair up in a knot. Two of them had University places, and another was going straight into a big chemical firm. These three talked together self-consciously while the other leaned against the wall, pushing the cuticles down her fingernails. This was Hilary Sanford who wore eyeshadow and had once been sent home for having her hair done up so high – it had a sort of sausage inside it with the real hair brushed over it, and people said she never took it down, not even at night. She was wearing nail varnish now, although that was forbidden, but as she was leaving there was nothing Miss Chatham could do about it. June studied her surreptitiously, for although Hilary Sanford was awful (in the winter holidays she wore *black* stockings and white shoes like skewers) she did actually look rather smashing, especially in contrast with the other three, with their queenliness and their ties a little crooked.

'Ah June, come in. Sit down, my dear.' This was special, you always stood if Miss Chatham sent for you during the term, even if it was about something nice. Across the honey-coloured width of the desk she smiled at June. Although it was fashionable to criticise Miss Chatham, June had always liked her. She smiled back now, despite her nervously thumping heart.

'Well, June. I'm very sorry this is your valedictory. Your mother telephoned me this morning and told me she had broken the news to you.' June nodded. 'I'm glad she did because otherwise I should have had to let you leave without an opportunity of talking to you, and that would have been a pity. You have done very nicely while you have been with Jervis's and I'm sure you will do equally well at your new school if you make up your mind to it.'

'Thank you, Miss Chatham. I'll try.'

'Do, June. Apart from the responsibility of making the best of the brains that God has given you, it means a great deal to your mother – to your parents,' she corrected herself.

June began to blush. It took a long time and she stared down at the clasped hands in her lap waiting for the embarrassment of it to finish.

Miss Chatham leaned forward on the desk. 'How do you feel about your father's return?' she asked bluntly.

'Well – nothing really. I mean, it's hard to take in . . .'

'Your mother said you were upset last night.'

'It was such a surprise. I mean, I think she ought to have warned me. She's gone and got a house and everything and never let on one word to me. Honestly, I couldn't believe it.'

'But you must have known that your father would return one day and that you would all be together again?'

'I never thought about it.'

'You can hardly blame your mother for your own lack of thought.' Miss Chatham's smile robbed the words of rebuke. 'It's a terrible truism, but there really are always two points of view. The same set of circumstances can always be approached in two different ways. Perhaps she should have told you as soon as it became possible that your father might be coming home, but think how unsettling that would have been – especially for you, with your rather romantic imagination. And how disappointed you would have been if, in the end, his plans had fallen through. Don't you think that then you might have turned round to your mother and said, "Why did you tell me if you weren't certain it was going to happen?"'

'I suppose so.'

'Your mother came to see me as soon as she knew it was definite and asked me what I thought. It was just before the examinations were due and I advised her to wait. It's unfortunate that there's so little time now before you actually do leave Havenport and go to your new home, but it can't be helped. In fact, it should act as a challenge. "Act, act in the living present" – who?'

'Wordsworth.'

Miss Chatham sighed. 'Longfellow. Of course, it's all rather a shock to you. You will all three of you have to make tremendous adjustments and allowances for one another. That's really what I wanted to say to you, June. It's going to be difficult for you to get used to sharing your life with a father you hardly remember but think how hard it is going to be for your parents.'

'But they're married.'

'But a long time ago. Twelve, thirteen years' separation. People change. In many ways it will be easier for you, not having known him before, than for your mother.'

'But how can it? I mean, she knows what to expect. And she's had letters all the time.'

'So have you.'

'Yes, but they never said anything.'

'Perhaps hers didn't either.'

'But they're *married*.'

Miss Chatham leaned back again in her chair. It was a moment before she spoke, for this needed care. 'June, I'm talking to you now not as I should if it were about your schoolwork, when I should be your headmistress speaking with authority, but as one friend to another, without any preaching or speechmaking but as somebody who really does know and understand young people in spite of being what probably seems to you very old.' She smiled faintly; she had been fifty last birthday, which still seemed ludicrous to her. 'People don't feel older because they get older – at least, not after their teens. Things still happen to them. They can be just as unhappy or happy and form relationships and start new lives just as when they were young. They can even fall in and out of love. They don't stop feeling emotions just because they have felt some of them before. This is one of the things one has to realise: one's capacity for suffering – or joy – doesn't grow any less, no matter how old you get. You just learn to bear it more quietly. That is what I want you to try and remember for your parents, especially for your mother. This will be a tremendous upheaval for her. Your understanding of that will be a test of your own maturity.'

What could she read in the delicate face across the desk, with its full mouth closed shut, the skin that held its blush like a glaze over the flesh, the surprisingly dark eyes now hidden by lids thin and stubborn as egg skin? June sat with her head a little bent, the wings of her hair swung forward, studying the clasped hands in her lap, thinking what? Understanding? Perceiving, perhaps for the first time, the possibility of compassion? Or just waiting for Miss Chatham to stop preaching at her?

'June,' she said sharply. The head came up and they regarded one another, the woman determined to compel response, the girl impenetrably defended. 'Try to imagine what your mother has been through these years your father has been away. She has brought you up single-handed from a baby, has provided you with a pleasant home and a good education and every possible love and care, without any help from anyone, not even financial. She has earned your and her own living by running the shop, with all the worry and responsibility that entails. Have you any idea what all this has meant to her?'

'Yes.'

'I wonder. I wonder if you're really able to put yourself in her place for a moment and realise what she must have gone through in these years. The separation and anxiety about your father – can you have any conception of what that must have meant?'

She was too wise to hope for more than an instant for a response; indeed, almost as she finished speaking she regretted having done so, for she knew one cannot penetrate the closed world of the adolescent by embarrassing her. So she smiled, warming her voice again. 'It's always hard to put oneself in another person's place. But do, June, try and show some of the understanding and love I know you do feel for your mother during the next few months. You can be of enormous help and comfort to her, you know. And I do hope you will buckle to and get really good O-Level passes next year. I know St Maud's, the school you will be going to, and they have an excellent record. Some of their buildings are more modern than ours too – I think they had to rebuild partially after the bombing. I expect you'll join their Dramatic Society?'

'I don't know.'

'I thought last night's production was one of the best I have seen,' and as she said this Miss Chatham really did think so, for time could never really wither her passion for English Literature which, when she was June's age, had been going to crown her with professorships and fill the shelves of libraries with her brilliant works, and which still – yes, at fifty – budded unseen in books of notes for a life of Mary Wollstonecraft. 'Perhaps you will send me the school magazine with a notice of whatever play they do next year. I should like to follow your progress.'

She pushed back her chair as a signal for June to rise, got up herself and came round the desk to shake the girl's hand. 'I won't say goodbye because I hope you'll come and visit us again one day. Au revoir, June – and try and remember what I've so often said to you – we are all members one of another. Especially of our families. I shall think of you very often during the next months and of the happiness I'm sure you will all find in your new home.'

'Goodbye, Miss Chatham. Thank you.'

She was at the door and out of it, it had closed behind her. The 5B moron was still waiting and looked questioningly at her as she went past. Although it was undignified, she rolled her eyes and pulled down her mouth in an expression of sufferance as the light above Miss Chatham's door went off and the elder girl moved forward to go in. Dignified or not, June no longer cared. She was out of Miss Chatham's jurisdiction now, she could run and shout in the corridors, kick up the grass on the front lawn, slam all the desk lids, undo her tie and wear nail varnish if she liked. She was free, free – free of the preaching and prying; and she was angrier than she had ever been before, an anger made bitter by embarrassment and shame. She had liked Miss Chatham, had loved the school, and now Miss Chatham had spoiled all June's good emotions by preaching and lecturing, telling her what she ought to feel. She was not a two-year-old child to be talked at and made to feel guilty; she was capable of understanding things for herself. And because in her heart she knew she had not really considered any of the aspects of her father's absence and return which Miss Chatham had put to her, she was full of resentment; embarrassment too at being made to look at grown-up people's emotions, which should not exist. Miss Chatham had forced her into guilt and anger, and she shut her mind on the love she had felt for her and for Jervis's as deliberately as she shut the lid of her desk and the door of her locker, leaving her school scarf in the dust at the bottom where it had fallen months ago. Someone else could find it, wash it, pin up a notice about it if they wanted to and sell it to some new girl if they could. It was no longer any concern of June's.

'Shall I see you up at the Lido tomorrow?' asked Marilyn (to bathe in the sea was common, June and her friends always went to the swimming baths).

'I don't know, I don't expect I'll have time.' Already she had gone beyond Marilyn and the rest, stuck down in their childish activities. 'I've got to go to Bristol to see the house and all, choose curtains and carpets and things. And I'm going to London to stay with my godmother . . .'

'Shan't we see you again?' asked Joyce, awed by the largeness of it all.

'I'll try. But there's masses to do. I'll give you a ring.' With a wave of her hand she turned and ran out through the swing door, the satchel of gleanings from her desk humped under her arm. They stared after her admiringly, yet glad it was not they who went.

The days after leaving school passed quickly, for there was much to do. Mrs Baxter needed help in the shop, for in preparation for its new owners she was trying to stock-take as well as run it during the last ten days of her ownership; but June had not much time to spare for that. The accumulation of her childhood was greater and more interesting than she had imagined and nothing could quickly be discarded or retained. Babyish things which her impulse was to throw away yet tugged at her affections, her sense of identity, so that she was constantly taking objects out of the rubbish box again and putting them, with straightened ears and scotch-taped bindings, into the box of treasures. She had not realised how full her past had been, nor how interesting she herself was, until she saw it all laid out around her in a litter which only with difficulty could be tidied sufficiently for her to get into bed at night. 'I just won't touch your room till you've tidied it up, June. It's like a pigsty,' her mother said; but it was not a pigsty so much as a memorial, and of course Mrs Baxter could not forbear to keep it clean, no matter how severe her face.

Slowly the sorting boxes filled. By the window, open to the sunny air in which she ought to be, June would sprawl engrossed in the diary she kept when she was nine, the autograph album full of signatures of her best friends, half forgotten now, old birthday and Christmas cards intended for a scrapbook never made; while in the other rooms and in the shop Mrs Baxter worked methodically through the detritus of her own past. There was not much; she was an orderly person and life in Havenport had not been so full that the boxes overflowed.

June knew she should not be loitering upstairs absorbed in what were solely her own concerns. But Miss Chatham's talk, though it achieved the right effect had the wrong result. Now, unless they were safely hedged about by domesticity, June was embarrassed by her mother. She did not want to think about Mum at all or to consider what she might be feeling, for that she might be vulnerable to feel anything would shake the image of absolute security that she had always presented. The future lay ahead of June, brightly lit like a stage set on which the action had not yet begun, and she did not want to think about the past or to consider a future in which she were not the central character. Mum was security, unshakeable, unchanging. She had no right to intrude emotions too large and personal for June to tolerate.

Yet, since Miss Chatham's talk, June knew she was at fault. That her mother must have a hidden emotional life she had always known, of course, with the intuition of an intelligent child who records but does not analyse tones of voice, expressions quickly changed, sentences half overheard, and with the jealous dependence of child for parent. She had not known what it was she knew; and as she grew older and more entranced with her own existence she had forgotten that she knew anything at all. She had gobbled her mother down whole with the greed of the fledgling for a worm – gulp, and it's gone, warm and solid inside, always renewable. Now Miss Chatham had destroyed her heedlessness and reminded her of what she ought not to have forgotten. Only deliberately now could she ignore that her mother was a person, not merely a symbol of security.

Covertly June studied her for some sign of stress, some trace of the emotional agonies which embarrassed but which might, perhaps, be turned into something romantic and unreal, given time and imagination. But there was nothing. Mrs Baxter's face was the same as ever, abstracted sometimes, sometimes anxious, but that was apparently because of some practical complication of which June knew – the removal date, a discrepancy in stock, the problem of washing curtains without which the bedrooms could not really be inhabited. These problems Mrs Baxter discussed with June as she had always done, as one woman to another, but now June could not respond. Instinct told her she was being fobbed off with trivialities even while she recoiled from the possibility of being involved in anything more serious. She shut her eyes on one aspect of the future and turned her back on the other; and all the while she surreptitiously searched her mother's face for reassurance that all was still secure and yet, finding it, could not believe. Save in the most trivial context, they did not mention her father.

As soon as the new people took over the shop Mrs Baxter and June spent two nights and a day in Bristol. It was an awkward journey, with a long wait at the junction, and June left her raincoat in the Ladies. They arrived irritable and took the wrong bus from the station yard, having to go back to the town centre for the right one. June could make no sense of the city. Roads in every direction crammed with traffic and walled with modern shops or what looked like warehouses; the blackened filigree of ancient churches amidst wastelands or the prim grass of municipal lawns; steep hills, slums, plain terraces of high-nosed Georgian houses; and in the middle of weltering chromium and traffic a huddle of small masts, hulls, muddy water – were these indeed the docks?

'Oh do wake up, June!' cried her mother. 'This is the one we want.'

'Why can't we take a taxi?' But Mrs Baxter was already pushing towards the bus.

It took them up a crowded hill at the top of which loomed a great tower, then on into wider streets of stucco houses, trees at the kerbside. Here they dismounted and walked to Fernleigh Private Hotel, where they shared a room. One of the taps had dripped a rust stain down the meagre basin and the only light was in the middle of the ceiling, cupped in an inverted glass tulip. Although the carpet in the corridors and on the stairs was thin, it seemed to dominate; the air smelt of carpet, the walls were papered with what looked like carpet, and the wan illumination on the stairs seemed the colour of carpet. It was the first hotel June had ever stayed in and she didn't think much of it.

It was a fine afternoon and the villas which replaced the stucco Victorian houses round Fernleigh glittered with cleanliness as though in seaside air. They were smaller than those among which the Baxters lived at Havenport, with less front garden and pinched façades, yet bright and self-respecting.

'Here we are,' said Mrs Baxter. She stopped and opened a wooden gate which had a sun with its rays cut out in its upper half. The privet hedge behind the fencing was beginning to sprout untidily and grass whiskered the central flowerbed. The front door was high waisted like a Regency lady's dress, the upper panels leaded in coloured glass. The smell of dust and plaster came to meet them.

'I'm glad the sun's shining,' said Mrs Baxter. 'The first time I saw it it was pouring with rain and the walls hadn't been stripped. It did look miserable. At least it's clean now.' Her footsteps echoing, she went into the front room. June followed. A pair of builders' steps and half a dozen paint tins occupied the middle of the floor, and in the grate stood a pair of boots. 'This will be the lounge. We get the sun in the back, so I thought perhaps primrose yellow for the paint in here and a pretty paper to warm it up. I expect we'll mostly sit in the back.'

They went out into the hall again and into the second room. The sun filled it and through french windows could be seen a narrow garden, hardly neglected yet. 'Look, there's the apple tree I told you about. My word, I believe the apples are turning red already. Look, dear.' She put her arm round June as they stood looking out. 'It's a nice size, isn't it – not too much grass to cut. We'll have Daddy to do that now. I thought we'd use this room mostly for ordinary living, have the wireless in here and that. The kitchen's next door.'

June followed her out and into the kitchen. A large pail encrusted with whitewash stood in the sink, which was splashed with tea leaves and plaster drums, and three dirty cups and an unrinsed milk bottle were on the draining-board. A tap dripped. 'They might at least leave things clean,' said Mrs Baxter. She rinsed the bottle and sluiced out the sink. 'They can do their own dirty cups. We'll bring our own cooker down, of course, and I thought we'd have one of those really gay papers, you know, the ones you can wash down, make it look like something out of a magazine. The same curtains will do and there's room for your oak tree on the windowsill when it's all cleaned and painted. What d'you think, dear?'

'Yes.'

'Come and see upstairs and then you can tell me what you think about wallpapers and so on.'

They went out and up the stairs. The balustrade had hearts cut out of the wooden struts.

'That's the bathroom. I thought we'd leave that as it is, it's only been done a few months and it's quite pretty.' It was green and white, with a panel of goldfish paper over the basin. The bath appeared to have been used for mixing size. 'And this is your room.'

Like the one downstairs, it was full of sunlight and looked out onto the garden. It was completely empty, walls and paint stripped down, sweet with the smell of sun-warmed boards. A cupboard was built into one of the alcoves, its door half open. It and the room seemed waiting to be filled.

Against her will, pleasure came into June's face. 'It's nice.'

'You can choose your own colour scheme, dear, only we must keep the same carpet.'

'I'd like pink and white. White walls and pink paint and a lilac cover for the bed. And candy-striped curtains, pink and white, that shiny kind.'

'Pink, in a sunny room . . .?'

'You said I could choose.'

'Of course. Pink's always pretty. And your beigey carpet will go quite well.'

'And I'll make the bed up like a couch, with masses of scatter pillows all different colours, lemon and black and red. And I'll have a frill round my dressing table of the stripes – or perhaps of the lilac? No, the stripes, and lilac to cover the chair.'

'What chair?'

'I'll need a chair, to sit in and listen to records or have for my friends. And I could have one of those contemporary desks, just a couple of drawers long, on thin legs, one side of the window and a great big rubber plant standing on it and an Anglepoise lamp . . .'

'My goodness, you make your plans fast!' Mrs Baxter was laughing.

'Well, you said.'

'I know, dearest. It sounds lovely.'

June came to her mother and for the first time for many days put her arms round her, kissing her cheek. 'I like it, Mum. It's going to be a real proper bedsitter where I can have my friends – records all over the floor and Coca-Cola . . .'

'We haven't got a gramophone.'

'Honestly Mum, they're not gramophones anymore, they're record-players! We could get one. I could save up.'

'We'll see.' Smiling, Mrs Baxter rested her cheek against the warm hair, feeling the ribs going in and out, the deep-buried heart beating near her own. 'We'll go and see the builders tomorrow and choose the papers. They'll be shut now.'

June broke free and went to the window. 'You can see the apples ever so plain from here. And look, next door there are gnomes. Look, Mum.'

Together they peered at the neighbouring gardens, the one on the right uninterestingly full of golden rod and bolting Michaelmas daisies, the one on the left like a sampler, each bed stitched in with a scalloped edging, filled with a petit point of plants, a birdbath with a concrete bird perch on its rim, flanked by two plaster gnomes with red caps. The gardens backed onto replicas of themselves but these were masked by small trees full of birds; even with the window shut Mrs Baxter and June could hear their warblings, for the sun was beginning to decline.

June turned from the window, looking again round the room already hers. 'Will it be done in time? Can they ever get it all done?'

'They say so. There's nearly three weeks. As soon as we say the word tomorrow they can get straight at it.'

'I'm ever so hungry.'

'Let's go then. We'll find a café in the town.'

'Could we go to the pictures?'

'We might.'

They left the room, June reluctantly. On the landing Mrs Baxter hesitated. 'And that's our room,' she said, nodding her head towards the front room. 'Shall we just peep inside?'

After the sunshine of the other this one seemed dark. A trestle-table bore rolls of lining paper and the grate was full of half-burned rubbish. 'I'm just having a plain floral paper here and the paint's all right as it is. Perhaps we can do it up ourselves later on if we feel like it.'

June said nothing, hardly inside the room. Mrs Baxter glanced round it, her face suddenly closed. For a moment she was totally absent, as though before June's eyes she had vanished, leaving June deserted. Then with a smile she turned and came out onto the landing. Together they went downstairs. The tap was still dripping. 'I must get a new washer for that,' said Mrs Baxter. 'In fact, I must make a list of all the things that want seeing to.'

They pulled the front door shut behind them and found a bus that took them back into the city.

Now June had something to work on. Now she had seen the house (and a house is better to live in than a flat), could visualise her own room (larger and prettier than the one at Havenport), had walked a little along the asphalt paths on the Downs, peered through the gates of her new school (all concrete and glass, far more modern than Jervis's), fantasies could begin to colour the plain fact of upheaval. In this new house and city she would cease to be a schoolgirl. Life would open up for her here; she would have a job, go to dances, buy her own clothes, even marry. From that house the whole pattern of her life would change and grow, who knew in what direction? A secretarial job among the test pilots, honours at the University, the Theatre Royal, marriage at eighteen – any of these could happen to her here. At Havenport all that had ever happened was that she had grown.

And her father. Impossible to imagine him in the rooms where she and Mum had lived their women's lives but easier in the house in Hellebore Road. He would sit in the back room reading the newspaper, would mow the lawn, would walk up the front path banging the gate with its sunrays behind him, whistling. June had seldom heard anyone whistle, girls don't, but it was something fathers did. A joking, confident father, indulgent but firm, understanding, smelling of after-shave, nice-looking rather than handsome.

She begged the wedding picture from her mother and studied it, creating what she could out of the image there. He was not tall; well, that was all right, too big a man would dwarf them and the house. He was fair, with hair brushed back in a faint wave; it might be thin by now but he would not be bald. She would not countenance a bald father. He had a pleasant face, a squarish jaw, a nose that looked straight in the photograph, and Mum had often spoken of the blueness of his eyes – forget-me-not blue, she had described them – and June felt they should have laugh lines round them, crinkles of good humour and wisdom, and perhaps partly due to scanning the skies and prairies of Australia. Of course he would be older than in the photograph. He was the same age as Mum, and while she had got thicker since the wedding picture, he would be thinner because he had been ill; but perhaps, with the sea voyage and the excitement of seeing them, he would have filled out a bit. A father should be solid. And he would have a lovely tan.

In the last few days at Havenport she did her best to help her mother, washing china and dusting their few books ready for the removal men, doing her own packing and, on the last morning, taking down the curtains in her room and stripping the bed without being asked. The pictures she had created for herself of the kind of father that was coming home, the kind of family they were going to be, her mother's serene efficiency in dealing with the upheaval, made it easy to forget what Miss Chatham had said and to accept again the stability of which her mother had always been the source and symbol.

She rushed in and out of Shirley and Marilyn's houses to say goodbye, too big with change to do more than leave her address and show off; and the day before she went to London she bought her mother a brooch made of Havenport shells and gave it her with gestures of love that were perhaps just a shade overdone, as was her excitement about going to London for ten days. On the station platform she hung on her mother's arm, peeping out of the corner of her eye to see if people were noticing her, acting young, loving, ingenuously excited, chattering down the apprehension that waited to pounce.

'I'll think of you tomorrow, Mum, eight o'clock and the moving vans driving up, and hope it won't rain. I hope they don't break anything or leave anything behind. Won't it be a business! I wish I was staying to help you, Mum. D'you think people will notice the vans and all come and stare at our things going out . . .?'

'Give my love to Auntie Norah, dear, and thank her.'

'Will she recognise me? Supposing she doesn't? Whatever shall I do, shall I wait at the ticket collector's or go to the Ladies or what?'

'She'll recognise you,' smiled Mrs Baxter, 'and anyway you've got her address in your pocket.' The shell brooch was pinned to her coat. She put her hand over June's clasped round her arm. 'Take care of yourself, dearest. You've got two pairs of panties and another slip, just in case. Put your ticket in your purse safely, I would. Tell Auntie Norah I'll write.'

'What time does the train get there? I wish I could have dinner on it.'

'You've got your chocolate and apples in the hold-all. It's only just over two hours, three fifty-six.'

'What will you do, Mum?'

'I shall go to bed early. There's still my desk to sort out. I'll just make myself an egg and a cup of tea and get to bed early.'

'I hope Auntie Norah and me have our supper out somewhere. I'd like to go to a real expresso and see all the beats. Is Gloucester Road near Chelsea?'

'Not far.'

'If I spend all my money d'you think I can ask Auntie Norah to lend me some?'

'You must buy her a bunch of flowers when you leave, Junie.'

'I know and I may not have enough left.'

'You must put some aside.'

'I bought your brooch, you see.'

'It's so pretty.'

Steam, porters, a tea trolley rattling by, the stink of soot merging with the crisp sea air under the green roof that looked like part of a pier with its ornamental edging, slot-machines and pale boards scoured by salty winds. There were not many passengers leaving

Havenport midweek, and those that were looked grumpy and over-heated, cross to be leaving the seaside at which others still lingered.

'Mum?'

'What, dear?'

'D'you mind if I get in? I want to get settled.'

'Of course.'

June jumped into the compartment, plumping down in her corner seat and hugging the holdall against her. The man in the corridor end already had his eyes shut, the woman opposite June drew in her feet. The guard walked along the platform, his flag under his arm.

'You've got your magazines, haven't you, dear? Don't leave them in the train, Auntie Norah might like to see them. Did you put your ticket in your purse?'

'Ugh, the sill's all dirty!'

'Be sure and thank Auntie Norah for having you, won't you.' Doors were slamming along the train. 'You're just off now, I think. Goodbye, my darling.' June leaned forward and they kissed through the open door. Mrs Baxter gripped her hand, her face suddenly strained. 'Junie darling, you don't mind?'

She pulled free. 'Careful, Mum, he's slamming the door.'

Mrs Baxter stood back. The door crashed shut, the whistle blew. With a jerk the train began to move.

'Goodbye, Mum. Goodbye, goodbye!'

'I'll write. Take care. Give her my love . . .'

The train moved off, slowly, faster, swiftly out onto the open track, fringed with a few waving hands, presenting soon only its square diminishing rear.

TWO

AUNTIE NORAH WAS a Ward Sister in a large teaching hospital, a job which needs a cool head and administrative ability, and at first June was not certain that she really liked her. The only times they had met before were on Auntie Norah's annual visits to Havenport, when June had been so occupied with her own affairs, the two women so occupied with each other, that June hardly noticed she was there. But in London Auntie Norah stood against her own background, a little aloof, friendly but not particularly affectionate, treating June as though she were an adult. This was the first time anyone had ever done this, and although of course it had its disadvantages (it was nice to be indulged, given treats, have everything done for her like Mum did) yet gradually her wariness of this compact, finedrawn woman grew into liking. Because she was expected to be a young woman, not a child, she began to think of herself so; she began to find pleasure in realising that where a child might be taken by taxi and bought ice-cream, a friend of Auntie Norah's would go by bus and eat only at proper meal times, and that on the two mornings when Auntie Norah had to give classes at the Nurses' College, in spite of being technically off duty, it was perfectly reasonable that June should wash the breakfast things, tidy her belongings, and go out to do the shopping for the day with Auntie Norah's purse. Coming back with the basket full, reckoning up the account, setting the table and putting the frozen peas in the refrigerator, June imagined that this was her own flat and this was how she would live, sensible, responsible, independent.

It was a tiny flat, no more than one room with three cupboards off it, one the bedroom, one the bathroom and one the kitchen, which was simply a sort of alcove. In the last two it was possible to perform all necessary actions by merely revolving on one spot; even in the bedroom you could not open the wardrobe door if someone were sitting at the dressing table. June admired very much the way in which everything was compressed into the least possible space and the efficient way that Auntie Norah kept order. She had given

June the bedroom and herself slept on the couch in the living room, yet once the bedclothes were folded and put away you would never know it. Hospital training, Auntie Norah said, and for a moment June wondered if she should become a nurse . . . But vomiting, bedpans, blood?

'You learn not to pay too much attention to what the poor old body does,' said Auntie Norah, slicing tomatoes.

'Do you? I don't see how you can. I had a whitlow once and Mum had to poultice it – ugh, all that yellow stuff, it made me feel sick!'

'The longer you stay in the wards you see it's not the bodies that matter but the people inside them.'

The people inside them? Apart from your body how could you be you?

Lying in Auntie Norah's bed later on, June wondered about her. She had seldom really wondered about anyone but herself before, for no one in Havenport was the least mysterious or interesting. But Auntie Norah was both. Why had she never married? She was thin and a bit dried-up looking now, with that brisk untouchability which clothes women in authority – June knew it from her schoolmistresses; but she must have been pretty when she and Mum were first friends, with her dark blue eyes and faint brogue. She had a brother married in Belfast, his wedding photograph stood on the dressing table in a double frame, and there was also a little brownish picture of a woman with her hair looped up in what June thought was the fashion of the first world war. This picture was on the bedside table in a dented oval silver frame, standing lopsidedly beside the travelling clock and the drinking water, and June supposed it was of Auntie Norah's mother. Otherwise the room was impersonal; even the books told nothing she did not already know about their owner although they told her a great deal she did not know about other things. Auntie Norah left her to read in bed if she liked (Mum used to come in and make her put out the light because of school next day), and June pored over the medical books, with their diagrams that looked like macaroni, finding first all the sexual bits she could. Of course she knew how it all worked; Mum had always answered questions, though in a reluctant sort of way, and they had done Biology at school. But the fascination never weakened and to read about what went where and turned into what, see the sectioned private parts and the foetuses curled like walnuts . . . well, it was scientific and never palled. Viewed like that, a matter of pipes and tubes and tailed invisibilities, how could it possibly be all that the films and some of the books said it was? Yet as she looked, turning the pages under the bedside lamp and the patient gaze of Auntie Norah's mother, June felt her body long and slim and silken like a stocking, stretched and filled with possibilities of which these diagrams were the blueprints, capable of she did not know what. After these books she sometimes dreamed hot dreams, forgotten on waking but leaving a bemusement behind, a sense that something was being kept from her.

They went about a good deal: to Greenwich on a steamer, by Green Line to Windsor, to the Zoo and Regent's Park, taking sandwiches and apples and buying only cups of tea. There was hardly any atmosphere of 'treat' about it, but it was much more of a compliment really. Some of the places Auntie Norah had never been to before, and in her brisk way she drew June into her own enjoyment, assuming June's equal interest. She hardly ever went to the theatre either, and equally dizzy they clung like gulls to the Gallery cliff-face for *My Fair Lady* and *Oliver* and golden Vanessa Redgrave – oh, if June Baxter could be like Vanessa Redgrave! Daydreams in which she both sat in the Royal Box and was the actress on the stage mingled with night dreams of fleshy passages, ova, and losing the housekeeping money. She was so absorbed that everything else seemed to have been wiped clean from her conscious mind, and it was astonishing to get a letter from her mother. The Bristol address was at the top, and seeing it a blade of terror pierced June for an instant, as though it had been written by a ghost. But the words were Mum's, in her clear handwriting, telling about the move and the house and how the Gas Company still hadn't delivered the water-heater for the bath. Automatically she passed it to Auntie Norah, who waved it away. 'I don't want it, unless there's any message for me.'

June looked at the letter again. 'She says "Give Auntie Norah my love and tell her to make you wash your own stockings." Honestly!'

Norah laughed, resting her elbows on the table and holding her cup in both hands. 'Is she settled in all right?'

'Yes.' She read out the bit about the Gas Company, and another funny bit about losing the kettle and finding it inside a coal scuttle they never used.

'Does she say if she's going to Southampton tomorrow?'

'Southampton? What for?'

'To meet your father.'

The blood swept into June's face, her whole body. Norah asked drily: 'Had you forgotten?'

'Of course not.' But she had pushed it so far into the back of her mind that she had been able to forget it. 'She doesn't say.'

'I expect she will. I don't envy her the journey.'

After a moment she said: 'Auntie Norah?'

'Mm?'

'You knew Daddy, didn't you?'

'Considering it was I practically brought you into the world and answered for you at your christening, of course I did.'

'What's he like?'

'You've seen his picture.'

'I don't mean to look at.'

Norah drank slowly before replying. 'He was the kind of man your mother would fall in love with.'

'What does that mean?'

'Oh, it's impossible ever to see exactly what makes two people fall in love with each other. Imagine falling in love with that old devil Khrushchev, for instance, but Mrs Khrushchev did.'

'But Daddy's not like Khrushchev.'

'Of course he's not, I'm only codding.'

'What is he like, then?'

'Och, it's all so long ago, thirteen, fourteen years, I can hardly remember. I never saw a lot of him anyway, it was your mother was my friend.'

'He was a salesman, wasn't he?'

'That's right.'

'And before that he was in the Air Force. Mum's told me.'

'That was before she knew him.'

'Yes I know, but he was in it.'

'"Twas the tail end of the war. He was ground staff of some kind. He didn't fly.'

'Didn't he? But he must have known how to.'

'I wouldn't know about that.'

'What's he like, Auntie Norah?'

'I told you, I never knew him well.'

'Is he, you know, a jokey sort of person or stern or what?'

'I should say, jokey – at least, as I remember he was. He used to butter up your old Gran like nobody's business, pulling her leg, calling her his best girl. She'd toss her old head and skip round like a two-year-old. He used to jolly your mother along too. He knew just the way to bring out the best of those two.'

'Didn't you like him?'

Norah reached across and laid her hand over June's. 'Ah June, don't run away with that idea. I tell you, I hardly knew him. It was your mum I was fond of, and it's often hard for a woman to see what her friend likes in a man. No one knew your father like Esther did. They had something for each other that no one else could know about. It's like that sometimes.' She withdrew her hand and poured some more tea. 'Eat that last piece of toast now, I don't want it wasted.' As June began to pile it with butter and marmalade, Norah cried, 'Easy now, for God's sake – we're not fattening pigs!'

'Auntie Norah, why did he go off?'

'It couldn't be helped.'

'Why couldn't it? I mean, if he and Mum – if they thought so much of each other, why didn't she go with him?'

'She couldn't. There was you to think of and your Gran, her so old and you so young. Esther had to think for you both. She couldn't uproot your Gran.'

'But after she died? Why did we go to Havenport, why didn't we go out to Daddy?'

'It wasn't possible. Hasn't she told you he was ill already?'

'Yes. But if he really wanted us . . .'

'It wasn't up to him. June, it's no good questioning what was done all that time ago. Perhaps the decisions were right, perhaps they were wrong. Your mother had to decide what to do. There was no one could really help her there, the decision was all on her and she did what she thought was best. She didn't know if she'd ever see your father again. The best she could do was make a good life for you. And she's done that, hasn't she?'

'Yes.'

'Then don't fret her and yourself about what's in the past. Thirteen years is a long time. She deserves all the credit she can get for being willing to start all over again.'

'Why, what else could she do?'

Norah gave her a dry look. 'Have you never heard of divorce, child?'

'Divorce? Mum?'

'I agree it's not exactly her style. And to do him justice, you and your mother were the only two creatures Raymond ever cared a row of beans for.'

'He's written me a letter every month, ever since I was tiny.'

'He was like a dog with two tails when you were born.'

'Auntie Norah, will he be an invalid?'

'Of course he won't. He may take a while to adjust himself to being back in the world again – to being a normal family man. You must try and help all you can.'

'People keep saying that. I'll have to adjust myself too. He and Mum aren't the only ones.'

Norah pushed her chair back, looking at June with eyes in which asperity was tempered by affection. 'That's true, they're not. Only for them it's the rest of their lives. It's only a little bit of yours.'

'Mum wants me to stay at school until I'm eighteen, but I think that's silly.'

'What would you rather do?'

'Oh, I don't know. Get a job, I suppose. I don't want to hang around at home swotting at O-Levels that aren't any use. I'd like to be an actress. No, don't look like that.' Her voice sharpened. 'Everyone always laughs, as if I was simply a two-year-old child, but it's in my blood, isn't it? I mean, Mum's mother was on the stage and Great Grandma too. Why shouldn't I be?'

'They were singers. Your Gran was on the music halls.'

'Well, I could be a singer. I could be on television. Or I could train at the Theatre Royal and do Shakespeare and Wesker and that. I was Sebastian in the end-of-term play, did Mum tell you? We did *Twelfth Night* because it's the GCE set book next year, and it was smashing. We did it medieval and I wore a lovely sort of greeny-blue tunic and tights and a pointed hat with a feather. They had all our names in the local paper, did Mum send it to you?'

'No,' Norah rose and began to clear the table. Amid June's chatter, the serious subject was abandoned.

That afternoon Norah had exam papers to correct and June went by herself to the Classic in Chelsea's Kings Road to see an old Alec Guinness film. She had schemed for several days how she might visit Chelsea alone, for although she seldom did more than glance at newspapers she knew that Chelsea was the place from which 'playboys' eloped with heiresses, lords' sons slept on piles of brown paper and parties went on for days unless broken up by police or angry fathers. Chelsea, in fact, was as unlike Havenport as it was possible to be, and as she came out of the cinema into the warm afternoon and walked in what she hoped was the right direction for Sloane Square, where she was to meet Auntie Norah, her senses were astretch. The drama and darkness of the cinema, the cutting during the past week of all ties with everything she had known as she grew up in Havenport, so that it was natural but unreal that she should be walking now alone in this exotic district, made her senses vulnerable. She felt contained in her skin like milk in a milk-bottle, conscious of her physical self in a way that seemed new since she had come to London, as though the upheaval and all that lay behind it had concentrated itself not in her mind, for until Mum's letter had arrived she had genuinely excluded all memory of what was going on, but in her flesh, the envelope that enclosed her self. Her body was almost like a separate person, stretched long under the bedclothes at night beside the shelves of medical books, walking now arrogantly along the pavement, head up, breasts out, hips swinging just a little in a way schoolgirls at Jervis's did not know (unless they were the wrong sort of girl). The cloying dusty heat, smelling of petrol and curry (for odours of the evening menu drifted out through the grid of an Indian restaurant), encased her flesh as her flesh encased her self, and she stared at the faces of the people she passed as though they were all young men.

But they were not. They were mostly housewives doing their shopping late or elderly people getting home before the rush hour after a browse round Peter Jones. They carried evening papers or library books. The housewives pushed prams in which hot babies lolled under a cargo of groceries, and did not glance at the antique shops or art shops, hardly even at the dress shops, for it was near their children's teatime. They might all have lived in Havenport.

The side turnings down which June looked as she crossed were like rows of dolls' houses, flat-faced and often flower-boxed, prim and expensive. Surely no lordlings slept on brown paper there, no heiresses were flung screaming into sports cars and driven to Gretna Green? Where was it all? Where was the pulsing forbidden life of cinema, vaginal passage, drink and drugs, and Havenport gone for ever? Where was she, June Baxter, sleek in her skin? She stared at herself in a shop window, and saw what she had always seen, a schoolgirl with her hair hanging forward, no bust, the strap of her handbag slouched from her shoulder, ankle socks on untanned legs.

She stared, pushing the hair from her face, her envelope of flesh seeming to disintegrate. Where was it all? What was real and what was not, how she felt or how she looked, what people said or what they did? Despair choked her. Ankle socks in Chelsea!

She recoiled, looking round desperately for reassurance, saw an expresso café and plunged in.

Twilight, the smell of coffee froth and pizza, stifled her for a moment. She sat down beside a plastic rubber plant, her heart suddenly thumping. She had never been in a café alone, and as her eyes adjusted to the gloom she saw there were no other customers except a silent couple at a table by the window. Both were thin and shaggy, both despite the heat wore thick jumpers that stood away from their vulnerable necks. The man sat with his legs thrust though the spindle-legs of the table as though through stocks, hands in pockets, scowling. The girl sat with her hands in her lap, a sheet of dark hair obscuring half her face. An heiress and a playboy? Surely not . . . The place was totally unlike any café she had ever been in with Mum or sometimes after school with Joyce or Marilyn. There were no tablecloths, no menus, no cruets, only large pottery bowls of brown sugar hard as gravel. A man came out from behind the counter and she saw with another thump of the heart that he was a Negro.

'Coffee?' She nodded. 'Danish pastry?' She shook her head. The terrible snarl of the coffee-machine made her jump and the silence more oppressive afterwards. In its shallow glass cup the liquid under its tower of froth burnt her lip. The couple by the window did not speak, the Negro read the *New Statesman*, propping it against a plate of apple strudel. He was very beautiful, his jeans so tight June wondered how he could ever sit down. Perhaps he was a poet or an actor. Perhaps at night playboys and heiresses thronged the place, singing and doing the Twist, living their lives for kicks. Perhaps the whole of Chelsea came alive at night long after she and Auntie Norah had closed themselves up in the flat; while they both read and slept, the night stretched out thinner and thinner until morning and the playboys fell asleep with their clothes on just when everyone else, she and Auntie Norah, were beginning to wake up to the humdrum day. She had come at the wrong time. She would never be able to be there when the time was right.

The girl in the window raised a hand and slowly pushed her lank hair back a little. June saw with fascination that tears were running down her face, carrying streaks of mascara with them. She sat crying quietly, and after a moment wiped her nose on the back of her hand. At this the man drew in his legs sharply, pushed back the table, stood up and walked out. After a moment the girl followed him. Nobody paid. The Negro did not look up.

That night she dreamed, a glutinous dumb dream from which she struggled soaked in sweat and sobbing. The light from the living room made a widening dagger as Auntie Norah came in and June clung to her, returning slowly from the reality which had been the dream and which already she could not remember. Norah sat on the bed with her arms round her, rocking her slightly; she wore a candlewick dressing gown whose ridges pressed against June's cheek, and beneath it she could feel the collarbone and beneath her arms, the ribs. When you put your arms round Mum you felt nothing but flesh, solid and warm, but with Auntie Norah June was conscious, even as she shuddered and clung, that she was a framework only lightly masked in flesh and that the comfort that came from her was less tangible than that of body to body. Auntie Norah said hardly anything where Mum would have soothed and kissed. Her arms contained you and she waited for the terror to drain out of you without trying to hurry it on its way.

When June's shuddering had eased she said, 'I'll made a hot drink.'

'I feel so sick.'

'A drink will settle you. Have you a hankie?'

June nodded and drew away a little to get it. Norah lifted the hair back from June's forehead.

'Goodness, you are in a sweat. I'll get your face flannel. Pull the sheets up now, don't get chilled.'

She switched on the bedside lamp and went out. June lay back, shivering a little, and blew her nose.

She felt weak and purged, as though some crises had passed. Just so would Auntie Norah soothe the last moments of the dying, she thought, in a starched cap and apron, so certain, competent and strong. That kind of dream must be like dying ... What kind of dream? She could not remember anything but the terror of it.

Norah returned and wiped her face for her as she lay on the pillow, and June dried it on the towel she had brought at the same time. Then she came back again with a cup of warm sweet milk and a biscuit. 'Here you are. Put your dressing gown round you.' She drew it towards June and sat down again on the bed while the girl sat up and pulled the robe round her. 'Drink it up now, it'll not stay hot for long.'

June drew up her knees and rested her elbows on them, the cup between both hands. 'I'm sorry I woke you up.'

'You don't want to be on your own with a bad dream. We'll soon get to sleep again.'

'Is it late?'

'No. Hardly one o'clock.'

'I don't know why I dreamed. I never do. I usually go straight off and don't know anything till Mum wakes me in the morning. I don't remember what it was about either, it was just sort of all bogged down and trapped.'

'The really nasty ones are the ones that stay with you, so you can't be sure they weren't real after all. It's better to have your kind.'

'Do you have nightmares?'

'I used to.'

'What kind?'

'The bad kind. The bad things of the day keeping on at you in the night.'

'Gosh, that must be awful.'

'It's tiring. Drink up your milk now.'

June did so and ate the biscuit. The night was so still they could hear the clock ticking in the living room. It sounded cold and lonely, and round it the night and the flat, the streets outside, the world itself, seemed to expand in wider and darker dilations till the shape of things was lost in the black terror space . . .

'Auntie Norah?'

'Yes?'

'What train must I catch on Friday?'

'I should think one about noon.'

'Must I? Couldn't I go later?'

'It's never much of a day when you're all packed and waiting to go.'

'I suppose you've got other things to do.'

'It's not that. I'm not back on duty till Sunday morning.'

'Couldn't I stay, then? I wouldn't be any trouble.'

'You've been no trouble.' They looked at each other. Dumbly, June begged. Silently, Norah comprehended. 'I was wondering,' she said at last, 'Should I perhaps come with you just for a couple of nights?'

June's face flooded with pleasure. 'Oh, Auntie Norah, would you?'

'I'd not stay at the house – I don't think there's room anyway, is there? But there's bound to be a hotel somewhere near, just for a night or two.'

'There's the one where we stayed, Mum and me, it's just round the corner almost.'

'I'd like to see the house and your mother – and everything. And perhaps it's more enjoyable not to travel alone.'

'It's a smashing idea! Oh, Auntie Norah!' She seized her hand and caught it up to her chest. 'I'll show you everything, the suspension bridge and the Downs, it's just like the country, all high up, and there's my new school, it's all modern buildings and glass. And then in the centre there's the University, it's at the top of a hill with a great big tower and a bell in it you can hear all over Bristol. I'm glad we don't live near it. Mum and me were just near it looking for a place to have supper and it went off just over our heads, we nearly jumped out of our skins!'

'I'll send her a postcard and ask her to get me a room.'

'Couldn't you stay with us? You could have my room. I'd sleep on the floor, honestly, I wouldn't mind a bit . . .'

Norah smiled. 'I would. I don't like sharing a room. Come now, it's past one o'clock.' She got up and drew June's dressing gown from her shoulders, laying it at the foot of the bed. 'Settle down now and go back to sleep.'

June snuggled down in the bed.

'You will come?'

'Bar accidents.'

'Oh, thanks a million, Auntie Norah!'

Norah turned off the lamp. 'Sleep well now. Good night.'

The cup in her hand, she went out, shutting the door quietly. In the kitchen alcove she rinsed the cup, and put away the biscuit tin. The breakfast things waited, already laid out for the morning. She went to the bathroom, cleaned her teeth again; looked at her face in the mirror over the basin, all bones with her hair kirby-gripped down to her skull for the night; returned to the living room and held back the curtain, looking out at the deserted road, the curtained houses opposite with their rooms of breathing bodies, stacked like catacombs. As always, the sky was pink over the rooftops, not with dawn but with London, as though it burned steadily out of sight. She let the curtain fall and went, without expectation of sleep, to her bed.

The train was fairly full and they were able to get only one corner seat. Norah let June have it and, once the journey had started, rested her head against the upholstered back and closed her eyes, for she had not been sleeping well these last few nights.

For a time June skimmed the magazines they had bought but her attention was not held; she soon dropped them on her lap and looked out of the window to where the fields steamed by, or at the other passengers. They seemed to her old and ugly, just parcels of people tied together inside their clothes, the women sitting with their knees apart so that she could see the inside of their stocking tops, which made her feel sick, the men sunk into their crumbled jackets, their faces pouched in sleep. Even Auntie Norah looked old with her eyes shut; the vibration of the train shook the skin under her jawbone and the lines round her mouth and eyes showed up. In the strong light from the open sky tiny black hairs could be seen on her upper lip which were not visible at other times. The old woman opposite had yellow teeth which showed now that her mouth had fallen open a little; the inside of her lips was mauve, like the inside of her disgusting thighs. The man next to her, awake and absorbed in a gardening magazine, had dried blood on the edge of his shirt-collar and

hairs growing out of his nostrils. People were ugly, ugly
. . . the things they did, disgusting . . .

She turned, swallowing nausea, back to the window. The cows couched under the humid sky, the sheep cantering away from the never-familiar train, the sprinkled poultry, the cottages embowered in washing-lines and trellises of scarlet runners at least were not disgusting although they might be dull. Auntie Norah was only a few years younger than Mum; and the woman opposite was probably only a few years older. The man with the nose hairs was about Mum's age. But Mum was Mum; she did not sit with sagging knees and mouth nor have hairs on her upper lip or in her nose. Or did she? If she were sitting opposite now, halfway through a stuffy train journey, would she look like these people? When she was in bed asleep did her flesh droop, did she snuffle and twitch a little, would a man, an ugly man like the one with the nose hairs, notice it or mind it if he did, or would they just snort and snuffle together like pigs . . .?

The fields streamed by to the rhythmic hammering of the train wheels. There was a rim of black dirt like putty between pane and gritty window-frame, and from the encrusted ashtray set in the door came the sour stench of ancient tobacco. The man with the nose hairs coughed phlegm deep in his throat and vibrated his little finger vigorously in his earhole.

'Auntie Norah.'

It was a whisper but she opened her eyes at once. 'Mm?'

'I feel sick.'

Instantly professional, she turned to look. June was certainly greenish, and when she took her hand it was clammy.

'Have a barley sugar. Do you usually get trainsick?'

June shook her head. The hair flapped against her pale cheeks, she looked so young and woebegone that tenderness filled Norah, the first she had truly felt for a long time, and she said gently, 'Come outside for a bit.'

They stepped over feet and stood in the corridor. 'Trains always smell, I don't know why, and it's terribly stuffy too. Did you read the books? But there's not much in them to interest you, just the same.'

'She – they won't be at the station, will they?'

'I told her not. With the two of us it's simpler to go straight there and not trouble them to come all the way down to meet us. This must be Bath. We shan't be long now.'

The train slid into the grey ravine of the city. People with luggage began to push past and they had to return to their seats. The man with the nose hairs had gone, the old woman had woken up and pulled her skirt over her knees. Norah touched June's hand. 'You'll soon feel better,' she said quietly, 'don't think about it.'

June laid her head back against the cushions and turned her face towards the window. Her hands lay clasped in her lap and after a moment Norah took one of them. It turned into hers and grasped it; and so, not looking at each other, they reached Bristol.

Deliberately Norah did not take a taxi. It was better to occupy the child with buses and luggage and finding the right stop than to sit passively in a taxi with nothing to think about save the homecoming. It was around six o'clock and the city was pulsating, bicycles like mosquitoes in and out among the heavier traffic, streams of people in the streets. Queuing, their suitcases unwieldy, they got a bus to the Green; queued again, progressed slowly, achieved the right bus. Rising up the hill out of the whirlpool of the centre, a calmer, wider sky met them. Sunlight lay on the upper windows of the roads, for the clouds had cleared, and when they got off the bus and turned into the side streets they could hear the birds beginning their evening calls. The air smelt of privet. They came to Hellebore Road.

As they approached the house a man came down the path. He was out of the gate and had come a few steps towards them by the time they reached him. He was fair, the hair brushed into jaunty wings above his ears. On a face that was older than it looked a bushy

RAF moustache was borne as proudly as the horns of a hunting trophy on a wall.

Norah and June halted. The blood rushed into June's face and above the thunder of her heart she heard Norah say hesitantly, 'Ray – is it you?'

The man paused, smiling, 'No joy,' he said. 'You want Mr Baxter, I expect. I'm his next-door neighbour, actually.' He laid his hand on the gate of 'Marylea'.

Norah said, 'I'm so sorry.'

'Think nothing of it.' He unlatched the gate and went through. 'You'll find them in.'

'Thank you.'

'Good show.' He raised his hand in vague salute and went up the path.

'How silly,' said Norah. 'Of course it wasn't him.'

As their own gate clinked behind them the front door opened. Esther stood there, her face radiant. She held out her arms. 'You're late. We expected you half an hour ago. Norah dear!' They kissed. 'And Junie – how are you, dearest?' She held June close to her. 'We waited tea and then gave up. I'll make some fresh. Give me your case, dear. Did you have a good journey?' She took June's suitcase and they all went into the hall. As Norah explained about the buses and the queues June looked furtively round her. There was a man's raincoat hanging on the stand and a hat above it. The door of the front room was half open. She began to shake.

And now the two women were talking a little shrilly, standing in the small hall with the suitcases at their feet, and Mrs Baxter's face was flushed. She wiped her hand on the hip of her skirt, then held it out to June. 'Well,' she said brightly, 'we don't want to stand about out here, do we? Come in, dear. Come in and meet Daddy.' She pushed open the door and drew June into the sitting room.

Standing on the hearth was a man; a little, old, bald man who took a step towards her with his hand half out and a silly smile on his face. 'Junie?' he said.

She recoiled.

'Junie,' he said again. He dropped his hand, staring at her; and as she stared back she saw his eyes (they were blue, that had been accurate enough) fill with tears which spilt and ran down his cheeks. He turned away to the mantelpiece, fumbling for a handkerchief. His wife took a step towards him, then put her arm tightly round June.

'You're tired and hungry, poor lamb. Come close now and I'll turn the electric fire on, it gets chilly once the sun's gone down. Norah, come in, dear.'

He turned back to them, dry-eyed now and smiling. 'Norah,' he said and put out his hand again. After only an instant Norah took it. 'You're looking well,' he said, 'not a day older. Still a real Irish colleen, eh?'

'I wouldn't say that,' said Norah.

'And you're a matron now – I mean, matron of the hospital.'

'No,' said Norah.

'Not matron, dear, sister – I told you,' said Esther. She had switched on the fire and drew June to it, pressing her hand in both hers. 'Come near, dear, you're perished. I'll make some fresh tea. Sit down, Norah. She's Ward Sister, Ray, I told you. Did you have a nice time, darling? I kept all your postcards, look.' They stood on the mantelpiece beside the china crinoline lady and the photograph of June as a baby.

Her mother was wearing a new dress.

'This is a nice room,' Norah said.

Esther looked round it as though surprised. 'Yes. Yes, it is, isn't it? It's a nice little house and easy to keep straight. We settled in ever so easily, didn't we, Ray? I'll make the tea.'

'Shall I do it, dear?' asked Raymond.

'No, you sit down and talk to June and Norah. I'll do it. I won't be a tick.'

'Sit down, sit down – make yourself at home.' Raymond drew two chairs a little forward and they sat. 'Did you have a good journey? I suppose the train was full of holidaymakers this time of year.'

As Norah answered him June saw he was not really little, old and bald. He was short – Mum had always said he wasn't tall – but sort of shrunken as though he had been ill. He had been ill, of course. And he was grey-looking, which make him look old; even his eyes seemed faded. And his hair wasn't fair anymore, as Mum had described it, but grey like his face and not much of it, cut very short round a pale skull that glistened a little where the hair had left it. He was talking hard to Auntie Norah but every now and then his eyes flicked sideways to June and his Adam's apple bobbed as he swallowed.

The fire began to scorch her bare shins but she still felt cold.

'Who was that man?' She broke across their conversation.

'Mm?'

'We met a man.'

'At the gate,' said Norah, 'for a moment I thought he was you, Ray.'

Raymond laughed heartily. 'You mean the chap next door – don't know his name, Etty saw him. He wanted something about the garden, ramblers cutting back or something.'

'Who, Mr Townsend?' Esther came in with a tray and Raymond jumped up to help her. 'Thanks, dear. It's his mother lives next door – you know, Junie, the garden with the gnomes in it and the birdbath? Now tuck in, both of you. I brought it in here because of the fire. He comes down to stay with her fairly often, he said, but he works in London. I'll let it stand a bit before I pour yours, Norah.'

'Still like it black as bog water, do you?' Raymond teased.

'I do.'

'Australia's the great place for tea-drinking – tea and beer. I used to say they made up for all their dry territory by all the slosh they put away inside themselves.'

He told them about Australia. He was full of facts – population, rainfall, the composition of the Great Barrier Reef. He told them about the sheep farmers and the cane cutters, and how mother kangaroos throw their young ('Joeys, they're called') from their pouches when attacked and leap away to draw the pursuit after themselves. He talked and they listened, and when tea was over they left him with the evening paper and went upstairs to see June's room and show Norah the house. There were two beds in Mum's room, plaid slippers besides Mum's scuffed velvet ones, a handleless brush and a small leather box on the chest of drawers, a drip-dry shirt on a hanger on the wardrobe door. Shaving things were on the bathroom shelf, two toothbrushes in one glass.

June leaned out of the open window of her own room, out, out into the sinking sunlight falling sideways across the house. The grass of their garden had been cut; next door the gnomes stood like figures in a needlework picture, each flower and grass blade a stitch. On the paving stones in front of the house two deck chairs, one with a canopy, were set, but no one was in them. June leaned out and out, feeling the sun-warmed sill gritty beneath her folded arms, hearing the voices of Mum and Auntie Norah murmuring in the bathroom, on the landing, then downstairs in the kitchen. The french windows next door were open and from them she thought came voices – but not people's voices, the marshalled voices of a broadcast. Not Mr Townsend.

They had supper and listened to a quiz programme on the wireless. Raymond knew many of the answers and gave them before the contestants could. Sometimes he said, 'Come on now, Junie, you know that one, don't you?' but even when she did she never replied. Quite soon Auntie Norah said she must go to her hotel, and Mum said, 'I'll show you the way,' but Auntie Norah said sharply, 'No, you stay here. Raymond will show me,' and he put on his hat and took Auntie Norah's holdall and they went off together.

Mum stayed with June while she got ready for bed, telling her all about the move and the funny things one of the moving men had kept coming out with, how the gas hadn't been turned on when they arrived and the man had fetched a great jugful of tea, the colour of ginger, from some men digging up the road round the corner. With the house empty about them, just her and Mum on their own, little by little she thawed. The miniature guardsman she had bought in Trafalgar Square after seeing the Changing of the Guard was unwrapped, admired and placed on the mantelpiece, the scarf with London scenes on it was given to Mum, who knotted it round her neck. Without making any comment on it, June observed that her room was lovely. It was pink and white, starched and frilled like an illustration in a homes magazine, the china animals that used to be in the kitchen at Havenport were ranged along the mantelpiece, and Mum had put a posy of small mixed flowers in a vase on the dressing table. All June's clothes had been unpacked from the move and now hung in the cupboard or lay in the drawers as though they had always been there; even the Duke playing polo and Alec Guinness in *Tunes of Glory* (looking sternly down his nose at that actress) hung in their passepartout either side of the flower picture. When Mrs Baxter drew off the pink and white bedspread June saw that the sheets were pink too, the pillowcase frilled. 'Oh Mum!' she cried and threw her arms round her mother. 'Are they new? Are they mine?'

'It's only the one pair,' Mrs Baxter said, laughing and holding her close. 'I couldn't run to a change.'

'Let me get in quick.'

'You've not done your teeth.'

'Oh goodness . . .' She darted into the bathroom, scrubbing and spitting energetically. 'I went in an expresso, Mum,' she called, 'in Chelsea. When I saw *Captain's Paradise* and Auntie Norah couldn't come.' A moment's silence and the plug pulled. Smelling of toothpaste, like a Pierrot in her pyjamas short at waist and ankle, she came back and jumped into bed. 'They're slippery!'

'They're drip-dry. They can be washed at home.'

'There was a man and girl there, Mum, wearing thick jumpers even though it was hot.'

'Where, dear?'

'In the expresso. And they never spoke at all and the girl was crying and after a bit the man got up and just walked out.'

'Well I never!'

'He never paid or anything. I suppose they were artists. The coffee was ever so bitter.'

Mrs Baxter sat down on the bed and took June's hand. 'We'll go to the school on Monday and see the Headmistress. I made an appointment. The blazer's nice, dear, grey with a blue and yellow badge. We get it in the town.'

'Is she nice?'

'I expect so. I didn't talk to her personally, just her secretary. And tomorrow we'll show Auntie Norah the suspension bridge and the Downs and all, shall we?'

'When must she go back?'

'Tomorrow, she says. It's not long to come such a distance, but she says she's due back on duty. Did you . . .' she stroked the hand, 'did you get to know her, dear?'

'Of course.'

'She's a good friend. She's always stood by me.'

'Can I read a bit, Mum?'

'Just a little while.'

Downstairs the front door opened. They both turned their heads.

He called, 'Etty?'

'I'm up here, dear.' She made to rise but did not. The front door closed and they heard his feet on the stairs. The bedroom door was ajar but he knocked on it and asked, 'May I come in?'

June withdrew her hand from her mother's, leaning back in bed and pulling the covers up over her, watching as he put first his head, then himself round the door and into her room.

'Well, I've seen Norah safely to her nest,' he said.

'Was it all right, dear?'

'Yes, yes, they were expecting her.' He stood on the beige carpet looking at the frills, the flowers, the two women lit by the pink light of the bedside lamp.

'Say good night to June, dear. She's going to read a bit.'

'Good. Good-oh.' He moved forward, bent and awkwardly kissed her cheek as she pressed back on the pillow. He smelt of tea. 'Good night, Junie. My little girl.'

His voice was rough. He stood back from the bed and Mum looked up at him. She took his hand, looking up and smiling as she sat on the bed in her new dress, her hand with its wedding ring clenched, gripping on to his; and June saw with revulsion that both of them had tears in their eyes, although it was only his that spilt.

THREE

MRS TOWNSEND DID NOT believe in knowing her neighbours. A nod in passing in the street was quite sufficient; anything more might lead to 'popping in', a practice she detested. The daughter of a solicitor's clerk and herself a senior clerk in the Ministry of Transport, Western Division, she had married beneath her when she married Stanley Townsend, a railway worker who was destined never to rise above being second booking clerk at Temple Meads Station. A bomb fell near him during one of the last big raids and although at the time he did not appear to be much hurt he died a year later, having been, as it were, literally shaken out of himself. Their only child was Anthony, who got compassionate leave from his airfield in East Anglia and stood at the graveside very straight and splendid in his Royal Air Force uniform although he was not yet operational, having only just left school and been called up.

There had never been anything in the Townsends' lives to equal the miracle of Anthony, to be for his father so much more than he himself ever could, to be for his mother the step up that compensated for her own step down. Even for him to have met a hero's death would have been acceptable; but he did not, surviving to fill his mother's widowhood with pride and love, and by his weekend visits (for during the last years he had worked in London) enriching her life already full with bridge and tapestry work and rug-making, gardening, flower arrangement and supervising 'the woman'. 'My woman is excellent,' Mrs Townsend would say, 'but of course I have to keep after her,' and three mornings a week she did, while the woman, straight-faced and meek, rubbed over surfaces already shining, washed out lace curtains and teacloths still with their folds inviolate upon them, listened to *Music While You Work* and drank tea.

Dry and light as a cricket, her grey hair neatly waved, in twin sets of pale pink or beige with a string of crystal beads, Mrs Townsend lived her busy life without ever doing more than say 'Good morning' to her neighbours. Her friends were further afield. Even her woman came from the other side of the city and worked for no one else. 'My woman is very reliable,' said Mrs Townsend, 'but even so, running in and out of other people's houses, they can't help but gossip.'

Nevertheless it was astonishing how much Mrs Townsend herself knew without such a source of information, simply by being sharp-eyed, sharp-eared and a good deal at home. She had seen Mrs Baxter's first approach to the house, alone, looking tired, going up the path with the house-agent's key in her hand on a rainy May afternoon. Mrs Townsend had even heard her footsteps going slowly in and out of the bare rooms, for the party wall was not at all soundproof. She had seen the builders take over, had in fact complained to the foreman about lumps of plaster tossed over her fence and the singing (if you could call it that) of one of the workmen. To do this she had been inside the house itself and knew what at least some of the rooms were going to look like. She had heard footsteps again one day and voices, and had been able to see the same woman and what must be her daughter going away together, looking more cheerful this time. She had, of course, observed most of the moving in, as it took several hours, and could judge pretty well what sort of people these Baxters were (she had learned their name from the milkman); but owing to a flower arrangement class she had missed Mrs Baxter's departure two days later with an overnight bag, and the first she knew of Mr Baxter's existence was a man's cough, very distinct, the other side of her bedroom wall one evening, and then the sight of him mowing the grass next afternoon – and making rather heavy weather of it too, puffing and stopping to rest and making a dreadful mess of the ground when he turned the machine at the end of each run. Mrs Baxter came out once and told him not to overdo it. They seemed a quiet couple; but where had the daughter got to?

'It's the school hols, Mother,' said Anthony, home for a weekend. 'Why else would I be here?'

'Silly boy,' Mrs Townsend said tenderly. 'Yes of course, that must be it, she must be on holiday somewhere. But where was *he* when they moved in, I wonder?'

'Gone underground like a sensible chap, I expect.'

'And before, when she went over the house? Of course, I might have missed another visit.'

'Not you, Mother. Catseyes Townsend, that's you.'

'Don't tease, dear. Presumably they don't realise their rambler is overgrowing my trellis. I don't think they're real gardeners. Perhaps you could mention it to them while you're here, dear! It comes so much better from a man.'

'Will do, sometime.'

'Now, perhaps? I know they're in, I heard the tap running in their kitchen. Then perhaps he could get it done over the weekend and you could make certain the trellis is secure.'

He got patiently to his feet. She watched him fondly. In her eyes his hair had not thinned, his face lined, his suits become slightly shiny. He was still her handsome flyer son, the symbol of his service still growing so splendidly on his upper lip. He went out, whistling between his teeth just as he used to do when he did his homework, and presently she heard the bell ring next door. She did not need to go into her front room to hear from the window what they were saying, for presently he would come back and tell her. This he did, after a few minutes, adding, 'And some pukka gen for you too, Mother. The girl's just come back.'

Anthony returned to London and Mrs Townsend and the Baxters pursued their lives side by side, the Baxters hardly aware of Mrs Townsend but Mrs Townsend sharply aware of them. Mr Baxter pruned the ramblers, although very inexpertly – he seemed to be cutting out all the new wood and leaving all the suckers. When it was fine he sat in the garden a lot, shirtsleeves rolled up, eyes shut to the sun, getting quite a tan. Occasionally his wife sat with him, knitting or sewing, and he would read aloud to her; rather distracting, this, to Mrs Townsend, intent on her own library book. But mostly Mrs Baxter would be indoors, in the kitchen, judging from the sink and crockery sounds and the remarks husband and wife exchanged through the window (which Mrs Townsend knew was over the sink). The girl was not often with her father but spent a lot of time in what presumably was her bedroom; here again remarks were sometimes exchanged between the parents in the garden and the child upstairs, and the wireless there was on a great deal; Mrs Townsend presumed the girl had her own set in what would be the duplicate of Anthony's old room – so pleasant, getting the sun and looking over the gardens, always kept ready for his arrival, with a spare sports jacket and slacks in the wardrobe and a change of underwear in the chest of drawers, school groups and squadron groups on the walls with a rather vulgar cartoon involving Mae West, drawn by one of his friends (but she had to admit it was quite droll), and on the mantelpiece the model aeroplanes that were so difficult to dust (the woman was not trusted with them) and the terrible lump of metal that had torn through the fuselage over Bremen once and missed her wonderful, her only boy by inches. Sometimes in the autumn Mrs Townsend would take her tapestry or her rug and work at it in the window of Anthony's room, catching the weakening sun. But not very often; even though now he seldom lived there, she felt an intruder. Neither she nor her husband had ever gone into Anthony's room without knocking, once he had been confirmed; a boy's need for privacy must be respected.

Sometimes she would see the girl in the garden alone, pinching off flowerheads, picking apples off the tree almost before they were ripe, mooning about by the shed. She took a rug and cushions there one weekend and made herself a sort of arbour by pulling the branches of the syringa bush over as a roof and tying them to the shed door. What she did there Mrs Townsend could not see, but she did not do it long for the branches kept whipping upright and besides, as Mrs Townsend could have told her, the bottom of the garden with all that loose earth unattended was a favourite digging place for cats.

They all went out together once a week or so in the evenings, presumably to the cinema; and before school reopened they went out during the days if they were fine, sometimes with carrier-bags that looked as though they contained a picnic (apples and thermos tops). The school began and the Baxters were quieter than ever, with the girl out all day. She looked nice in the uniform. She was a slender child, not one of those unfortunate great lumps with busts and mottled legs, and she wore her beret sensibly on her clean-looking hair, not half falling off like some of them. She carried a handsome briefcase, obviously new, with her initials on it – J.B. Julia? Jane? Janet? When she came home at teatime Mrs Townsend could sense a stirring the other side of the party walls – taps running in the kitchen, crockery, voices calling from room to room, and soon the wireless turned on upstairs. Did she do her homework with it on?

As September waned the days grew colder and there was less to observe in the garden. When she met Mrs Baxter at the shops or by the gate they exchanged good mornings and that was all. Mr Baxter she hardly ever saw, yet he was not out at business. They must have private means, retired perhaps? Yet he seemed young for that – although it was hard to tell, when a man had lost most of his hair (thank goodness the Townsends all had good heads of hair). A war disability perhaps, and a pension; he seemed all in one piece but it might be internal, lungs, heart . . . Certainly he had made heavy weather of the lawn.

With the shorter days, closed windows and drawn curtains, Mrs Townsend's knowledge of her neighbours ceased to grow. She was conscious of them now mainly by sound, the unexceptional sounds with which he had grown familiar, that denoted a rhythm of lives without interest and holding no threat to her own convenience. But at the beginning of November she noticed a change. Mr Baxter did not cough there during the mornings and Mrs Baxter did not always rattle there during the afternoons, and something began to awaken Mrs Townsend at half-past five in the morning; not every morning, for she usually slept soundly, but two or three times during the week, perhaps when she had drunk coffee with one of her friends the evening before. But nevertheless it was most annoying, for once awake she could not settle again, despite the darkness.

One morning she woke before the noise that would awaken her. In the absolute silence of pre-dawn she heard a front door close quietly, quiet footsteps down a garden path, the faint squeak of a gate, footsteps receding with less care as they became more distant. Well now, what was that? Half-past five in the morning, cold and dark as Tartary? It must be someone going out. Mr Baxter? Why? To work – unless he were a burglar! – but what work? Was he not then retired? Only the lower types of work required people to leave the house at half-past five – factories, public services, the railways. Mrs Townsend remembered, as she had not remembered for years, getting up to see Stanley off to his booking office on winter mornings, cold nose, cold feet, no way of getting warm even if she had gone back to bed, which she had never done; and the summer mornings, light already and the birds singing as they never sang in the day and half her housework done before it was time to rouse Anthony to go to school. Surely Mr Baxter did not work on the railways, was not a hand in a factory? They had seemed such superior types.

All the people who lived in Hellebore Road were more or less superior types because, Mrs Townsend presumed, the houses were too small for families with a lot of children (fatal to the tone of a road, with all those tricycles and screaming up and down) or to be let off in rooms. The inhabitants were elderly or young, retired or newlywed, or childless couples who both went out to business and who might perhaps have, not as a lodger but as a paying guest, one very quiet, very superior lady such as Mrs Townsend herself had been. In the great patchwork that was Bristol, Hellebore Road was the pale blue of suburbia, the green country at its back with the chasm of the riverbed, white circlets of Georgian houses at its sides, the black and red and purple of slums and industries at its feet. At night, when the coloured lights of factories, streets and railways festooned the city, Hellebore Road lay decently obscure in the linked patches of old-fashioned lamp-posts and from its windows the huge sprawl of the valley could not be seen. Mrs Townsend seldom went down into it – to the theatre with Anthony or a friend perhaps, shopping for clothes or Christmas presents – but everything she needed for daily life was close at hand. There were Anthony's visits to look forward to and no need to be sad when he had gone, for he would soon be back again; and it was far more comfortable for both of them that he should have his life in London, she hers in Bristol. She did not pry, but her own life was so full and orderly that presumably his was too. He was her pride, her wonderful son who in wartime, straight from school, had served his country in the most gallant of Services, who was doing so well in his work at Fletcher's of Oxford Street, who was so dutiful in his attentions to her, and on whom she was in no way dependent. *If she never saw him again it would almost have been enough that he had once existed.*

He came home as usual for the Christmas holiday, looking tired, she thought, but she did not pry and he told her he had been to a party the night before. The RAF boys had learned to enjoy themselves during the war, when each day might be their last, and she was proud of him for having what she presumed must be a hangover, for knowing how to live life to the full. He mentioned names with which she had grown familiar over the years since he had lived in London, among them several girls. She did not wish to pry but was not sorry that he spoke of them all impartially. It did not do to rush into marriage (she had forgotten he was nearly forty). He fell asleep in front of the television, looking very like his father in spite of the handlebar moustache. She woke him gently and sent him up to bed.

She was watering the plants on the front room windowsill next day, which was Christmas Eve, and looked out to see Anthony in conversation with the Baxters' daughter. They were walking along together, Anthony carrying two Christmas trees and the girl Anthony's shopping-bag. At the gate they halted, the girl took one of the trees and returned the bag, Anthony smiled and bumped his way through the gate while the girl went on to her own house. As he reached the front door he called, 'Merry Christmas!' and faintly Mrs Townsend heard the girl answer, 'Same to you' before her front door closed and Anthony found the key to open theirs.

She went into the hall. 'Was that the Baxter girl, dear?'

He put the shopping-bag down and hung his cap on the stand. 'Catseyes Townsend strikes again,' he said.

'I didn't know you'd spoken.'

'We don't communicate by radar, Ma.' He always called her Ma when he was vexed; he knew she didn't like it.

She smiled placatingly. 'Such a dear little tree.'

'Would you believe it, seven and a tanner.' He held it out between both hands, surveying it. 'It's highway robbery.'

'Still, it wouldn't be Christmas without a tree, even though they do shed their needles so dreadfully.' She followed him into the kitchen with the shopping-bag. 'Did the girl buy hers at the same shop, dear?'

'I haven't a clue.'

'I thought you were together . . .?'

'She was walking along the pavement and I caught her up. Her tree was bigger than mine so I offered to carry both and she took the shopping-bag. OK?'

'So they're staying at home for Christmas.' It was a statement, not a question, and he did not reply, unpacking the basket with her and putting the things away. 'Did I tell you he leaves the house at half-past five every morning? It wakes me quite regularly.'

'The Stores only had small packets of peas so I got two. OK?'

'Yes, dear, quite right. She didn't happen to say what her father's business is, did she? Half-past five is so very early.'

'For Pete's sake, Ma!' He regarded her with exasperation tempered by affection. 'If you're so crazy to find out, why don't you get to know them?'

She bridled. 'One must respect people's privacy.'

'Come off it! I shall ask them in for a drink.'

'Anthony!'

'Tonight, after supper.'

'They may have other engagements.'

'They haven't.'

'How do you know?'

'She told me. And her name is June and she'll be sixteen next summer and she goes to St Maud's School and doesn't think much of it.'

'She told you all this today?'

'Yes. She's a nice kid.'

'I think you should have told me, dear.'

'Told you what?'

'That you thought of inviting them. After all, it does concern me.'

He grinned. 'What doesn't?'

'No, dear. It's not funny. I think you've been just a wee bit underhand.'

He turned away. 'What time shall I ask them for?'

'You haven't asked *me* at all.'

'I'm asking you now. Come on, poppet, don't sulk.'

'I know it's very dull for you here, especially at holiday times.'

'Dull? With your Christmas cooking tomorrow and the panto on Boxing Day and maybe bridge with the Sinclairs sometime?' He was laughing. 'Come on, Mother – before or after supper?'

'If they came before they might have to be asked to stay on.'

'After, then.' He put his arm round her as he went past. 'Cheer up, it may never happen!'

Mrs Baxter answered the door, in an apron with her sleeves rolled up. She seemed as disconcerted by the invitation as his mother had been. 'Oh – well, it's very kind. Won't you come in?'

'Thanks.' He stepped inside and she closed but did not shut the front door, standing there pushing a strand of hair back from her forehead.

'It's just my mother and I on our own and we thought a neighbourly noggin . . .'

'It's ever so kind of you but I'm afraid we can't. We're engaged.'

'Oh Mum!' From the landing where she had been listening June came halfway down the stairs. Her mother looked up at her uncertainly.

'Well, it's Christmas Eve and there's such a lot to do the last minute – and Mr Baxter won't be back till late. I'm afraid we'll have to say no. But please thank Mrs Townsend.'

'Oh *Mum*!' June came down the remaining stairs, her hair swinging round a face flushed with both anger and shyness. 'Why can't we? We don't have to stay in just because Dad's not home.'

'We can't let Daddy come home to an empty house, dear.'

'Why not? He's not a baby!'

'June!' said her mother warningly. 'I'm so sorry, Mr Townsend.'

He looked from one to the other, the chasm of Christmas Eve boredom yawning at his back. 'Would you let June come in on her own? She could watch the telly with us if she'd like.'

'Well . . .'

'Oh please, Mum!'

'TV's still quite a treat, Mr Townsend. We've not got one, you see, and it's a novelty. Are you sure it wouldn't be inconvenient?'

'Absolutely.'

'Well – but you mustn't stay late, dear. It's Christmas tomorrow.'

'Good show. About seven-thirty or so? The good programmes usually begin about then. And if you and Mr Baxter change your minds . . .'

'You're very kind.' She opened the door again and he went outside.

'Till this evening, then.' In the darkness of the hall June nodded.

'Send her home when you've had enough, won't you? Not later than ten anyway.'

'Will do. Merry Christmas.'

'Merry Christmas – and the same to Mrs Townsend.'

Crockery rattled in both kitchens a little earlier than usual that evening. As Tony festooned the tree with the tarnished tinsel he remembered from boyhood, he could hear someone running up and down the stairs next door and a voice calling – June getting ready, he supposed. In their own kitchen his mother was frying chips – cold ham, chips, tinned peaches and cream had always been one of his favourite meals – and above the sizzling he could hear her singing bits from *The Mikado* in a determined way. That was to show she was not in the least put out; she never sang when she was not. The fairy for the top of the tree was really past it, skirt squashed, wings askew, her small wax cheeks yellow. Hearing June's voice calling next door, his mother announcing she was three little maids from school, he tried to rejuvenate the doll with fingers deft from pinning shirts, tying ties, clipping on price tags in the Men's Wear department of the store in which he now worked. This little old doll was nearly as old as he was. Christmas after Christmas he and Dad had crowned their trees with her while Mother got supper ready. Christmas after Christmas until he joined the RAF they had opened the same chocolate-box with the picture of the kittens on the lid, lifted out the same tinsel chains, the same baubles, the same squashed bells made of silver paper and reverently, not speaking much, swathed trees which, as the years passed, were smaller as he grew bigger. He and his father had never had much to say to one another but in the ritual of the tree they had communed. It was ritual too that his mother should praise their work, each year the same, as though she had never seen it before, as now she did when she came to call him to supper.

'How very pretty, dear, you're always so clever,' but he saw she hardly looked at it. Her eyes were bright and she carried a plate of fancy biscuits in either hand. 'Supper's on the table, we mustn't dally. I suppose your guest will eat these.'

'She's not a guest, Mother, she's a fifteen-year-old schoolgirl.'

'Anyone coming to my house is a guest, Anthony. I only hope there'll be some left to tide us over the holiday.' She set the plates down, rearranged them, tweaked cushions, shifted a chair, humming *Tit Willow*. 'I suppose you had better turn on the other bar of the fire,' she said and went out.

June was almost as distracted when she arrived, wary, colour in her cheeks, her hair held back by a velvet Alice band. She handed Mrs Townsend an envelope containing a Christmas card, which Mrs Townsend admired coolly and placed with the others on the mantelpiece. The television was already on but with the sound turned down, and the mute gesticulations on the screen added to the atmosphere of confusion in the room. Tony arranged chairs for them and there was demur as to who should sit where. 'I'll fetch my own little chair,' cried Mrs Townsend gaily, 'you take the large one – Daddy's chair, wasn't it, dear?'

'No, please.' June hung back.

'She prefers the little one,' he said.

'I do my tapestry, you see. I can't bear to sit idle, just having entertainment fed to me as presumably so many people do nowadays.'

'Where is it, Mother, I'll fetch it.'

'No, no, dear, don't stir. I know just where it is. You start the programme going – I haven't a notion what it is.' She went out of the room, leaving the door open.

Tony patted the armchair. 'Come along.'

'Where will you sit?'

'Here.' He drew forward another chair. 'Go on. Really. She likes the little chair best, it's got no arms.'

Hesitantly June moved round and sat on the edge of the big chair. He was adjusting the set but she did not watch the screen yet, her eyes busy over the room, noting, marking down. As with themselves, the Townsends used the back room as the living room. There were flower pictures on the walls and over the sideboard a coloured reproduction of a flight of aeroplanes against a dawn sky. At one end of the mantelpiece was an old-fashioned photograph of a mild-looking man, at the other a larger one, smiling beneath tilted cap and twirled moustache, of a gay young man who had the day before attained the winged insignia displayed above his tunic pocket.

'Is that you?'

'That? None other. PO Prune himself, the very man.'

'Who?'

'Yes, that's me.'

'Were you a pilot?'

'No. Tailend Charlie.'

'What?'

'Rear-gunner – bupbupbupbup – you know, machine guns.'

'Oh.' She was awed. 'Were you ever wounded?'

'Burned my hand on the barrel once.'

'Barrel?'

My God, he thought, am I so old? Is it all such ancient history (the cold, the loneliness, only the intercom holding you from the sky with its malevolent moon and its stars that never came nearer and the probe of the searchlight, first one, then several, then the cold concentration of them heralding war). 'It was a piece of cake really,' he said. 'That's what we used to call something that was easy.' He turned off the central light, leaving only the standard lamp, and sat down. 'Haven't a clue what this will be like, it's some kind of variety.'

Eight young men and women in black leotards were dancing on what looked like ice. Their teeth flashed like icicles, especially the men's. Mrs Townsend came back with her tapestry.

'Don't get up, don't get up!' she cried, waving them back into their chairs. 'What have we here? How thin they are! Perhaps the screen distorts them.' She settled under her canvas and skeins of wool, leaned towards the lamp to thread a needle. 'Is it a little loud, Anthony? Perhaps you could just . . .'

He got up and turned down the sound.

'That's better, thank you, dear. Do you like dancing, June?'

'No.'

'No?'

'I mean, not to watch. I like plays best – I think.'

'There now, Anthony. Is there a play on the other channel?'

'Oh please – I didn't mean . . .'

Mrs Townsend quelled her with a smile as Anthony rose once more and turned a switch. The whine of gunfire deafened them and two huge men, sweating beneath ten-gallon hats, ducked behind rocks in an echoing canyon. 'Oh dear,' said Mrs Townsend, and Tony switched back.

Long ago, in Grammar School, Tony had learned how to suspend consciousness while appearing to be paying attention. He could sit at his desk, a seemingly alert, pink-faced schoolboy, but in reality simply a husk, no more a part of the activity around him than a bolster dummy left in a bed. Later the same process had served him well in those periods between take-off and attack, when encapsulated in the gun turret, nerves and body could do nothing but await whatever was to happen. Once you were ready, everything checked, yourself and your apparatus ticking over in what seemed perfect condition, it was better to opt out of thought for a while. It had worked well then; only on land again did tension catch him, make him rowdy and adolescent, clowning in the Mess, slotting back the beer as though he were sluicing a fire, roaring round the piano, a mug in one hand, the other round the shoulders of someone, a man or a girl, depending on where he was – if he knew where he was in those hours before the next sortie began to rise in the sky like the moon, and sleep and personal health became the orders by which not only he but the whole crew lived – or might not . . .

The same suspension operated often during his peacetime working days, the silent-screaming hours of boredom in a series of offices and shops, unable to find just the right job, just the right way of living, for going into the Air Force straight from school had not trained him for civilian existence. He did not know how to keep the even pace essential to jog through day after day. He chopped and changed, resigned, started afresh, was fired, tried something else. For four years now he had been a salesman in the Men's Wear department of Fletcher's, a long time, the longest he had ever stayed anywhere. Perhaps he had given up at last.

For much of the time he spent with his mother he was absent too, quite gone behind the blue eyes, the affectionate smile, the teasing and the thoughtfulness. Nothing Mother could ever say or do would take him by surprise and therefore long ago the need to give her his attention had gone. Affection he gave her and his presence; but much of the time it was the presence only of the dummy in the bed. Most evenings were like that. They would sit in front of the television, exchanging remarks, making tea in the natural breaks, and not until he rose to turn it off, kiss her good night, go to the loo quickly so as to leave it free for her, would he be really with her again.

Yet he was nowhere else meanwhile. Less and less did his liberated self visit, consider, plan within the freedom of his skull. In the beginning he had invented or remembered – wizard parties, wizard popsies; then he had planned – careers and holidays and girls. Lately he seemed to do none of these, his head seemed full only of a slack sea eddying to-and-fro, out of which emerged vague shapes and names: Frothy Forbes and Ginger and good old Polsky, Stella at the King's Head, Jennifer (ah, Jennifer!), that bastard Groupy who tried to make the Mess dry, the girl he'd met in an empty compartment on the way to Lincoln and how they'd nearly rolled off the seat (he often thought of that, even now) – these were rocks rising from the slack tide of his inertia, submerged little by little by time until, one day, they would have gone and nothing would be left inside his head but the grey sea slopping to-and-fro.

He had asked the Baxters in this evening as a half-conscious man will make a few feeble gestures towards life. Anyone, anything that was alive, different from Mother and her busy elderly friends! He knew her life was full of activity when he was not there, but the convention, started when he came on the leaves which might always be his last, was that all her friends withdrew, all her normal occupations were put aside while he was with her. Enclosed in a vacuum of affectionate goodwill, they got through the days somehow, helped by television and the theatre, an outing if the weather were fine, and his ability for absence.

Half gone behind his open eyes, he sat in front of the television, hardly conscious of his mother with her cascade of canvas, perched on the edge of her chair to catch the light from the one lamp, her mouth pursed; she always looked severe when she sewed. He was more conscious of June. She was new and young; freshness seemed to come from her like a scent, but of course he knew it was the Christmas tree he could smell, responding to the warmth of the room. June had relaxed now and leaned back in the big chair with her hands clasped in her lap, her knees sharp-pointed from a pleated skirt. They were quite good legs, he noticed idly, perhaps a little too thin. But thin with youth; she was all length and delicacy, limbs, hands, hair, young for her age. He thought of some of the girls at Fletcher's, hardly older than this child here yet acting ten years older, elaborate hair styles, skirts they could hardly walk in, married even, some of them, their youth showing only in the actual texture of their flesh. This was a nice child, of no interest to him whatever save that she was someone different, someone he had brought in to break the uncharmed circle of mother and son.

Sometimes June forgot where she was, carried away by the antics on the screen, but almost always she was aware of Mr Townsend in the chair next to hers. Without turning her head or letting on she was not concentrating on the programme, she could swivel her eyes and see him from the tips of his suede monk-style shoes right up to the folds of his yellow pullover. He smoked a lot – more, June thought, than he allowed himself here, for several times he had reached for the packet lying on the arm of his chair and then drawn back his hand, and his fingers were stained brown, even the nail on his right forefinger. Even so, five or six butts lay in the ashtray and to June the air smelt exotic and sickly, the scent of the Christmas tree coming through the cigarette smoke.

In the intervals Mrs Townsend urged June to eat the fancy biscuits and she took one out of politeness, although she would rather have sat quiet and watched the advertisements. Mrs Townsend took a ginger-nut and cracked it between her teeth like a squirrel with an acorn – crack, snap, crack, toss the husk away, turning the nut in avid paws, nibble, nibble, crack, crack. Mrs Townsend did not actually toss anything away but she brushed crumbs off her chest in much the same manner, and June felt she would have been quite happy to toss June away if she could. She did not see how somebody like Mrs Townsend, old and dried up and sharp, could possibly be the mother of somebody like Mr Townsend. Perhaps he was adopted . . .

It was a panel game now. 'Do you care for this sort of thing?' asked Mrs Townsend.

'I'm not very good at it. We did Top of the Form sometimes at my old school, different forms against each other. I was awful.'

'That must be a sound radio programme. I confess I don't very often listen to sound radio since we had this monster.' Mrs Townsend laughed, finishing off a woollen rose on the canvas with deft severity. 'But I keep our old set in the kitchen and my woman likes to listen. What did he say, dear?' as applause sounded from the screen.

'I couldn't hear,' said Tony, taking a cigarette.

'Oh dear, naughty me! I do so hate it if other people chatter while it's on and yet I know I do it myself if I have company. Now I really will sit mum.'

She's showing off, thought June contemptuously. She's pretending to be young yet making sure that I feel childish. It won't cut any ice with *him*. She took a quick look. He was staring at the television. His eyes were steady, hardly blinking, and the light threw funny shadows under them as though they had bags there. His nose was almost straight, with an interesting sort of little knob at the end; and his forehead was lined and thoughtful with the fair hair brushed into little wings at the side, like the crinkles on the top of a small wave just before it breaks. But it was the lower part of his face that was best; his mouth was firm and sensitive (that was how they were always described in magazine stories) but shadowed, made mysterious by the twin horns of his moustache. From the softness of cheeks and lips and nose it was wondrous how that double plume of hair sprang out, bushy, vital, twirled at the ends, brave as a knight's banner, thought June, who had done Tennyson for mock GCE. Yes, that was exactly what Mr Townsend's moustache was, a knight's banner whereby he proclaimed his chivalry and the proud past to which he belonged. It was all ages ago and she knew very little about it, but every September there was something called Battle of

Britain Sunday and quotations from a wartime speech someone had made, and there were programmes on sometimes about how the RAF beat the Germans and even films with Kenneth More with no legs, reissued at the Classic in Havenport, and she knew that the RAF had been brave and glorious and that for some reason a large moustache was the badge of those who had belonged to that heroic band. He had flown. He had been a pilot-officer. He had diced with death and been a hero, not like people who wore the uniform but just did clerking on an airfield . . .

When ten o'clock came June said good night politely. Tony saw her out, walking with her down to his front gate, shivering a little for it was a cool night, the stars shining sharply. He opened the gate for her and stood with both hands leaning upon it.

'Well, thanks ever so much,' she said.

'Think nothing of it. I'll see you again, I expect.'

'Yes.' She hung her head and shifted away.

'It's a fine night.'

'Yes.'

'Good visibility for Father Christmas. Whang, crash, bang on the target every time.' She giggled. 'If it's fine tomorrow, we might go for a walk.'

'Oh yes!'

'Walk off the Christmas pudding, eh? After lunch?'

'I could come in the morning if you liked.'

'Mother likes to go to church in the morning.'

'Oh.' She was ashamed not to have thought of that, and that they did not go to church themselves.

'Say about half-past two?'

'Yes.'

'Bang on. I'll call in for you.'

'All right.'

He smiled at her in the darkness and held out his hand, knowing she did not know how to go, and feeling cold. 'Good night, June, sleep tight.'

Her hand was soft and cold as a paw. He put his other one over it. 'You're freezing. Run in quickly, poppet.'

'Oh yes!' She withdrew her hand and ran to her own gate and up the path. He watched her find the key and open the door, raised his hand in salute before she went inside, stood for a moment more alone, looking at the stars, then turned and went back to his mother.

'Going for a walk? Going for a walk where?' asked Mr Baxter, putting down his spoonful of Christmas pudding.

'I don't know. On the Downs, I suppose.' Her plate was empty, she was anxious to get to the crystallised fruit and then be off. It was five past two already.

'On the Downs? Whatever for?'

'It's lovely there, Ray, you know it is. I think Mr Townsend should have asked me first, Junie.'

'How could he? Honestly! It was late last night and this morning they've been to church.'

This morning had been the first Christmas with *him* here, breaking the tradition of Christmases June and her mother had always had together, the getting into Mum's bed to open the parcels, the slopping round in dressing gowns, the laying of the table while the goose grew tender in the oven. This morning they had all got up and dressed, and the presents had been opened after breakfast, in a room as yet hardly warm.

'Still, your Mum's right. He ought to have asked.'

'Oh honestly! He's not a sex maniac or something!' She flung down her serviette and got up.

'June!'

'Well, it's silly. I'm not a baby.'

'You're our baby,' said her father.

'It's nothing against Mr Townsend, dear. It's just – well, Christmas Day I think we all ought to stay together.'

She tried to speak patiently. 'It's only a walk. I'll be back in an hour. We've been together all morning and we'll be together all evening and all tomorrow too. Honestly!'

'You'll miss the Queen.'

June did not even answer that but went upstairs to get ready. Watching for Mr Townsend from behind the coloured glass panes in the top of the front door, she had it open before his hand reached the bell, hoping to get away before her parents could appear; but Mrs Baxter heard them. With her apron on, she came out from the washing-up.

'Oh – Mr Townsend.'

'Hullo, Mrs Baxter – merry Christmas.' He peered in at her from the doorstep. He was wearing a windbreaker and a flat cap pulled low over his eyes and looked, she had to admit, very gentlemanly.

'You're just off, are you?' she said hesitantly.

'Too right. A brisk constitutional to shake down the Christmas fare, eh, June? Would you and Mr Baxter care to join us?'

'Oh – well, thank you very much but we're not . . . You and June go.'

'Another time, perhaps.'

June began to pull the door shut but her mother called, 'Where are you going?'

'Oh, round the Downs a bit, I reckon – look at the bridge.' He gestured vaguely.

'Oh yes. Be careful, won't you, dear.'

'I'll look after her.'

June pulled the door shut again but through the crack her mother called, 'Shall you be long?'

'No, not long.' The door closed sharply.

It was a moist and blowy afternoon, with white clouds racing across a ceiling of grey. Not many people were about, a few fathers with children and dogs racing ahead of the wind, and the dead leaves that had been trapped in the grass rattling like teeth.

After deciding which way to go June and Tony Townsend walked in silence, Tony because he had almost forgotten she was there, June because she did not know what to say. He was so mature, so tough in his jerkin and cap, she could just imagine him all muffled up in flying kit, boots and scarves and oxygen masks and lifejackets, carefree and unafraid, with a row of little swastikas painted on his aeroplane to show how many he had shot down, like in that Kenneth More film. She had recalled as much of the film as she could in bed last night, and as she walked beside him now she tried to remember the tune of the march they played on Battle of Britain Sunday, so that her steps should keep in time to it, but it eluded her. This is me, she thought, walking on Christmas Day with a hero, a man who has shot people and had love affairs and never known when tomorrow's day will dawn . . . And Mum humiliating me by clucking round as if I was a baby of two years old!

'Had a good Christmas?' he asked idly.

'Yes, thank you.' One could hardly say No, it has all been spoilt until this walk . . .

'Lots of loot?'

'Yes, thank you,' she repeated, more stiffly this time, for that was a question you asked a child. He glanced at her from beneath the peak of his cap and smiled.

'Lots of parties?'

'Well – no, none really. We don't know anyone, you see.'

'No school chums?'

'No. I don't like any of them. They're not like they were at my old school. I had masses of friends there.' Her eyes suddenly stung and through the tear-sparkle it was as though she saw the sparkle of the huge Christmas tree always set up in the Assembly Hall, and all of them standing round by candlelight, singing 'Holy night' . . . 'I expect you go to lots of parties in London, don't you?'

'Well, we whoop it up now and then, you know. New Year's Eve's the night, actually, pretty dead till then, everyone gone home to Mum.'

'Where do you live?' she asked shyly.

'Where do I live?' He laughed, remembering the oilcloth stairs, the landing windows that never opened, his room with the divan under a rug coverlet, the corner curtain concealing the double gas ring, the basin, the shelf of groceries. 'I live in Pevensey Terrace, Bayswater, in a furnished room. My name's on a little card by the bell, with about a dozen others.'

'Is it nice?'

'It's convenient and there's a pillar box just outside, a pub round the corner. I can walk to business if I have to.'

'Are you at the Air Ministry?'

He laughed again. 'God, no!'

'Where, then?'

'Guess. I'll give you twenty questions.'

She blushed. 'I couldn't possibly.'

'Go on. Have a go, Joe.'

'A travel agency?' He shook his head. 'Cars? Advertisements?'

'Nothing so glamorous.'

'I give up then.'

'I'm at Fletcher's – you know, the super department store, a household word.'

'A shop!'

'You could call it that. Why so amazed?'

'We've got a shop too.'

'You have?'

'Yes. We had a lovely one in Havenport, where we lived, all greeting cards and china animals and dainty things, you know? But now it's horrible.'

'How so?'

'Oh . . .' She hung her head, pushing her hands into her pockets. 'It's just newspapers and cigarettes and trashy magazines. It's right down in the slums. I've only been there once, it was horrible, I wouldn't go again. I don't tell anyone about it.'

'What's horrible about a shop?'

'Oh, not one like Fletcher's or the one Mum and me had in Havenport. I mean, Fletcher's is known all over the world, isn't it? You must meet all different sorts of people and sell such lovely goods and everything. And being a head and everything . . .'

'I'm . . .' but he did not continue.

'It's absolutely different – our beastly little slummy place and Fletcher's. I mean, it's simply a difference in degree so great as to be one of kind, you know?' Miss Chatham had once used that phrase about the stories of H.G. Wells and horror comics, and June was pleased to find so good a use for it.

He looked at her, smiling beneath his handlebars. 'Still, let's face it, a shop's a shop. They both sell things.'

'Oh yes. It's a bond between us.' As soon as she said it she could have killed herself, the blood colouring her face and neck, sweat breaking out in the palms of hands she clenched deep in her pockets. She was so embarrassed that she reeled slightly, stumbling away from him over the grass verge to the path which led them to the cliff's edge. An asphalt crescent lay between them and the gorge below, and they crossed it in silence and looked out over the wire netting to the bushy cleft and the tiny cars creeping and the Meccano grace of the bridge, grey in the grey light. The wind beat at them, whipping the hair from under June's woollen cap and across her eyes. She brushed it back, holding it in place with both hands over her ears, looking at him covertly. He stood gripping the top of the fence, staring up and out rather than down. The height gave him a queer feeling; not like being up in a kite but a glimpse, a nostalgia for the air which, as he was earthbound, was almost unbearable. The aircraft had always been solid around and beneath him, he had never had any sense of being insecure, only of severance from something that clogged, that anchored him against his aspirations, of being enclosed in a pure small world of absolute . . . what? No freedom, for the crew were bound by rigid interdependence, their speech, actions, future existence itself strictly subject to events they could not control. Never perhaps at any other time did they have so little individual choice as when rising from the earth to drive across the sky and drop their bombs and turn homeward again, machines drumming along lines ruled on charts in underground Operations Rooms, all liberty suspended. The wild adventurous early days of the war were over by the time he was old enough to get into it; it had been a milk run for him and his fellows, a suburban train with bombs instead of briefcases. But death had paced them just the same, they had grown from the legend and carried it on, and it had been freedom. It had been free and gay and clean – God, the cleanliness of life then! The beers, the popsies, the parties that in furnished rooms in Bayswater were shabby subterfuges, they were beautiful, part of the bravery of living. Drunk, hung over, shagged out, still you were inviolate in the purity of your calling, the male world of war. No emotions save fear, joy and discipline; no responsibilities save each man for the other; no decisions save possibly between dying or living. And everyone building you up into a legend, a legend that would never fade. Only the men of whom it was made up had faded.

Christ, the cleanliness, the freedom, steady up there, each doing his appointed job! The peace, the space – the space going on and on, no end, is that where they were now, swanning about, Frothy and Polsky and the others? Free, clean, gallant for ever, absolved from the need to go on being men to be proud of, they shall not grow old as we who are left and all that cock, but Christ, it was true, it was true . . .!

'Don't you fly anymore?' she asked shyly.

'What? No.' He turned his head, smiling automatically, coming back to the ground they stood on. 'No, I don't fly anymore. Strictly a penguin now.'

'Penguin?'

'Ground type, earthbound. Too old now, anyway.' He took his hands from the fence and thrust them into the pockets of his windcheater. They turned from the chasm and began to walk homewards before the wind.

'Couldn't you have stayed in the RAF?'

'What? Oh, possibly. I don't know. All we thought of was being demobbed, the form was that only absolute clots stayed on in the Service.'

'Couldn't you have been a test pilot at one of the factories?'

'I told you, I wasn't a pilot. No, that wouldn't have done. I didn't want to get bogged down at home again.'

'I want to get away from home.' Her voice was wistful.

'Most people do,' he said idly.

'Do they? Honestly? Home's so awful, and school and being treated like a two-year-old child.'

'You'd better come up to London, get a job.'

She sighed extravagantly. 'Ooh, I wish I could! You'll laugh, but I wanted to be an actress once.'

'Did you?'

'Yes. You don't think it's silly?'

'Why should it be?' He was not really listening.

'My grandmother and great-grandmothers were on the stage. They were singers. So it's in my blood, isn't it? I was Sebastian in *Twelfth Night* at my old school and the paper gave my name. They gave a whole list and I was the second one they printed. But I don't know,' her voice dropped again, 'I've gone off it now. They don't bother with drama much at this crummy school and anyway Sandra says everyone's being models now.'

'Who's Sandra?'

'A girl at my school. She's awful, but she's terribly bright. Not school bright, she doesn't bother with all that stuff, but about, you know, life and that.'

'Ah, life!' he said. 'You want to get out and see life some time, live it up, live for the day – like I do!' He laughed, full of contempt for the self to which he had dwindled, but she gazed at him with large eyes.

'Do you really? Do you know lots of models?'

'Of course. I eat 'em for breakfast!' He caught her serious gaze and said abruptly, 'I'm shooting a line, poppet. Pay no attention.'

'I bet you do, though – in Fletcher's and all. Is it hard? Could I be a model?'

'You'd have to leave school first and come to London and learn all about life. Your parents wouldn't like that.'

'Oh, parents! They want me to stay at school and take A-Levels and all that rubbish. He's always on at me to make something of myself, be a librarian or something, but it has to be something *he* wants, they don't pay attention to what I want, as though I was still a child . . .'

'Parents are like that.'

'Well, I'm not going to. I'm going to make up my own mind.'

'You do that thing.'

A wave of boredom seized him, at this babbling child and at his mother waiting at home, stitching her tapestry before the television, tea, scones, his favourite pudding for supper, and tomorrow, the silent wastes of Boxing Day. . . . There were trains back to London and its depopulated streets; but he knew he could not take an earlier one than, year after year, was ritual.

They had left the Downs and now turned into Hellebore Road out of the wind, walking in silence, each absorbed in rebellion. They halted at her gate.

'Well, here we are,' he said.

Her candour left her, she was an awkward child again, fiddling with the latch. 'Well, thanks very much, Mr Townsend.'

'My friends call me Tony.'

'Do they?' She flushed, pink as coconut icing, he thought, seeing her suddenly. Fresh from the wind, her skin would feel as cool as a sherbet ice. Fresh and clean, clean . . .

'In the Raff I was Trigger.'

'Trigger? That's funny.' But her eyes were round, imagining heroism.

'Yes.' He laughed, remembering. In his golden youth, clear-skinned, eyes blue as the uniform which bore the sacred insignia of his destiny, vigorous and free from school and subservience to his parents, blood, muscle and semen taut in a body which was never handsome but was beautiful because of its youth, one heroic leave they had nicknamed him Trigger-happy, quick on the draw, and the name had stuck. He had made it stick, boastfully. Trigger Townsend, with his horned moustache and his inexhaustible loin proud not to be mortal . . .

'Trigger Townsend,' she said solemnly. 'That's lovely.'

'It's a long time ago. Well – be seeing you.'

'Yes. Thank you very much.'

'Thanks for coming.' He raised his hand in half salute, the way he always did, and turned into his own garden.

June opened the front door carefully, hoping no one would hear her return. She wanted to go upstairs to her room without interruption and there relive the afternoon, sorting it out into shape. But as she reached the stairs the living room door opened and her father came out, a magazine in his hand.

'That you, Junie?'

'Yes.'

'Did you have a nice time?'

'Yes.' She began to go up the stairs.

'Just had a walk round, eh?'

'Yes.'

'I'll put the kettle on, you'll relish your tea.' She did not answer any more but went up the stairs. He called after her, 'Don't be more than five minutes, dear, there's crumpets.'

She was a long time in her room, brushing her hair slowly, choosing what shoes to change into, washing her hands dreamily and massaging them with hand lotion, until her mother came to the foot of the stairs and called, 'June! Your tea's spoiling.' She loitered a few more minutes, then descended. The room seemed hot to her air-freshened cheeks and her parents looked stuffy, one on either side of the fireplace, he in the new slippers Mum had given him, Mum in her old spread house-shoes. Mum had the trolley beside her with the tea things on it, currant bread and butter, biscuits and a big pink and white cake with paper holly stuck round it and a papier-mâché robin, and crumpets on a covered plate on the hearth. Her father sat holding his cup and saucer close up under his chin, his thin hair ruffled, a *Reader's Digest* open on the small table by his chair. Behind him the tree, overdecked in tinsel and crackers, loomed like a clown's hat.

She sat down far from them, sprawling her legs.

'Here, dear.' Her mother handed the crumpets. 'Take a plate, you'll drop butter on everything.' She did so, lolling back again in the chair. 'Did you have a nice walk?'

'Mm.'

'Where did you go?'

Butter ran down her chin and she tried to lick it up.

'Answer your mother when she speaks to you, dear.'

She mumbled deliberately, 'My mouth's full.'

'We ought to have come with you. Done us more good than staying indoors over the fire. Here's your tea.'

'You needed a rest after cooking that smashing dinner, Ett.'

She smiled at him. 'It wasn't much work, not with all the veg got ready yesterday. You had a little snooze, Ray.'

'I may have closed my eyes for a moment.' They laughed together. 'I'm not used to all that good food, that's what it is.'

Her mother turned to her. 'Was it cold out, dear? It looked ever so blowy, as though it might rain.'

'We ought to have snow at Christmas time. I seem to remember when I was a kid snow on Christmas Day.'

'I don't know when, dear. Bar that awful winter after the war, I can't remember more than a scatter of snow for years.'

'That's a thing you never get down under – snow. Used to make me real homesick just to think of it. Is there another cup, dear?' He passed his cup and she filled it.

'Junie? I'll cut the cake.' She lifted the plate onto her lap and began to cut it awkwardly. The icing broke and bits went into her lap and onto the floor. Raymond put down his cup and sank to his knees on the hearthrug in front of her, steadying the plate. They were both laughing.

'Mr Townsend was in the RAF,' June said.

'I know. Oh, hold it steady, Ray, you're no help at all!'

'He was a rear-gunner.'

'Tailarse Charlie – if you'll pardon my French.'

'Raymond!'

'He went bombing all over Germany and once he was shot down in France and escaped in a rubber dinghy.'

'That was clever of him, wasn't it?' Her father glanced at her, then back at the cake.

'He was a pilot-officer.'

'Still wears his wings, I notice.' He got back into his chair, brushing the knees of his trousers.

'His wings?'

'On his face.'

June sat up so suddenly the tea slopped into the saucer. 'At least he's the right to!'

'Everyone who was in the RAF has the right to,' her father said carefully.

'Not *penguins*!'

'We all wore the badge on our caps.'

'But he *flew*! He went straight from school and flew.'

'He was lucky to be so fit,' her mother interposed.

'He seems to have been telling you the story of his life,' said her father. He took a sip of tea, not looking at her.

'At least it's worth hearing.'

There was a moment's silence, then her mother said, 'I'm sure it is, dear. He seems a nice man. Now let's get tea cleared away and we can settle down to a nice game of something. I don't expect any of us are going to feel like much supper. Let's try out that Scrabble Auntie Norah sent us. Where is it, did you leave it in the lounge?' She began to tidy the tea things onto the trolley, drawing them both into her activity.

Later, when they all sat round the table under the central light, spelling out words with tiny squares of wood, June looked at her father. She looked so steadily that he raised his eyes and looked back at her. As her mother pondered and sighed over her rack of letters, June and her father stared for a moment into each other's minds. He looked away first; and with a stab of joy June knew he was afraid of her and that she hated him.

FOUR

ALMOST FROM THAT MOMENT she felt better. It was like having had a general jaw ache and then the dentist told you which tooth it was. Now each day she could admit and identify; could look frankly rather than with veiled eyes; could lie in bed at night between the pink and white striped sheets and think, I hate his voice or I hate his feeble jokes or even, with exaltation, I hate him because he and Mum laugh together – but this was a dangerous hate, often bringing tears. She would lie sobbing into her pillow, quietly yet hoping perhaps to be overheard; and then her nose would get so stuffed she would have to sit up, and the abandonment of warmth and pillow would anger her so that her sobs would end and she could lie down presently secure, almost happy, in hate again. Then she would think of Tony, enacting in her imagination scenes in which he confessed to her that he hated his mother, or that he produced undeniable proof that June was not in fact the child of her father at all but – who? Not Tony himself, for her fantasies needed him for more than mere substitute father, although that had sprung from her first sight of him coming out of their gate. Perhaps, then, of one of his comrades, double VC and bar, Legion of Honour, moustachioed as Tony was but higher in rank, an Air Vice Marshall who went to his death smiling – better jump out, chaps, we're losing height, I'll keep her steady till you've gone and then try to miss that school down there full of pregnant mothers, tell Marie-Celeste I loved her, not knowing that even at that moment Marie-Celeste lay in agony on the hospital bed, the bombs falling, Nurse, Nurse, something has happened to my lover, I know it *here*, striking her breast with her clenched fist. Nonsense, cherie, you imagine things, be patient only a little moment and your baby will be born, and in that instant the crash, the flames, the crew safe, the school avoided, and a tired mother looks down at the fatherless baby in her arms . . .

Often June was asleep before she reached this point; and in any case, she did not really believe it for she could not deny that Mum was her own mother and who, then, would be Marie-Celeste? But that Raymond was not her father was a fantasy which took hold and grew in the darkness until, wilfully, she half believed it.

For it was feasible. They were not alike. Already she was almost as tall as he was and although they were both fair, she had not blue eyes as he had. Noses were noses and her chin was her mother's, and it was not true that the whole top of her face, temples, eye-sockets, and the way her hair grew, resembled him in the wedding picture put away in Mum's japanned box. Between herself and this middle-aged, baldish little man she could see no similarity; and more significant than all this was the fact that she hated him. Yes, hated him, hated him! You couldn't hate your parents, could you? You might be exasperated, frustrated, scornful, resentful, but you still loved them, didn't you, because that was natural, just as they loved you no matter what. That he loved her there was no doubt; he had shown it in a hundred ways since his arrival, wooing her, sucking up to her, cringing to her. He longed for her to love him back, and because he needed it so much he feared her, was afraid of losing what she, looking at him with hard eyes, knew she would never give him.

Over the years, through his letters, his love had come to her in the stilted words of someone who did not exist, since she could not remember ever having seen him. She had accepted the words as she would accept the words of a story and the figure of 'Daddy' who wrote them as an image of that male whom all children seem to possess. As his return came nearer she had clothed that image in character, handsome, firm, understanding, a symbol of those qualities of which, even though nervous of his intrusion, she sensed she had been deprived. She had done without him for most of her life and she could do without him for the rest of it; but if he must come then, if he were acceptable, she could have accepted him.

So she told herself, full of self-pity. Perhaps it was true. They would never know, for he was not acceptable.

Little, bald, old, timid, with a false gloss of authority on him that dimmed at a silence, master of a house which had never been his, third leg in a structure that needed only two, interloper for whose sake Havenport with its sunny villas, the shop full of pretty things, Jervis's, school friends, her established place in her own known world, had been abandoned – how could he be her father? How could he be anything? How could he be anything to Mum?

Here June's thoughts could not take form. Up to that point she could think clearly in hatred, but about her mother and this man coherence dissolved in emotion that was not sensible to scrutiny.

She could not help but see how her mother had bloomed since his return. Outwardly she seemed the same as ever but she was irradiated from within by a light which June had never seen before and which she sensed she herself could never have lit. She hated it, she feared it as an animal fears fire, not understanding what it is but recognising its power. Her mother glowed with something her child had never been able to give her, and it came from him. When they talked together, even about ordinary things, sometimes something would happen; their words would go on, words anyone could listen to, in which they included June, and yet they were speaking only to each other. Under the words they were saying something else, something private to one another. When they looked at each other sometimes it was as if everyone else were outside, in the darkness; when they laughed together it was at things no one else would smile at, things hidden from everyone but themselves. They seldom touched each other; there was a special care in the way they kept themselves apart in front of her. Nothing they ever did or said could shock her or be out of place, but their care was more wounding than their negligence might have been, for behind it were the hidden impulses, the gestures held back, and when sometimes their hands touched or a kiss was exchanged at meeting or parting, it was so heavy with understanding that it affronted more than a gross movement might have done. And always, when it was made, he or her mother would draw June into it, kiss her too, put an arm round her too, drawing her into that closed circle into which there was no entrance save for the two of them.

When June came home from school in the afternoon the shop was shut for early closing, there was always a great welcome; yet she knew they had been perfectly content before she came. She sensed that in some way her existence merely intensified what was between them. Without her they would have been different people, less complete; but when she was with them, she was not often necessary. Before he came she had been the sole focus of her mother's love. Now that love had grown another head. Mum loved her no less but she loved him as well.

She went into their bedroom as little as possible (at least there was not the obscenity of a double bed) and she spent more and more time in her own room. At first she made the excuse of homework or a radio programme chosen deliberately because she knew it would not appeal to them; but after her admission of hatred she made no explanation, giving them simply a blank face and silence. It was cold up there in the winter, even with the gas fire on; both of them talked to her about fuel bills and when sometimes they insisted she join them in the living room she did so sullenly, sitting sprawled in a chair, refusing to read or join in anything, until even her mother's temper began to rise and June could see (grinning within herself) that he was quite baffled. Somehow he ought to have been able to make her behave better. She despised him because he did not even try, held back by his own and his wife's fear that if he did June would not love him. That was a laugh!

In her own room she turned the radio on loud, and she began to nag for a record-player, for Sandra had one and although June could keep up with the brag and chat about pop music by listening to it on the radio, it was not the same as having it on records, spending one's pocket-money on the discs which moaned or beat incessantly in Sandra's room whenever June had been there. Discs were a prestige symbol among Sandra's set. Already June suffered by not having television, but it was possible to mask this deprivation by affecting scorn at the quality of the programmes. Nevertheless it was humiliating not to be able to discuss the latest *Maverick* at break on Monday mornings or know what *Candid Camera* had been up to. Why was he too mean to buy a telly? Why should Sandra have everything?

Except, of course, looks. She was big and fat and pasty and her hair got greasy in a day. In her school uniform, her thick legs in ankle socks, her beret on the back of her head and her hair divided into two plaits closed by elastic bands, she looked a complete St Trinian's type, scuffing along, whispering to her friends, peering out of the corner of her eyes in case she missed anything, a half-eaten bar of something sweet seeming always in her hand. The teachers were most of them rather sorry for Sandra, for she gave an impression of plodding mediocrity which was sometimes rewarded more highly than good work would have been. 'Tries hard' was a phrase often appearing on her reports; only one or two of the staff (and all her friends) knew how hard Sandra tried to achieve just what she had: the indulgence of her mistresses to do just enough work to leave her in idleness most of the time.

But at home Sandra was transformed. Her hair was shaken loose and hung like seaweed over her shoulders and much of her face. Hairy jumpers down to her thighs almost concealed her thickness, and tight slacks hid her legs. When she opened the front door to June the evening before school started again, June saw immediately that her lips, fingernails and toenails (for her feet were bare and looked rather cold) were all painted a mauvish opalescence which, with her black jumper and the strands of hair from between which she peered, gave an impression of striking decomposition. A large silver label engraved WHISKY, slung from a chain round her neck, lay between breasts which, liberated from a gym tunic and naked beneath the wool, seemed to radiate magnetism.

'Hi,' said Sandra. 'Long time no see. Come into the pad.'

Sandra's parents lived in the bottom half of an early Victorian terrace house and the front basement room had been turned into what Sandra's father called the Den. It was now full of the usual rhythm of pop music and the smell of cigarettes, and half a dozen young people were sitting around with mugs in their hands. Sandra had said it was a party and June had dressed accordingly; not as her mother would have liked, for June did not expect Sandra's party to be quite like those at Havenport, but in what she had thought would be suitable: dark nylons and her long-toed pumps and a blue dress that made her waist look about twelve inches round. But now she saw with horror that three of the other girls were wearing slacks and jumpers like the boys and that the fourth girl wore a skirt so vestigial as to hardly count. Her hair was wound into not so much a beehive as a wasps-nest and her eyes were rimmed with blue. June had never seen her before, but two of the others were from Sandra's set, although she hardly knew them.

She hardly knew anybody at school. She refused to, because it was not Jervis's. Jervis's was a golden dream that had forsaken her; all that the uprooting had left her of it was a Christmas card from Joyce, who had not been her favourite friend, and a calendar with warm words written on it from Miss Chatham. Jervis's had forgotten her but wilfully she would not forget Jervis's, contemptuous of everything in the new bright buildings of St Maud's, with its bigger, more urban classes. The buildings were ugly, the staff mad, the girls common. She had closed herself against it all and therefore had herself been excluded. The teachers watched her with reserve; they offered no incentives or rewards, for she did nothing to merit them. It was GCE this summer and she did not care. None of Sandra's set really cared, and because Sandra was so awful, so everything her friends at Jervis's had not been and that her mother would be shocked by, June had fallen into a kind of friendship with her.

Sandra did not introduce anyone but merely made a vague gesture and said, 'This is June.' The girls stared, the boys drew in their legs as well as they could in their tight trousers, and June wished she were dead. When Sandra put a mug into her hand she took a gulp of its contents and nearly brought it all back again, for it was beer. She sat down on a hard chair and wondered how soon she could leave.

They listened in silence to the record, the wasps-nest girl jigged her shoulders in a knowledgeable way. Sandra had sat down by the thinnest boy, who wore a small Christ-like beard round the rim of his jaw, and was fondling his hand. The other boy stared at his shoes, smoking in sharp puffs, and June saw with astonishment that he was the assistant who served at the cold meats counter at the grocer's in the main street. He wore his hair differently there. When the record ended Sandra got up and put on another one, the other girls began to talk to each other and the front door bell rang. It was two more boys.

With their arrival things livened up a little. One was the boyfriend of the wasps-nest and they began to dance motionlessly together in a corner. The other produced a carton of potato crisps and a small bottle which he said contained whisky. He was absolutely mad and insisted in pouring some into everyone's beer, and then he took Sandra's tennis racquet and pretended it was a guitar and sang to the record in various styles, Cliff and Helen and Adam, and then he stuffed handkerchiefs under his jumper and pretended to be Shirley Bassey. He was really very clever. One of the other girls from school – Jeanette, June thought her name was – had persuaded the cold meats youth to dance and they were locked in catalepsy; but they looked bored, which wasps-nest and her partner did not. Sandra fetched a plate of cocktail biscuits and offered them round. 'Where are your parents?' June whispered.

'Out,' said Sandra. 'They always go out when I have a rave. Don't yours?' and she returned to the bearded boy, laying her head on his shoulder. He was talking to the other girl and paid no attention.

The lively boy came up to June and squatted on his haunches in front of her.

'Hi,' he said. 'Who are you?' He had clever eyes close on either side of a big nose and a mouth wide enough to devour or laugh.

'June. June Baxter.'

'Phil Barber. I'm a riot, aren't I?'

'Yes.' She could not help smiling.

'Have some plonk.' He held out the small bottle.

'No, thank you.'

'Go on, don't be a mouldy fig.'

She allowed him to pour some into her flat beer. He sat down and took a deft swig direct from the bottle.

'I could be on telly.'

'Yes.'

'I don't rehearse my stuff, you know. It's all spontaneous. I can do anyone. Play me a record and I can do it.'

'Can you do classical? Harry Secombe and that?'

'I can do anyone. I could be professional.'

'Aren't you?'

'No. Apprentice machine-toolmaker. This is only a hobby. What do you do?'

'I'm still at school.'

'You're what?' His incredulity shamed her. 'I'm still at school. So's Sandra.'

'Yeah, but she don't act like it.'

He took another small swig from the bottle, looking at her over the top. Then in one movement he got to his feet and left her.

Surprise, humiliation, but mostly sheer rage overwhelmed her. To be so *rude*! They none of them had any *manners*! They were simply *rabble* who didn't know any better! Through the hurt and sense of inadequacy she drew comfort from remembering Tony Townsend and their worldly, civil conversations together. Only older men knew how to behave, these were simply ignorant children. With elaborate but sincere disdain June picked up a copy of *She* from a pile on the floor beside her and began to look at it.

Time passed so slowly that there seemed no reason why the evening should ever end. The air got smokier, the records continued to beat out their rhythms until they became as unnoticeable as the beat of one's own heart. The clever boy was occupying himself by trying to cut his friend out with the wasps-nest, and two of the girls were dancing together for want of a partner. After a little while the remaining one slid over to June.

'She ought to have more boys,' she said, 'it's not fair not having enough boys.'

June shrugged. 'It's all the same to me.'

The girl looked at her suspiciously. 'Don't you like boys?'

'Not much. They're childish.'

'I don't think Ceddy's childish. I think he's dreamy.' She looked across at the bearded one on whose lap Sandra had now managed to sit. 'Sandra's mad about him.'

'Sandra's crappy.'

The girl looked thoughtful. 'She's awfully sexy though.'

'She's a warthog.'

The girl was shocked for a moment, then began to giggle. 'Are you at her school?'

'Yes. So are those other two.'

'I'm at the Comprehensive. I wanted to leave but Dad said I must stay till I'm seventeen. He's stuck on education. Ceddy's taking A-Level Science. He's terribly intellectual. He writes slogans on walls.' They looked across at Ceddy, of whom little could be seen beneath Sandra save his head and the lower half of his thin legs. Sandra was nibbling at his ear, and with a sudden rush of blood June saw that his hand was underneath her jersey. She shut her eyes quickly, turning her head away, the music and her thundering pulses roaring in her ears; and when he opened her eyes again she thought for an instant's panic that she had been struck blind, for the room was dark. Then she saw the clever boy moving away from the light switch, back to the girl with whom he had been dancing. Only a table-lamp remained, in a warped orange shade. Wasps-nest and her original partner were leaning against each other in a corner.

The girl beside June whispered, 'She's quite old – twenty or twenty-one. She only comes here because Nigel does. Sandra says they have sex together.'

June could say nothing. Her mouth was dry, her throat hurt, and the palms of her hands were sweating so much she wiped them unknowingly on her skirt. She was terrified; terrified and aroused.

The girl whispered, 'Sandra says she has sex with Ceddy too but I don't believe it. I think it's just talk. I don't think Ceddy really likes Sandra much.' The girl looked out through the murk at the scarcely revolving couples, the immobile pair in the corner, the sprawl of limbs in the chair, her face peaked and sad despite its eye-black and cascading hair. 'It's not fair not to have enough boys,' she repeated. 'I read in the paper there were more boys than girls now but it never seems like it. Do you know a lot of boys?'

June shook her head. Waves of repugnance and longing beat about her, only in silence could she retain her identity. She dared not look in the corner, dared not look at the chair, her eyes sliding again and again to the great mound of Sandra's buttocks, the bony peak of Ceddy's knees, refusing to check the whereabouts of the hand, admit the bare breast beneath the wool, admit that front to front in the corner something unspeakable grew in silence, while in her own body throbbed pulses that she had hardly known existed.

The front doorbell rang.

Only June and the girl heard it, but they all heard Sandra's mother calling down the stairs, 'Sandy! Sandy dear!'

'Oh crap!' said Sandra and got quickly off Ceddy, shaking the hair out of her eyes. She went and opened the door. 'What?'

'It's Mr Baxter, Sandy. He's called for June.'

June jumped to her feet. The room seemed to have grown eyes, all turned on her amazedly in faces pale and expressionless as balloons floating in the gloom on the waves of rhythm and heat.

'Did you tell him to come?' Sandra hissed accusingly.

'Of course not. I'm not a child.'

'You'd better blow then. We don't want *them* down here.'

'You said they were out.'

'They've come back, stupid. Now I suppose the crowd'll break up. You are a creep, June.'

'It's not my fault. I didn't tell him to.'

'Oh well. See you . . .' She turned away, switching on the main light. Under its sudden brightness the children looked thin and sad, getting up and gathering in a group for the first time round the record-player. When Sandra's mother called down, 'Would you all like some frankfurters?' they looked at each other and nodded, suddenly alive.

As soon as the door shut behind them June said furiously, 'Why did you come?'

'Why? You can't walk home by yourself at this time of night.'

'It's only half-past ten!'

'It'll be eleven before we're home.'

'You've humiliated me!'

'Humiliated you?' He stared at her as they walked along the pavement. She could hear the smile in his voice. 'Don't talk soft, dear.'

'It isn't. None of the others are fetched.'

'Then they've got parents who don't care so much.'

'Oh!' She stamped her foot as she walked. 'No one ever goes home at half-past ten. It goes on all night.'

'Not with my girl it doesn't.'

'Your girl! Your girl! I'm not a baby.'

'You're our baby, Junie.'

Hopelessness engulfed her. The complacence of his tone, with its undercurrent of yearning, sickened her. God knew she was glad to be rescued but not by him, not like this. How they would all be laughing!

She thrust her hands into her pockets and drew away from him. Soon they would be in the main street where they would have to keep fairly close together, but here between the already sleeping terraces she could have the illusion of repudiation.

'You friend's mum and dad seemed good sorts. We had a bit of a chat in the hall while you were getting your coat. Was it a nice crowd? Did you have a good time?' She did not answer. 'You were dancing, I expect. I could hear the gramophone. We used to have the piano when I was a kid. And not many parties either, only Christmas and maybe a birthday, just for the House group. I was in an orphanage, you know.'

She had not known and the news gave her a pang of pity and curiosity so that she glanced at him, anger forgotten for an instant but returning when she saw his eyes begging her. She swung away from him again, but they had reached a crossing and he took her elbow to halt her while a bus went by. She pulled free as they crossed.

'They did their best,' he continued. 'The House mother used to ice a cake and make all the other kiddies sing Happy Birthday. But a lot of us didn't even know when our birthdays were, so it was a bit of a farce really.'

Shut up, she wanted to say, nothing about you interests me, why should you think it does? What do I care who you are, you're nothing to do with me, nothing to do with me . . . Her footsteps marched to the declaration while her thoughts went back to the basement, Ceddy's hand, the rigid boy in the corner.

It was strange to see Sandra next morning, fat and sallow in school uniform, and all through Assembly and later in class June found herself watching her out of the corner of her eye, trying to see in the lumpy schoolgirl the sex elephant of the night before.

She caught a glimpse of Jeanette too but they were in different sets and did not meet.

That morning as she dressed June had stared at herself in the mirror, envisaging her eyes blue rimmed, her lips mauve, brushing her hair forward to obscure her face; but even when she raked it with her fingers it was too fine to fall into the proper strands. She seized it in both hands and dragged it back, piling and twisting it on the top of her skull in an attempted wasps-nest. It was too short for this but she stared, for it was as if a curtain had lifted and revealed a girl where before had been a child. The delicate neck soared from the shoulders, the piled hair was like a headdress, the lines of jaw and temple and ear showed clearly. She gazed entranced, seeing like phantoms behind this revelation the long legs, long backs, long hands of Ceddy, Nigel, clever Phil, the bold moustache of Tony Townsend. She gazed, thinking of perfume and mink, huge mohair jumpers, winter sports, moonlit nights beneath the tropical stars . . .

'June!' called her mother from downstairs, 'you're going to be ever so late, dear. Do hurry up now.'

She dropped the hair back, obliterating the vision. Our Baby! My girl! She turned from the mirror in disgust.

And now at school here they all were, hidden in juvenility again, princesses disguised as peasants. It made her feel better that they were all schoolgirls once more, but still she could not forgive Sandra the fawning sprawl of her lumpy body or what Jeanette had whispered about having sex; nor could she forget that from that frightening anteroom of the future she had been whisked like a bundle of laundry by a man who talked about gramophones and thought that parties – 'raves' – ended at ten-thirty, and that because he had been an orphan she had to be wrapped in cotton wool. If she had stayed, Ceddy might have reared up from beneath Sandra and laid his hands – his hands! – on June's waist and talked to her about the Bomb. Phil might have invited her to dance (or was that as old fashioned now as being fetched?). The boy in the corner might have become sickened with wasps-nest and realised that

June, with her fastidious, patrician grace – patrician grace, that was it – was the girl for him. And smilingly, coolly, she would have held herself aloof, saying, 'Do you mind! I only like mature men.' And all the girls would have gone mad with jealousy.

She kept away from Sandra, only her eyes returning to her again, but at break Sandra sought her out.

'You were crappy last night.'

'I wasn't. You were.'

'I wasn't. You just sat there.'

'What was I supposed to do? I didn't know anyone.'

'Pooh, who cares about that? It's not a church social. And breaking it up like that.'

'I didn't.'

'You did. Once they knew Mum and Dad were in it was dead, just dead.'

'They couldn't have been having much fun, then.'

'They were! It was you, sitting there like a dummy that spoilt it, and being called for by your old man. I could have died.'

The colour was high in June's face. 'I told him to come and fetch me because I knew I'd be bored silly by you and your crappy friends.'

'They're not crappy!' Sandra's eyes seemed to get smaller than ever with rage.

'A lot of silly kids trying to be beatniks. I haven't time for that sort of thing, my boyfriend's mature.'

'Yeah – mature like nothing!'

'Mature like thirty. He's thirty years old.' She was breathless with rage and recklessness, triumphant at the gleam of respect in Sandra's eyes, extinguished by malice as she sneered, 'Yeah, and I bet he's too old for sex.'

For a moment June thought she would hit her, but instead tears blurred her sight and she swung away, pushing through the small group of girls who had begun to loiter near them, attracted by the raised voices and hostility. One or two asked, 'What's the matter? What's happening?' but she walked away without answering, into the locker room and through to the lavatories beyond. They were all common, common and hateful like him and his horrible shop that she told no one about, selling to common people in a common part of the town.

She bowed her head against the wall of the cabinet, letting the tears run down her face but making no noise lest some girl enter outside and hear her. Where was Havenport, sunny and fresh, where Mum's pretty shop with the china animals and the anniversary cards, where the familiar buildings of Jervis's, as known as her own home, and Miss Chatham's firm bosom and her voice making announcements? And her friends, her social life, going out to tea, playing tennis, parties in pretty frocks and the furniture all pushed back in the lounge, the radiogram, the prize for the best hat made out of newspaper, and brothers in blue suits or blazers from the grammar school? Where the dignity, the comfort of belonging? All, all gone because he had come home.

Gradually, as term went on, walking to school and back, doing homework, up in her room with the wireless on, sitting at table not looking at him, the fantasy that he was not her father strengthened. At first she had known it to be fantasy like all the rest of the daydreams with which she passed the time, but it took hold. She wanted it to be true, she encouraged herself to believe it was true. He was utterly unlike what June's father must be – and what real father would have left his wife and child for all those years? Surely he must be a stranger, meeting Mum somewhere (had she not always spent a day each month in Southampton, buying stock, she had said), getting some hold on her and marrying her, foisting himself on them?

But the letters that came so regularly from Australia? Never mind about them; how did she know they were from Australia anyway, they had always come enclosed in ones for Mum, they could have been from anywhere.

Why should he want to go to all that trouble, pretending to write and all? Because Mum was good and kind and he – he had this hold over her (her heart thudded as she refused to acknowledge what she could see was between them). And because he was an orphan and wanted a family.

She took to putting questions to her mother casually, one here, one there. 'Mum, where did you and Daddy meet?'

'In a teashop. He borrowed my paper.'

'How old was I?'

'Brush your brains out, Junie! You weren't born.' Or, 'How old was I when Daddy first saw me?' Mrs Baxter hesitated before answering and June knew she had her. With a straight face Mrs Baxter said, squeezing the washing-up mop, 'Exactly three hours and twenty-five minutes, dear.'

Of course, there was all that Auntie Norah had told her, about the wedding and Great Grandma being so old and him going to Australia and then getting ill; but that could have been her real father and this one a stranger. The answers Mum gave her could be about her real father, for Mum always told the truth; but this man's origins could be concealed, the truth about him evaded because never directly questioned. Mum could speak about June's real father and assume June identified him as this man, this second man. The dual lie and truth would never be revealed save by direct demand and proof.

If only she could find proof! If she could prove he was not really her father she might even be able to stop hating him. He would be nothing to her and she could dismiss him from her thoughts; healing indifference could take the place of hatred and he would be no more than a lodger, an aberration of her mother's. If only it could be proved . . .

Clearly, calmly, one morning during French, she remembered the deed box.

It was kept in the bottom of Mum's wardrobe. There were a dozen better places for it, especially now they lived in a house, but just as the fuse wire was always kept in with Mum's handkerchiefs, so the deed box had always been at the bottom of the wardrobe. It was locked, but the key, as June remembered it, had looked like one of those which opened suitcases; it should not be very difficult to find one that would fit. Inside the box Mum kept the things she valued, and among the photographs, locks of hair, letters tied with tape, June remembered Post Office Savings books and documents in envelopes which had held no interest for a child without need for curiosity. Among these must be proof.

She knew that she must do it. She had never in her life done anything against her mother, not even the filching of a penny from her purse, and she approached this act of treachery with a misery which made her sweat and a cruelty which kept her mind clear. She planned, and inwardly screamed; secretly collected keys from suitcases and her school briefcase with hands that sweated but were steady. She chose an afternoon when she was home early from school and her mother helping at the shop. Her tea had been left in the kitchen, bread and butter under a plate, chocolate biscuits, the kind of doughnut she particularly liked, with a note in her mother's writing saying, 'Crumpets in bin if you want. Stove only needs raking. Love.' She took two biscuits and went upstairs into her mother's room.

The deed box was in its usual place but under a row of shoes – his shoes. There were three pairs, all fairly new, with trees in them. She lifted them aside and took out the box, kneeling down on the floor with it to try the keys. Her palms were sweating so much she had to wipe them on her skirt.

The first one would not go in.

If none of them fitted, it would be a Sign. It would mean there was no proof inside, might almost mean she was in fact his daughter and she might put the idea that she was not out of her head for ever, accept him and love him and be part of a happy family. She would consider that, if none of the keys fitted.

The next one turned but did not grip. If none of them fitted she would never try with anything else, like a hairpin or a nail file or the blade of a knife . . .

even as she thought this, looking round in her mind for such implements.

The third key fitted.

The familiar souvenirs lay there neatly like a picture of her childhood: the sunny room at Havenport, the box open on Mum's knee, herself leaning against the warm thighs and breast, arm-encircled, watching Mum's fingers select the lock of Great Grandad's hair, a baby tooth, earrings that sparkled like drops of rain as she held them up to the light, the photograph of Mum's mother in *The Gondoliers*, listening to the familiar explanations (Gran always wore these earrings, that's my first tooth, dear, and see the big hole in it, not like yours; even when he was old Grandad never lost his hair) told in the familiar voice, like a spell cast for love and remembrance.

There was the bundle of letters, the Post Office books, some certificates called War Damage, a Householder's Insurance Policy, and a foolscap envelope. She took out its contents.

The wide pink and white form opened between her fingers: Certified Copy of an Entry of Birth; Second July 1947, Camden Hospital, NW; June Victoria; Girl; Raymond Cavendish Banks . . .

Banks! Her head spun, her eyes saw swirling blackness that cleared to confirm what she had seen. Name and Surname of Father, Raymond Cavendish Banks.

She was not his. Her name was Banks. She was free. Name and Maiden Surname of Mother, Esther Winifred Banks, formerly Wilson.

Banks. Banks. She was June Banks. She did not like it much, June Baxter sounded nicer. But she was free. She read it all again, carefully. Raymond Cavendish Banks. Raymond? That was *his* name. Cavendish she did not know. Lots of men are called Raymond . . . Raymond, Ray . . . She could not think of one other. But her father's name had been Banks, it was here, set out in the pink columns of her birth certificate, legal, irrevocable. She was not Baxter.

Fumbling, for her hands were cold, her head giddy, she took out the other documents. A Certificate of Marriage – Raymond Cavendish Banks, trader – Esther Winifred Wilson, spinster – St Peter's Church, NW . . . She was the child of this Banks and this Esther. This Raymond and this Esther?

There was a third paper, thick, white, folded lengthwise. Statutory Declaration by Esther Banks. She opened it. 'I Esther Winifred Banks hereby declare that as from this twelfth day of January 1950 I shall be known as Esther Winifred Baxter . . . and also for my Infant Child June Victoria . . .'

She did not understand. Mum had married a man called Raymond Banks and they had had a child who was herself. She was June Banks. When she was still a baby this Raymond Banks, her father, had gone to Australia, become ill – and died there? And in 1950 Mum had changed their name to Baxter, which was this man's. Why? When had she met him? Her father, Raymond Banks, had scarcely been gone a year, could not have died so soon, from all Mum and Auntie Norah had told her – they had told her Daddy was in Australia nearly a year before he got ill and went into a sanatorium.

Supposing it was all lies? Supposing he had gone to Australia and died at once, been murdered or killed in a train smash or something? Then how, so soon, could Mum have changed their name (not only her name but June's, her infant child, without consultation)? She could not have been untrue to Daddy when he had scarcely gone, was scarcely dead. Mum would never be untrue to anyone, not Mum . . . But if Daddy died, why change their name? If she met this Baxter (but when, how so soon as to change their name to his so quickly?) why did she not marry him? Perhaps he was married already. And if Mum changed their name to his in 1950, where had he been all the years in between? Why had he not insinuated himself little by little into their life instead of suddenly appearing so long afterwards? Why had Mum not told her Daddy was dead, how could she have hidden this Baxter from her? And if Daddy was dead, who had written his letters?

The questions whirled in her brain like birds in the sky, and against as great an immensity. Betrayal lurked behind a web of lies, for something was wrong somewhere, someone had lied. No, not someone: Mum and Auntie Norah had lied. The two rocks.

A great coldness began to creep on her.

The world slowly, silently withdrew around her, leaving her in space; that world whose warmth she had drawn on greedily, whose nourishment she had devoured without thought, which had surrounded her solely so that in her self-absorption she might disregard it, now was withdrawing from her. For the first time in her life she began to feel absolutely alone. She sat alone in a vacuum of her own making. Her body was cold, her heart, her mind. She thought, There is only Me.

Deliberately she read the Declaration through again, then folded it, replaced it in the envelope with the others. She untied the tape which held the bundle of letters and looked through them. They were all very old, notes from Mum's mother dated from provincial theatres, stiff letters from Great Grandad, scrawls signed 'Gran', nothing of interest – nothing from him. She tied the tape again and put them back, lifted the souvenirs in their worn wrappings and went quickly through the brittle photographs beneath: Grandad, herself as a baby, Mum as a baby, Auntie Norah in her

Sister's cap, the wedding. She took this one out and scrutinised it. Mum in a costume, wearing a fur cape with carnations pinned to it; and beside her, him.

She looked at it a long time. Then she put it back among the others, closed the box, locked it, replaced it in the wardrobe with the three pairs of shoes on top of it. She closed the wardrobe door, turned off the light, went into her bedroom and shut the door.

FIVE

TONY TOWNSEND CAME as usual to spend the Easter weekend with his mother. Fletcher's was open on Saturday mornings so he could not get away until the afternoon. It was better really; trains were not so crowded, and in any case two days with Mother were enough. You could fill two days with affection and leave before boredom bit through to the bone. Besides, on Good Friday there had been Jacky.

One of the ant-stream, he left the Staff entrance of the store, carrying his tartan weekend bag, and queued for a bus to Paddington. With any luck he'd have time for a beer at the station bar. The wind was cold and the sun, which pounced and retired again behind fast-moving clouds, probed through his thick fair hair to the incipient bald patch developing in secret. The springing hair, the springing bold moustache, the pink face with its short nose and gentle lips, all gave an ageless impression of youth. He jumped eagerly on the bus, dropping his case into the luggage cavity under the stairs, letting a woman precede him down the aisle. She was an elderly woman and she smiled at him, vestigial memories of brave wartime days stirring in her at the sight of his moustache, and he smiled back boyishly.

Oh Jacky – oh Jacky! There was hardly any joy in his thoughts of her, for the happiness of living was overcast by the difficulties of every aspect of her life. Not his; his life was nothing, a husk, a furnished room, a counter at Fletcher's, a pub or two, a party or two, and recently the Tallyho Club, two rooms and a bar in a street near Queensway. He had gone there with one of the chaps from the Squadron reunion, Dusty Miller, whose left hand and arm had been badly burned when his aircraft caught fire over Bremen. Jacky was the Club's cashier and hostess. People talked to Jacky not simply because she was always there but because she was sympathetic. Her pale legs wound round each other on her stool, a jacket thrown over her shoulders, the charm bracelet (on which only two charms were real gold) jingling on her grasshopper wrist, she listened, chatted, accepted a shandy, refused to cash cheques but sometimes lent a pound, excavating for it in the huge crate of a handbag she always carried, stuffed with letters and cigarette-packets and Kleenex and lord knew what besides. She had been doing this when Tony first saw her, standing on the high heels that still made her only five feet two, her platinum hair like a small chrysanthemum. Her thin hands, the charms bumbling on one wrist, delved and scrabbled in the enormous handbag as though she were a squirrel looking for a nut; and when she looked up her eyes were a squirrel's too, bright and strikingly dark beneath the whitened hair, the face peakily pretty. She was tiny, light, yet with small buttocks that curved her tight skirt and small breasts looking you straight in the eye. He knew now they were not so aggressive, released from the wired and strung suspensions.

Jacky, ah Jacky! So much a thing of artifice, brave jut, gallant paint, indomitable bleach and bag and bangles, and within it all, a muddle. Loyalty, weakness, generosity all confined within one trim female body to make an insoluble mess of her life and the life of anyone who loved her. It was her virtue that ruined her; the generosity that wanted to give, the loyalty that forbade it, so that all Tony knew of her after that Good Friday (the first time she had been able to escape and be with him alone) was that her breasts were small and sad without their buttress, that she smelt of cigarette-smoke, gin and sharp savoury sweat that intoxicated him, that probably she loved him and that there was no hope, no hope at all of her ever extricating herself from the dreary labyrinth of her relationships.

The bus reached Paddington and he got off. Of all the London stations this was the one he liked best, its steam-tainted air still seeming to smell of straw and horse piss. The brown train lay along No. 1 platform, stewards in their monkey-jackets standing at the dining-car doors. Not for me, chum, he thought. He found a seat far down the train, set his bag on it and went out again to have a ham roll and a bitter in the station bar. The big, reading soldier of the Jagger war memorial touched him with sadness as it did each time he saw it, reminding him not of death but of the intense living of wartime days strung like beads on a string which might momently break; and so, because of living, of Jacky again. She came between him and the newspaper he meant to read, between him and first the suburbs, then the fields through which the train plummeted, between him and the strangers amongst whom he sat; but not between him and sleep. He laid his head back against the prickly cushion ('Never rest your head on a railway seat, Anthony, you might catch something'), and behind closed eyes saw again her tousled head on his divan pillow, the little breasts erect above the half-abandoned underclothes, her thin hand gripping his wrist in denial. And the feel of her afterwards curled up on his lap, her tensions spent in tears that were warm in the hollow of his neck but his turned back upon themselves. Ballache and heartache, he thought wryly, shifting with closed eyes between the strangers. And for what? A lover with a wife who would not divorce him. A lover whom she no longer loved but took too many sleeping pills if she tried to leave him, with whom Jacky had lived for four years and with whom she had not slept for several months. And even should she succeed in leaving him, whether she would marry Tony or not was far from clear, for her own divorced husband said he would not continue his payment for Moira, their child, if Jacky remarried, and then her mother, with whom Moira lived, would not be able to keep up the payments on the bungalow they had been buying when Dad died, so Jacky paid them out of her allowance for Moira . . . It was hard to think of any complication which Jacky had not got. And yet, since meeting her five weeks ago, his life had regained its core.

His mother greeted him with her light, dry kiss on each cheek and the news that the sink was blocked up. 'Of course it would happen at Easter, just when all the plumbers have gone off.'

'Not to worry, Mother. I'll see to it.'

'Have a cup of tea first, dear. You look so tired, such circles under your eyes.' She touched his cheek gently and he gathered her to him in a hug – uncomplicated mother-love that knew nothing! For a moment he longed to be free of any other, simply a son again with no will or life of his own. Little Mother, who had never seen a divan with its covers half kicked aside, had never sniffed armpits, had never . . . 'It's my woman,' she was saying. 'If I've told her once I've told her a hundred times but she will continue to empty the tea-leaves down the sink.' With his arm about her shoulders they went into the living room, but behind his filial indulgence a seed of irritation sprouted – like a match-flame held for Jacky's cigarette . . .

There was television, when he could absent himself behind his eyes. There was the night, when he longed to possess Jacky in his sleep but was denied her even there, dreaming instead that he was packing for a journey and his mother had hidden all his clothes. There was the waking too early; the first cigarette, lying in bed; the shabby clamour of his body dragging him back to schooldays and a handkerchief stuffed guiltily out of sight in his tartan case; Mother's rap on the door and entrance with a cup of tea, her hair in a net, her lips dry on a forehead surely even she would feel still sweated; the tea going down, soothing, smoothing out, till it hit the bowel; and rising, he began the day.

And breakfast, brightly served and deliciously cooked, pleasurable beyond belief after the Bayswater gas-ring, sliced loaf and Nescafé. No one can fry bread like you do, he thought; and then, because he loved her, he said aloud. 'No one fries bread like you do, Mother.'

'The fat must be smoking hot,' she answered, but he knew she was more pleased than if he had told her she was beautiful.

After breakfast he shaved, absent again while his eyes oversaw hands and blade paring the soaped cheeks and jaw on which the skin was growing flabby. Those lips through the soap had still power to rouse; if he had gone on, kissed more, kissed somewhere else, not been denied, he would have had her. He had been too gentle with her. Women were all alike; they liked to be overpowered, that girl in the train to Lincoln, those girls at the party where Trigger Townsend was born. ... Jacky had laid her thin finger on his moustache (which now he wiped delicately with a Kleenex), had stroked it, giggled, rested her forehead on his cheek, her finger still on his moustache so that he caught her hand and kissed its palm smelling of cigarettes, and she had said, 'You're so sweet to me, Tony.' How could he force her then?

'I'll mow the lawn, Mother,' he called and stepped out into the east wind of Easter Sunday.

Press and walk and tug, turn, press and walk, avoiding the gnomes and the birdbath, arms braced and shoulders square, still muscular enough despite four years at Fletcher's and beer and furnished rooms. Still Trigger's body if no longer Trigger, worthy of Jacky, capable of Jacky . . .

'Hullo.' A voice called him and raising his head he saw June at her bedroom window. He halted, lifting a hand in salute.

'Hi. Happy Easter.'

'Same to you.'

She leaned her forearms on the sill and he saw that her hair, instead of hanging in two wings either side of her face, was coiled on top of her head. She was also, he thought, wearing eyeshadow and a great deal of lipstick.

'You're looking very glam,' he said.

'D'you like it?' She fingered her hair uncertainly.

'Terrific.' From this distance it made her look grown up; he had preferred her as a schoolgirl. He gave the lawnmower a push.

'I wondered if you'd be coming this weekend.'

'It's expected,' he answered and thought, like every bloody thing else, unstop the sink, be good, Tony, sweet Tony, understand, be the one to give way . . .

'Can I see you?'

'See me?' He halted again. 'Oh, I get you. I'm going back tomorrow – early.'

'Oh.' Her disappointment was disarming enough to draw him a little out of his sourness.

'Tell you what, come in for a cuppa this afternoon.'

'Ooh, can I?'

'Sure.'

'Ooh, thanks.'

Mrs Townsend appeared at the french windows. 'I'm almost ready, dear. You had better come in and tidy yourself.'

'Will do.' He looked up at June again. 'Be seeing you.'

He rattled the lawnmower into the shed and entered the house. His mother was settling her coat on her shoulders.

'Who was that, dear? The Baxter girl?'

'Yes.' He went through to rinse his hands in the kitchen and she followed him.

'I don't know what's got into that child lately, such a change. High heels and her hair in one of those dreadful erections. I wonder her parents allow it.'

'I've asked her to tea.'

'You've what?'

'Asked her to tea. OK?' He faced her aggressively, drying his hands.

She stood quite still, her face and neck slowly turning a purplish red. 'You shouldn't have done that.'

'Come off it, Ma. She's a nice kid.'

'In my house it is I who should issue the invitations.'

He turned away to hide his own rising blood, saying lightly, 'Then do it, dear.'

'I have no intention of doing it. I have to live with my neighbours, Anthony, you do not. I have no intention of having that child constantly running in and out . . .'

'Oh, for Christ's sake!'

'Anthony! Today is the day of Christ's Resurrection.'

'I'm sorry. But of all the nonsense . . .'

'It may seem nonsense to you but you're only here occasionally. I daresay it seems very dull here to you after all your London friends, but I have no intention of being at the mercy of some young girl who feels she can ring my bell whenever there's something she wants to see on television. I have quite enough to occupy my days without that.'

'All she's doing is coming in for a cup of tea . . .'

'No, Anthony.'

He stared at her as she stood putting on her best grey gloves with shaking hands. She refused to look at him and her face, chalky now above her mottled neck, was set inflexibly. He felt himself go hard with hatred.

'Right.' He turned away to the cupboard, got out a tray, set two cups and saucers on it.

After a moment she said, 'There's no need to do that now. We're going to church.'

'I'm not. I'm having June in for coffee.'

Now she looked at him, panic-stricken old eyes in an obstinate elderly face. 'I don't wish it, Anthony.'

'I know.'

She clicked open her handbag and shut it again, finding employment for fingers that shook and eyes that did not for the moment see quite clearly. Neither of them knew quite how all this had happened. 'This is not like you,' she said at last and turned away. He heard the front door close.

He went back into the garden and whistled up at June's window. After a moment she appeared.

'Hi again,' he called. 'Like a cup of coffee?'

'Now?'

'Yes. Get cracking.'

'Oh yes!' She vanished.

He returned to the kitchen, filled the kettle and set it on a high gas, added to the tray the sugar-bowl and a packet of biscuits intended, no doubt, for tea. The bell rang and he opened the front door to June in tight blue slacks and a crudely knitted black jumper. Her piled hair was sagging a little and she was out of breath.

'I came just as I was.'

'Good show. You look like Brigitte Bardot.'

'Honestly?' She bloomed, putting a cautious hand to her hair. At the nape of her neck and over her ears it hovered in tremulous wisps too short to brush into the main edifice. Her eyelids were bright blue. The make-up, the hairdo, the coarse jumper gave her an air of great fragility which he found funny and touching. She followed him to the door of the kitchen, watching while he made the powdered coffee. 'Mum wouldn't buy me a jumper so I got the wool and made it myself. It's not very well done.'

'It looks bang on to me.'

'Honestly?' After a moment, she asked, 'Isn't your mother in?'

'No, she's gone to church. There we are!' He poured the milk with a flourish so that froth rose. 'The Townsend Cappuccino Expresso Coffee Bar. Bring the biscuits, will you?'

They went into the sitting room. He was conscious of the house empty of his mother's presence yet full of her disapproval, hollow above and around them. He turned on both bars of the electric fire his mother had thriftily turned off. 'Sit you down,' he said, 'and get warm.'

'I am warm.' And he could see, now that he looked at her properly, that she was, her skin plump with the warm flow of youth, pearly beneath the extravagant make-up. At twenty-six Jacky's skin was not like that. Even though twenty-six was youth to his forty, Jacky's life had worn her skin as it had worn her gallant, crazy virtues. He suddenly hated youth that cheated its possessors so soon.

'You've got the whole lot on today, haven't you?'

She was puzzled. 'What?'

He gestured. 'All the war paint.'

'Oh.' She blushed, looking down and pulling at the hem of the jumper. 'I feel bolshie. Everything's so boring.'

'At your age?'

'What's age got to do with it?'

'Sorry.' He pushed the biscuits towards her. 'What about your acting? Isn't there a school play?'

She answered sulkily, 'I'm not in the school play. They said my marks weren't good enough and I ought to work harder for GCE or I haven't a hope. I don't care.' She added quickly, 'I'm not interested in their boring play. It's only for cretins really. The whole school's only for cretins. I wish I could leave. I'll be sixteen this summer. Do you think I could get a job in London like you said? That's what I wanted to ask you. They go on and on at me, pass your GCE, get a training, get some education . . . What's the point of it?'

'What indeed? Except that parents like to turn round as though they'd laid an egg and say, "Look how clever I've been!" My son's so good, so devoted, does all the jobs round the house, visits regular as clockwork, never goes against me, never married, is never uncouth, my son on the mantelpiece, a hero, a credit to me . . .' He lit a cigarette.

'Sorry,' he said, smiling his sweet smile under the handlebars. 'Come again?'

'Why do people change their names?'

'Change their names?' He was bewildered.

'Yes. Why do they?'

'Because they don't like them, I suppose. How would you like to be Miss June Sidebottom?'

'No, I mean seriously. What reason would they have?'

'I haven't a clue. Could be because of a will – you know, you inherit a million pounds if you take Uncle Jasper's name. Or you might have a murky past and be trying to hide it, make a fresh start and all that. Or you might be living in sin.' Like Jacky and that man—

'What's that?'

'Not properly married, or bigamous perhaps.'

'Could people find out?'

'I suppose they *could* . . .'

'How?'

'Well, if it was a crime I suppose they might be able to turn it up in old newspaper files or someone recognises them or they read about it in Famous Trials or something.'

'Is Famous Trials a book?'

'A whole lot of books, all the gen about big trials like Christie and Crippen and so on. Or of course you could just go up to the chappie and say Excuse me, old man, but why did you change your name from Smellie to Stinks?' He laughed, but she did not join him. 'What's this all in aid of?'

She took a long drink of coffee. 'Nothing.'

'Come on now, tell Uncle Tony.'

She gave him a cold, slow look. 'I'm not a child,' she said quietly.

Outside someone called her name. 'Is that your mother?' She shrugged. 'Doesn't she know you're here?'

'I don't know. I just came straight out.'

He stood up crossly. 'You shouldn't have done that. She'll be wondering where you are.' He opened one side of the french windows and stepped outside. 'She's here, Mrs Baxter.'

'Oh – good morning.' They could see each other over the fence. She was standing a little way out in the garden, a teacloth in her hand, her hair blowing over her cheeks. She smoothed a strand as she turned towards him.

He went to the fence, resting his hands shoulder-high on the top. 'I'm sorry she didn't tell you where she was. We're having elevenses. Won't you join us?'

'Oh – thank you, it's very kind. But I'm in the middle of my morning.' She glanced beyond him into the house but June was invisible. 'It's just I wondered where she'd got to.'

'She should have told you, or I should. I saw her up at her window and just asked her in on the spur of the moment.'

'That's quite all right.' Her glance came back to him, weighing him up. 'I heard her run out but she didn't say anything. They're thoughtless at her age.'

'At any age, I'm told.'

'Perhaps.' She smiled. There was something composed and gentle about her despite her faintly troubled air. 'Don't let her be a nuisance. She gets so wrapped up in what she's set on, she doesn't think whether she's welcome or not.'

'She's a sweet kid.'

'Well . . .' She smiled again. 'She's grown up a lot in these last few months, I don't hardly know her sometimes.'

'Sure you won't change your mind?'

'I can't, really. I've got my husband home today and the dinner to get. Just send her back when you've had enough.'

'I'll do that thing.'

Closing the window behind him he said, 'You should have said where you'd gone.' June shrugged. His voice sharpened. 'Let's face it, it's common courtesy.'

'Oh, that! I'm old enough to look after myself.'

'You're old enough to get into trouble.'

'What sort of trouble?' She glanced at him from beneath her blue lids, a glance of pure sexuality yet quite impersonal, directed not at him, Tony Townsend, but solely to his male presence. Instinctively he stared back, accepting the challenge. He felt his gaze grow hot, felt the blood begin to draw to the surface, wishing, in that brief surge of basic response, for his mother to come back and find them on the hearthrug, on the couch, in her chair, wallowing, grunting, unbuttoned, this straight draught of sexuality in her tight slacks and badly applied makeup, raw and unsuitable in every way to his mother's eunuch life . . .

Unsuitable, my God, to his too. He drew back within himself with a start. This was June from next door, a sweet kid but a schoolgirl in whom he had no interest whatsoever beyond that of boredom and casual friendliness. Christ, he wasn't a Lolita type! His response had been solely automatic, old Trigger Townsend on the job again, built up from irritation and the throbbing pressure of Jacky – Jacky . . . For perhaps half an hour he had forgotten her, and the memory of her now thrust back at him.

He took June's cup and put it on the tray. 'Your mother said for you not to be long.'

'She's always nagging.'

He made his voice light. 'All mothers nag.'

'Not when you're grown up.'

'Especially when you're grown up.'

'But at least you can get away. I hate this place. I hate school and the house and everything.' Her face had suddenly thinned and tears rose in her eyes. 'I'd like to go away and never come back, forget it all, everything, every single thing!'

'Who wouldn't!'

She clenched her hands. 'Don't joke! I'm not making a joke! You don't know . . . You're the only person I can talk to – my only friend . . .'

Christ! he thought, steady, men! Hold back. Play it cool . . . He rose and picked up the tray. 'I'm not much help,' he said lightly. 'Open the door like a good kid.'

She stood up slowly, her half-fledged woman's body erect in an effortless movement of childhood, staring at him, but he avoided her eyes. She was slight and light like Jacky but still in the egg, still in the bud, dynamite, tedious. . . . 'Ta,' he said. 'Switch off the fire, will you?'

She did so, then followed him into the kitchen. Busy clearing the tray, he said, 'Sorry to turf you out now but I've got to meet Ma out of church in ten minutes.'

'That's OK,' she said quietly.

'And about this afternoon – I've made a boob, I'm afraid. Ma's got some friends coming in, two old girls – we'll play bridge, I expect. I'm afraid I forgot.'

'That's OK,' she repeated. 'I expect my mother'll want me in anyway.'

'Well – see you sometime, then.'

'Yes.'

He edged her out and opened the front door.

'Thanks for the coffee,' she said.

'Think nothing of it.' He smiled too warmly.

Still she hesitated. 'That book – where would I find it?'

'What book?'

'That trials book.'

'Haven't a clue, poppet. Public library, I suppose.'

'Oh. Well, bye-bye.'

He watched her run suddenly to the gate, her small buttocks shifting beneath the rim of the jumper. As he shut the front door solitude swept through the house like a wind, howling down the long hours between now and train-time tomorrow. They would pass over his head as all hours passed if you went limp and let them. He would ring Jacky from Paddington station . . .

He put on his cap and windbreaker and went slowly to meet his mother out of church.

SIX

SINCE THE OPENING of the deed box June had retreated into the cell of her own skull and locked the door. The implications of a deceit so vast that it ranged far beyond the mystery of changed names, tainting every aspect of her known world, were locked outside. Her mind refused admission. She would not think about it; but within the prison of her elected cell she was frantic and lost. Outside was menace unimaginable but inside was the bleak aridity of isolation.

She shut herself into her room as she shut herself into her exile, retreating to it as soon as possible when she came home, coming out of it only when she must. Lying on her bed or staring out of the window, she sensed her parents' presence, their bafflement at her withdrawal, as though they actually stood outside her door, waiting, waiting for her to come out. When she came home from school her mother greeted her with love, and things she liked were put before her to eat. She consumed them in silence, picking and crumbling the scones she could have devoured in a gulp, leaving the second cup of tea she need not have had to grow scummy in the cup. Mrs Baxter put aside whatever she had been doing and had tea with her. She talked quietly of this and that, asked about school. It was only the two of them then, he was at the shop. Sometimes June forgot and they sat together in accustomed amity until something reminded her – her mother's glance at the clock, a reference to him, almost anything would do to snap the lock of June's cell again. She would fall silent, go upstairs, leaving the tea things for her mother to clear away, and shut the door of her room. She would drop off her school uniform, put on the tight slacks and baggy jumper, pile her hair on her head, experiment with make-up, the radio turned full up against her mother's quietness downstairs. When she was called for supper she did not go at once but made them call again, become irritated, so that when she did slide down into her chair the atmosphere was already fretful.

'When your mother's taken the trouble to cook a nice supper it seems a pity to let it get cold,' he would sometimes say, jocular because afraid to be cross.

'I didn't hear her call,' she would mutter, not looking at them.

'If you turned the wireless down a bit you might hear better,' he persisted.

'Well, if her supper's cold she'll have to put up with it,' interposed her mother briskly. 'Like a bit more, Ray?'

Sometimes he would ask her about school or pull her leg about her appearance. 'My word, who've we got to supper this evening, Ett – Marlene Dietrich?' trying to wrap his disapproval in a joke. Once, in the beginning, he had spoken out: 'You'll have the skin off your face with all that stuff, look like a proper clown,' and she had flounced out of the room in noisy tears, running upstairs and slamming the door of her room. Since that time he had only made jokes.

Once a week or so they all went to the cinema and June went with them because they paid for her and bought ice-cream in the interval, and because the isolation of herself was almost more than she could bear. But she always walked a little behind them, and she never sat beside him; sometimes they tried to put her in the middle but she never would. She sat beside her mother, and knew that in the darkness they held hands – held hands like teenagers! When they came out her mother would take her arm and draw her close; but he took her mother's other arm and soon she manoeuvred herself free, to walk the half-pace behind.

At such times as she had to give a reason for her withdrawal to her own room she pleaded homework. But she spent only enough time on homework to get the requisite number of pages covered in writing which she no longer bothered to make legible. Her exercises became more and more scored over with red ink, and at each poor marking she became more stubborn, refusing to pay attention, concentrate, do her best, for what was the point? She did not care if she passed GCE, did not care for the opinion of her teachers, for this school, like Hellebore Road, Bristol itself, was simply part of the hell she had been condemned to since he came back.

They had not said very much at the bad report she brought back at Easter, and what they had said she had been able to shut away. The evening before summer term began she was in bed turning the pages of a magazine when her mother came in.

'Here's your school dress for tomorrow, dear. I've put a little starch in it, so it ought to keep fresh for the week if you're careful.' She hung the dress on a hanger on the side of the cupboard, shaking out its skirt critically. 'You've put everything ready for the morning, have you?' June made a vaguely acquiescent sound, flicking the pages of the magazine. 'Well, have you, dear?' Mrs Baxter repeated. 'For goodness' sake turn that thing down a bit.' Sighing noisily, June turned down the radio. 'You don't want to have too much of a scramble in the morning, do you?'

'It doesn't matter if I'm late.'

'Of course it matters. You want to start the term right.' She picked up June's jumper from the floor and hung it over a chair, looked inside the satchel that bulged on the table. 'You've got all your books packed, have you?'

'Mm.'

'There's some on the floor there, oughtn't they to go in?'

'What? Oh, I suppose so.'

'Well, I can't do it for you, I don't know which you need.'

'I'll do it in the morning.'

Mrs Baxter sat down on the edge of the bed, absently reaching forward to lift a strand of hair and tuck it behind June's ear. 'Junie, you do like this school, don't you?'

June did not lift her eyes from the magazine. 'It's all right.'

'It always takes a bit of time to settle down but you've had two terms now.' Silence. 'Daddy and I were a bit disappointed your report wasn't better. Isn't it the same work it was at Jervis's?'

'I suppose so.'

'Only you were doing so well at Jervis's, weren't you, and it is a bit disappointing. And you've got your big exams coming on this term, haven't you?'

'It doesn't matter if I don't pass.'

'Well, not in a way it doesn't. You're a year young and you can take them again next year, I know. But it would be nice to get some of them out of the way.'

'Exams are a waste of time.'

'They're not, dear. They set the standard.'

'Standard – crap!'

'June! That's not at all nice language to use!'

'It's what we say at school.'

'Well, I don't want to hear it at home. Only rough people speak like that.'

'OK, so I'm rough. It's a rough school.'

'Some of the girls, perhaps. But there must be a nice type too . . .' June shrugged, riffling the magazine pages. 'All the more reason for you to do well, then. Daddy and I do so want you to do well.'

'Why?'

'Why? Because we want you to have all the things we never had. If Daddy'd had a proper education he might have – everything might have been different.'

'How?'

'Well – more opportunities. He wouldn't have had to make do when he was young. We want better things than that for you.'

'Tony says parents are like birds who've just laid an egg.'

'Who?'

'Tony. Next door.'

'Mr Townsend?'

'His nickname was Trigger in the war, because of all the planes he shot down. He says parents are like hens with eggs, always wanting you to admire what they've done.'

'I don't think that's a very nice thing to say.'

'Well, it's true.'

'I don't know whether it's true or not. All I do know is it's natural for parents to want the best for their children. Exams are important nowadays. After all, you don't go to school for fun.'

'You can say that again!' She threw the magazine on the floor and lay back, staring up at the ceiling, making her face as bored as she could, for her mother's presence sitting on the bed as she had done all through June's life undermined June's isolation. So she had often sat in the flat in Havenport, in a bedroom which had not been as nice as this one but which love and security had made perfect. Now June lay longing for her to go before the habit of love found some vulnerable place.

Mrs Baxter's voice was gentle. 'June, don't you like this school?'

'It's all right.'

'It's convenient, isn't it, and it's got a good record. There's bound to be more of a mixed type of girl in a big place like Bristol than there was at Havenport, but Miss Chatham spoke ever so well of it, didn't she, and I'm sure the teachers are good. Aren't they good?'

'They're all right,' she repeated indifferently.

'And there's nothing wrong with your brains, dear, is there? I mean, they can't have just suddenly gone off because you've come to live here, can they? So it's up to you to make the most of them, isn't it? You can do it if you want to, Junie. Can't you?'

The pain of tears cut suddenly at June's throat. She threw up her arm and laid it across her eyes as though the light hurt them, swallowing, mute. She felt her mother lay a hand on the bedclothes over her thigh; heard her mother's quiet voice.

'I know it's all been an upheaval. It's been an upheaval for all of us. But we've settled down, haven't we, dear? It was worth a bit of unsettling, wasn't it?'

The voice, the hand, the gentle questions that pleaded not for answers but for reassurance, the nest-familiarity of bed and mother and night-time, pressed in unbearably so that in desperation for escape she reared herself up sideways and turned the radio full on again.

Mrs Baxter withdrew her hand.

'You'd better get to sleep,' she said.

'I've missed half the programme already.'

'Then you won't mind missing the rest.' She stood up. 'Turn it off now.'

'Oh honestly! There's only twenty more minutes!'

'Not tonight. There's school tomorrow.'

'Oh, crap!' She flung herself down in bed again, turning her back, pressing her face into the pillow.

Mrs Baxter turned off the radio. The silence seemed unnatural. 'Good night, dear,' she said, bent and kissed the unbrushed hair that was all that was offered her, switched off the bedside lamp and slowly made her way through the darkness to the door.

School was abominable. The summer term was always one of mingled hysteria and determination, the implacable demands of the important examinations superimposed on the restlessness of the end of the school year, freedom at the far end of July, and the summery sensuousness of cotton frocks, blossom, holidays. Even the clever girls were prey to these conflicts: the laburnum blowing outside the study window, the scent of talcum powder and skin through their own clothes, the anxious scrutiny of dates to see whether they would have the curse at the time of the exams. For the ordinary girls, bored with or unable to compete in schoolwork, the summer term was a torment, not only a waste of time but a blasphemy against it when the world, shimmering with sunshine and pay packets, was only just beyond the school walls.

Therefore an air of yeasty ferment pervaded the school which the staff tried to suppress but were themselves affected by in various ways. For them too five weeks' freedom glowed at the end of July – Greece with a student group, Yugoslavia with the WEA and rucksacks, Scotland and the Edinburgh Festival, Cornwall in Mary's adorably primitive cottage. For them too cotton replaced worsted under the cardigan and the laburnum distracted from Latin. For some of them this was the last term of engagement; next term would find them married, perhaps even pregnant, removed for ever from spinsterhood. And on all of them was the pressure of a system whereby every girl under their charge must be shoved and pulled through the groaning labours of competitive examination, the bright ones spurred to scholarships, the medium ones hoisted onto the safe side of a pass, the hopeless ones prevented from infecting the others or despairing themselves; and all of them female, subject to headaches, backaches, fits of crying, wounded feelings, sleeplessness, skin blemishes that caused misery that led to inability to concentrate, nausea, stomach cramps, menstruation.

This atmosphere made June at once wilder and more withdrawn. Her work became more careless, for she did not care. She had no desire to do well in the exams for she had no desire to cause either her school or her parents pride. Why should she work hard in order to bring credit on those she distrusted or despised? She could not be a credit to herself, work for her own sake, for she did not know who she was. When her sixteenth birthday came she had hardly said Thank you for her presents (a record player at last), refused an outing. What was the point? She was nobody, a non-person, the egg had shattered round the naked fledgling. By rudeness, idleness at school, make-up, hair-does, clothes at home, she was trying to build up a self that was her own, who would be armoured against whatever truth lay locked in her mother's deed box.

Sandra had come up to her a few days after term started, for they had fallen back into a wary contact again, and looked her up and down with her small eyes.

'Hi,' she said. 'What have you done to your hair?'

'I'm growing it, do you mind?'

'Miss Rush'll make you put it in a plait. How are you going to wear it, in a French plait?'

'I might. It depends what Tony says.'

'Who's Tony?'

'My boyfriend. Didn't you know?'

'I've never seen you with a boyfriend.'

'We probably don't go where you'd be.' She turned away disdainfully but Sandra stayed by her side.

'Tony who, June? Where's he from?'

'He works in London. He's a Sales Manager.'

'Go on!'

'He's much older than the kids you lot go around with. He's mature.'

'Ceddy's twenty. And Michael that my friend goes with is twenty-three.'

June shrugged and walked away. Nonplussed, Sandra called, 'Did you see him at Easter?'

'But natch. He comes down most weekends.'

It was true, wasn't it? He did come down at weekends, he was her friend. And he was a man, mature yet boyish too. Just as a child will create a personality for its teddy-bear, knowing it to be only fabric stuffed with kapok, with button eyes and an embroidered smile, so June could fashion a man for her necessity out of Tony Townsend, a father, a lover, a confidant, a privacy for Them. Mum had not liked what he had said about parents, *he* had been uneasy about their going out together. Tony could be a stick to beat Them with, a boast against Sandra, a teddy-bear to cuddle for herself. He was so worldly, living in London and in the RAF and all. He knew about all sorts of thing, like changing one's name . . .

Turn the radio full on, answer back, plaster your eyelids with green shadow, stare at the boys going home from the Grammar School, wiggling your bottom, laugh so the whole roof of your mouth showed in the middle of Scripture and take a detention with a flounce and a shrug, four out of ten, twelve out of twenty, 'This is shoddy work' in red ink, run up the stairs and slam the door on the uncleared table, the half-eaten meal, the baffled faces that did not tell the truth.

Sometimes whatever she was doing went away from her, leaving her with nothing but her thought. In class or walking home from school (for the fine weather and her disinclination to get home at the time she was expected led her to take the bus no longer) she often found herself cut off from everything but thought. Why Baxter now, Banks then? Why Australia? Why thirteen years? Why? Why? Why had Mum hidden whatever it was from her, why had she lied and lied, not by saying but by not saying, not by doing but by not being? Why would people behave like that, what would make them? Auntie Norah too. Was Mum ashamed of him, was that it? Because he was little and silly and not in the Havenport class, came from an orphanage and had no education despite all his reading? But Mum wasn't like that. Mum was never ashamed of what she believed in, and she believed in being married to this man . . . They were married, married, married? Looks, voices, acceptance, all were marriage. Mum wasn't acting. Mum never did what she didn't believe . . .

Didn't she? Then why? Why Baxter now, Banks then? Why nothing ever said? Why . . .?

When the questions grew too insistent she sought more definite methods of evasion. On her way home from school she would go for a bus ride or into a café, go down into the city centre and wander round the shops. When she got home she said it had been Games or the Film Club or special revision. One day she did not go to school at all but took a bus to Bath. It was beautiful there, she liked it. Another day a little later on she spent at Clifton Zoo, but this time she had to write a note in her mother's name saying she had had a chill. Several times between beginning of term and Whitsun she did this, wandering the outskirts of the city or the nearer neighbouring towns, going to the cinema at lunchtime or to the swimming baths. In the cinema once she held hands with a man whose face she never saw, for when he presently pressed her fingers to his flies she pulled away from him and hurried out into the street, terrified he might follow her. In the swimming bath she stared out of the corners of her eyes at the naked men with water dripping from the bulges in their trunks, smoothing the wet hair from their faces, rubbing their wet hands over their wet smooth bodies, springing into the water again to come spitting and gasping to the surface, naked and streaming, their bulges softly revealed. Sometimes they tried to sport with her, putting their cold wet hands on her in the water, but she would kick away from them to the side of the bath and haul herself out, and they would laugh at her from the water, the hair and the water streaming down their wet faces.

She was happy during these truancies, alone but not lost, herself a new person in a world created by herself. Free from everyone's knowledge, she was free also from thought. Away from the background that contained her problems, she could forget them for a time. She knew it would not last. Someone would find out and in any case she would have to sit the exams. She gave herself till Whitsun. At Whitsun Tony would come down and she would tell him the whole thing. What he had said already about – reasons – did not really count, for he had not realised that she was serious. He had just thought it was a joke. When she explained it all to him properly, he would tell her what to do. Perhaps he would even say, 'Why don't you ask your mother?' and then perhaps she would. And there would be some simple explanation.

She could hang on till Whitsun.

Half-term and Whitsun coincided. It was, she knew, no good looking for Tony before Saturday. The time passed somehow, but from Saturday teatime she began to watch and listen, leaning out of her bedroom window where she would be able to hear a man's voice if it spoke in Mrs Townsend's living room. Nothing sounded. The french windows remained closed. Perhaps he was not coming till the evening.

But there was no sign of him next day. The Townsends' house felt dead. The day was fine and all along the gardens deck chairs were put out during the morning. *He* went out and read the paper in the sun. But nothing stirred next door.

A terrible restlessness crept over June. He would be gone again tomorrow. If she did not catch him soon the chance would be lost for she did not know how long, perhaps for ever, for by the time he came again in the August holidays they might all be dead. She might as well be dead, for she could not carry the mystery about with her in secret much longer. Someone must tell her it was not a mystery after all, and the only someone was Tony. If she did not see him this weekend she would die.

They made her come for a walk in the afternoon, trailing behind them under the trees to look down on the suspension bridge among the parked cars smelling in the sun and the lolly-licking children. She remembered the blowy Boxing Day when she and Tony had stood here and how his eyes had seemed to be looking into space as he looked out over the bridge, not like *him*, who was full of facts and figures, as though anyone cared. When they got home Mum took tea out into the garden, but June ran upstairs to her bedroom window. The french windows next door were open and one empty deck chair was outside them.

She ran downstairs and out of the front door, down the path, along the pavement, up the path to the Townsends'. Only when she stood by their front door did she pause, smooth up her hair and settle the wide belt round her waist more trimly before tinging the bell. She heard the chimes, then silence except for the thudding of her own heart. She was wondering whether to ring a second time when Mrs Townsend opened the door.

'Yes? Who is it?'

'It's me, from next door.'

'Oh. The light's behind you, it's difficult to see.' She was spruce as ever, cardigan, beads, hair neatly waved, but she seemed very small. Perhaps June had grown. Mrs Townsend stood with her hand on the latch, making no move.

'I wondered – I mean, I'm sorry to trouble you but is Mr Townsend in?'

'No, he's not.'

'Oh. Oh, I just wondered. He asked me to find something out for him, you see, from school. We were talking and I said I'd find out for him so I came round to tell him. Will he be in soon?'

'No. He's not here.'

'Not here? Not at all?'

'No.'

'But he always comes at Bank Holidays.'

'He usually has done in the past, yes.'

'Is he all right?'

'You mean is he well? So far as I know, perfectly well. He has just made other arrangements.'

'Oh. Well, I'm sorry for disturbing you.'

'Not at all.' Mrs Townsend closed the door.

June went back down the path and into her own house. Her parents sitting in the garden did not even know she had been out. She went automatically to the window and looked out on their two heads. Mum was making a blouse and he was reading aloud to her from a library book. On the other side of the fence Mrs Townsend came out. She shifted her deck chair slightly to face the sun and sat down, opening a magazine on her lap. It lay there for a few moments, Mrs Townsend immobile. Then she took a handkerchief from the sleeve of her cardigan and blew her nose. She wiped first one eye, then the other, blew her nose again and picked up the magazine.

June went and lay on her bed. Her mind was perfectly blank, as though from shock. She had leaned on a prop which now was not there. There was no point in thinking, for she had been going to think only what he told her to and so now there was nothing. Just a blank. Nothing. Forget it all. She lay on the bed as mindless as though she were asleep.

Next day the weather changed, it was cool and rainy. Denied the outing which he always liked to take on Bank Holidays, they went to the cinema in the afternoon like almost everyone else. Over supper, she said, 'Haven't seen that chap next door this time. Perhaps he's got a young lady.'

'Come off it, Ett. He must be my age.'

'Well, that's not so old.'

'Old enough not to be much catch for young ladies. Only nice cosy middle-aged ones, eh?'

'Be quiet, Ray!' They were both glowing and smiling at things beyond spoken words.

'He's much younger than you,' June said rudely.

'Not all that much, dear, I don't suppose. He was in the war.'

'Can't forget it either, to judge from all the face fungus.' He laughed.

'He went straight from school.'

'Well, he can't be much short of forty anyway, can he? It's a matter of simple arithmetic.'

'Have you finished, June? Can't you eat up a bit more salad?'

'No.' She pushed back her chair and got up.

'We haven't finished yet, dear. There's some pudding.'

'What is it?'

'W and S, we were always told in the orphanage. In plain English, wait and see.'

'It's treacle tart. We haven't had it for ever such a long time and I know you both like it.'

June sat down again grudgingly, letting Mrs Baxter carry the tray into the kitchen. He looked at her, opened his mouth, decided to say nothing.

'The wind's getting up again,' said Mrs Baxter. 'It's rattling the kitchen window.'

'We've had our summer. Can't expect more than two fine days a year, can we?'

'I get sick of it, blowing all the blossom off the trees. We shan't have so many apples as we had last year, I don't think, because of those awful cold winds round Easter, remember?'

'It was before Easter. More end of March. I remember thinking I hope it warms up a bit for Easter and the Bank Holiday.'

'Was it? Yes, I believe it was. I know we didn't seem to have the tree in blossom more than a day or two. It doesn't give it a chance really, does it?'

'That's one thing you don't get in Australia. You get the winds, of course, blowing all across the outback but it's a warm wind, none of your biting north-easters. Those warm winds, you know, they can be nasty too – dust, grit, gets properly on your nerves blowing day after day. And then, of course, there's the danger of bush fires. That's what you've got to be careful of.'

'Would you like some more, Junie?'

She held out her plate in silence.

'Of course, you do have the sunshine. I will say that. Cobbers used to say to me they got sick of it day after day, the same blue sky, same old sun blazing down, but I used to say they didn't know when they were well off. If you've ever lived in England, with grey skies four days out of five, I used to say, you'd know when you were well off.'

'They do say June is the best weather now, but I always think September's nice – and October can be lovely. Remember those lovely hot days we had last year, just before we opened the shop? It seems such a shame to get the bad weather just when people are taking their holidays.'

'Now that's something we ought to discuss,' he said, pushing his plate away and wiping his lips on his serviette. 'Holidays. I don't know about us but we ought to get little Junie fixed up with something. What d'you say, dear?'

June shrugged, crumbling the last bits of pastry with her spoon.

'Daddy and I had a bit of a talk about it the other night and we decided we'd better talk it over with you too.'

Thanks very much, she sneered, but not aloud.

'You see, the trouble is your mum and I can't both leave the shop at the same time.'

'Why don't you shut it?'

'We can't really do that, with that type of business, dear, especially when it's not been open long.'

'It's all casual trade, you see – at least, sort of regular casual, people rushing by on their way to work pop in for a paper or a packet of fags. They could just as easy pop in somewhere else if we wasn't open, and the habit'd be broken, see?'

'We used to shut at Havenport.'

'That was a different class of customer, dear. They all knew us. And anyway, it was never more than just the week.'

'So what your mum and I thought was you and she had better go off somewhere and leave me to hold the fort.'

'That was what *you* thought, Ray. It might just as well be you and Junie go off somewhere.'

'No, no, it's you that needs the break, Ett. After all, I've had my rest cure, haven't I?' Again something passed between them which June could not decipher – was it bravado from him, warning from her, an assertion from him, a reproof from her, all in the exchange of a glance from which she was barred as though behind bars.

'I want to go on my own,' she said loudly.

'On your own? Don't be silly, dear.'

'What's silly about it?'

'Why, just about everything, I should have thought.' He laughed unconvincingly.

'Where could you go, dear?'

'Butlin's.'

He made an impatient gesture. 'I never heard such rubbish.'

'It's not rubbish! Lots of the girls at school go.'

'But not on their own, I'm sure . . .'

'Why shouldn't they?'

'I don't know anything about why shouldn't they, all I know is you're not going.'

'In any case,' interposed Mrs Baxter, 'it's ever so expensive.'

'But it's all included. Absolutely everything's paid for.'

'Your mum's right. We couldn't run to as much as that. In any case, the two of you's going.'

'I want to go to Butlin's,' she repeated sullenly.

'We couldn't run to it, Junie. There's been a lot of expense this last twelve months. Wherever we do go will have to be reasonable. I wondered – would you like to go back to Havenport?'

'No!' She sat upright violently. 'I'd rather die than go back there!'

'I thought it might have been nice to look up your old friends . . . Still, there's plenty of other places. We might find somewhere in Devon. I've heard Exmouth's nice.'

'You need somewhere with a nice beach and something to do in the evenings,' he said.

'Well, you'd get that in Exmouth. It's all sand there, I believe, and a proper holiday place so there's bound to be plenty to do. The only thing is, I expect it gets booked up.'

'Yes, we have left it a bit late. It's all your fault, not making up your mind.'

'Well, it's not easy, Ray, having to leave you on your own. Don't you really think we could close up just for a week? Even just for a long weekend, so you could join us?'

'I can't see it, dear. It's too risky.'

'Or couldn't Miss Turner carry on by herself for just a few days? After all, she's been helping a few months now, she ought to be able to manage it on her own.'

'It'd take me a month to get straight again. No, dear, you and June go.'

'I want to go on my own!' she cried, banging the table with her fist.

'June!' her mother said sharply, 'you'll have the china off!'

'I don't want to go with you, I want to go on my own!'

'It's out of the question,' he said, 'you're much too young.'

'I'm not, I'm not!' She was almost screaming. 'You keep on treating me like I was two years old, talking in front of me, fixing things up behind my back, having secrets! Why don't the two of you go on holiday and leave me here!'

'That's enough now.'

'You mum needs a holiday . . .'

'Let her have it without me, then. I don't want to go on holiday with Mum and have her wondering how *you're* getting on all the time! If I can't go on my own, then I'd rather not have any crappy old holiday!'

'I won't have that language, June.'

'I don't care what you'll have! I'm sick of being treated like a baby, the pair of you smiling behind my back, fixing up what to tell me, thinking I'm too young to know anything or do anything you don't think's quite the thing. I'm sixteen years old! I could be out at business, I could have a baby, and all you can think of is where to send me with a nice sandy beach and hang around with Mum all day long!'

Her mother began to stack the crockery. 'You'd better go upstairs, June. There's no sense in talking to you when you're like this.'

'I don't know what's got into her, Ett.'

'You don't know anything, you don't! You think I'm just a dear little girl to be drooled over and lied to because I don't know any better. You're stupid, that's what you are, stupid and wicked!' Even through her hysteria she saw his face go white, then flood with red.

His eyes, which for a moment had seemed blindingly blue, turned from her to his wife.

Mrs Baxter stood up. Her voice shook. 'You're not to speak to your father like that. If we can't have sense we'll at least have some respect.'

'What for? Him? What have I got to respect him for?'

Her mother put out a hand. It trembled. She made to speak but could not. Tears began to run down her cheeks, quite suddenly, without a sob. Raymond pushed back his chair and went to her. He put both arms round her and held her tightly against him as though to absorb her trembling into himself. 'Don't, Ett. Don't. Don't take any notice. Don't upset yourself, Ett – don't, my sweetheart, Etty love . . . don't, don't . . .'

The pain was so intense she nearly screamed. She turned and ran upstairs, into the security of her prison cell, across the room, to stand panting, pressed against the wall in the far corner. The wall felt cool against her cheek, solid against the length of her trembling body. She was gasping, dry-eyed, her mouth open as though she had died of thirst. She pressed against the wall, stilling herself against its hardness. After a little while she drew away and went very quietly into the bathroom. She opened the medicine cupboard and searched the shelves: TCP, Elastoplast, inhalant, talcum powder, vegetable laxative, suntan lotion, calamine, iodine, Vaseline and, in a powdery bottle, aspirin. She emptied them into her palm but there were not enough. She put them back in the bottle, and the bottle back on the shelf, closed the door and went quietly back to her room. From downstairs she could hear the quiet catch of her mother's breath, the tender murmur of his voice, hesitant, low, infinitely private.

She shut and locked her door and lay down on the bed.

A long time later she heard them come upstairs. She heard them moving about in their room, then one, then the other go to the bathroom. Her mother spoke her name outside the door, but she did not answer. Her handle turned impotently. 'June – say good night?' She did not answer. Her mother went away.

She was cold and drew the eiderdown and coverlet over her, lying in the dark which made the square of the window seem quite light. Her window faced the city and the sky over it was faintly tinged with green from the arc-lamps that fringed its industries. At Havenport the lights had been yellow, and not so many of them. You could feel the sky at night over Havenport; somehow the sea seemed to spread up out of its bed and merge with the sky, so that the whole town and the dark country beyond was enlapped in the dark water. She had not often been awake as late as this at Havenport.

There was a soft knock on the door. She froze.

'June.' It was his voice, very low. 'June, let me in.' She did not answer, but her heart began to beat in big leaps. 'June – I don't want to wake your mother.'

Slowly she uncovered herself and got up. She staggered a little, having lain for so long in one position. She unlocked the door and retreated several paces back into the room, wrapping her arms across the body. He came inside and closed the door softly. She could see him quite well, accustomed as she was to the dark, but he peered about for her.

'Where are you? Ah, there. We don't want to wake your mother.'

She retreated again to the bed and sat down on it. He came a little towards her. He had his dressing gown on over pyjamas. 'Shall we have some light?'

'No.'

'Just as you like. I want to say this, June. I won't have you upset your mother. Whatever you feel about me can't be helped, but I won't have your mother upset.' There was silence. 'It's not easy for any of us. I'd hoped we'd settle down as the happy family I'd remembered, but I reckon that was too much to ask for. It's only natural. Your mother and me – time seems to have stood still for us two, but of course it couldn't have been expected for you. I still see you as the little kiddie you were when I went away. That's silly, of course. You're a girl, a young lady. It's hard to realise.'

She spoke in a whisper. 'Where were you all that time?'

He did not answer at once. 'Those thirteen years are between your mother and me,' he said at last. 'I couldn't be with you. But you were always there in my dreams, the two of you. Always there.'

There was another silence. Then he said, 'I just came in to tell you this – I love your mother. I always have and I always will. I love you too, whether you like it or not, because you're my girl. You ought to have grown up with me, then we'd have got on all right. I couldn't expect to come back and have the two of you just the same as if I'd always been here. Ett's miracle enough. But I won't have her upset. For her sake, you and I have got to make a go of it, see? Whatever you think or feel, just keep it to yourself.' His voice softened. 'Get to bed now, eh? No sense in stopping up all night.'

He moved to the door. 'Good night, dear. Sleep tight.'

She sat for a while without moving, then got up and began to undress. As she sloughed off her clothes the tears began to fall, pouring down her face, splashing her hands, her garments, then soaking into the pillow. She cried with relaxed abandonment, letting the tears wash right through her, sluicing, cooling, leaving her resolution hardened. If he had come to her sooner, if he had spoken thus to her months ago, she might have come to love him. She could have respected him. Now it was too late. She would not forgive him for being too late. Newspaper records, Tony had said, or books of trials. Raymond Cavendish Banks, sometime between 1946 and 1950 . . .

Notable British Trials . . .

The Trial of
RAYMOND CAVENDISH BANKS
edited by
Justin Edgeworth, CCB,
Barrister-at-Law
Trial
within
Old Bailey
London Summer Assizes

on
23 June 1948

Judge:
Mr Justice Dickson
Counsel for the Crown:
Mr Haynes Barrett, KC
Mr Arthur Herron
(Instructed by the Director of Public Prosecutions)

Counsel for the Defence:
Mr Dominic Haylett, KC
Mr Stuart Shirley
(Instructed by AF Fortescue, Solicitors, London)

INTRODUCTION
by Justin Edgeworth

It was fortunate for Raymond Cavendish Banks that he chose to emulate his somewhat more notorious predecessor, George Joseph Smith, over a period which brought him to trial during that brief interregnum of seven months in 1948 when the death penalty was temporarily suspended. Had this not been the case, his crime would have carried the penalty of cessation rather than mere interruption of that state of being which both men held so lightly in the case of their unfortunate victims. George Joseph Smith suffered the full penalty of the law for his callous if businesslike removal of those ladies who might well be described as the geese who laid the golden eggs; but for Raymond Cavendish Banks only the nominal sentence of 'Life' rewarded one who, for cold expediency, would otherwise, before the passing of the Homicide Act 1957, have well merited 'a sudden taking off'.

The two cases present an irresistible comparison, even to the fact that Banks, like Smith, had his devoted 'Miss Pegler' who knew nothing of his sinister activities and for whom he appears to have felt some affection . . .

She left the book open on the table and walked out through the swing doors, out of the vestibule, out of the building into the mellowing afternoon, impelled by a revulsion so total that she was unconscious of haste or movement, conscious only that she must get away, out, escape, a reflex of horror, a retching of the spirit. Instinctively she turned away from the direction of Hellebore Road, walking into narrow streets where she had never been before, until she reached the river. She walked blindly along it, fast, as though she were going somewhere. She had to keep moving, for if she did not she would collapse. To keep moving was like holding one's breath in air so foul that to take it into one's lungs would suffocate. She walked fast, fast, the wind lifting the hair from her cheeks, the satchel thumping on her hip, walking away from knowledge too unspeakable even to be remembered, the numb vacuum of her mind gradually filling with small, feverish planning. Away, anywhere. Not home – never, never again. The river, a rope in a barn, South America, but never again home. Never. London. London was far and vast. Trains went to London all the time, and she lifted her head to see where she was and in which direction Temple Meads Station lay.

But it cost pounds to get to London. She stopped and, turning into a corner, counted the money in her purse. Seven and three-halfpence – you didn't take much money with you to school for sometimes it got pinched. She had money at home, some cash and about three pounds in Savings stamps; but at home it might just as well be on the moon. She would stow away on the train, take a platform ticket and lock herself in the toilet and somehow evade the ticket collector at the other end. But she would be caught and sent home.

As though stung, she began walking again, desperately. How did one get money? One earned it or stole it or sometimes men gave it to girls who let them have sex with them. There was no time for any of these; she must get out of Bristol quickly before they missed her. There might be time to steal some, but where from and how? Or had she something she could sell? Nothing, nothing, dressed as she was in school uniform, not even a locket hidden under her dress like some of the girls wore.

Sandra. Sandra wore a locket which she claimed contained a lock of Ceddy's hair. If she told Sandra some sexy story about why she was running away Sandra would lend her some money. Sandra was so awful she was the only person she could go to.

She took her bearings. The foliaged peak of Brandon Hill was to her right; if she cut through the streets at its foot between the river she would get to Sandra's terrace. But she must be quick, for they would miss her before long, accustomed though they were these days to her being late back from school.

Music was sounding from the basement room of Sandra's house, which might mean she was down there and alone. June found a shard of flowerpot and threw it gently against the window, but it fell short. She could not find another. The gate at the top of the steps leading down to the area was stiff, only the dustmen used it, and it gave a terrible groan as she got it open. She crept down the steps and peered in through the window. She could see nothing but the music was loud. She tapped on the glass through the bars.

After a moment Sandra loomed, looking astonished. She mimed a question and June mimed back to open the window, but it was stuck and would not budge. Sandra disappeared and from a door beside June, beneath the front steps, came grinding noises and bangs. At last it opened a little way, Sandra tugging at it.

'It sticks,' she said and stared at June. 'You do look queer. What's the matter with you?'

'Let me come in.'

'All right. But why down here?' She stood back and June slid through the opening. The record-player was full on and the noise beat about June's head. She suddenly felt weak and half fell into a chair.

'What's the matter with you?' Sandra repeated.

The darkness and coolness of the room, the jazz, Sandra standing there already changed into slacks and a striped over-blouse, seemed like the setting for a play, altogether unreal. The whole thing was unreal. June pulled off her school beret, eased the satchel from her shoulder, letting her breath go.

'Swear not to let on to anyone you've seen me.'

'Why?'

'Swear.'

'All right. But why?'

'I'm going to London.'

Sandra gaped. 'What for?'

'To be with Tony.'

'Tony? Your boyfriend?'

'Yes.'

Sandra's expression of astonishment changed to interest. She sat down, clasping her hands round her tightly encased knees. 'Go on! Why?'

'We want to be together.'

'Don't your parents know?'

'No. They think I'm too young. So I'm running away to join him.'

'They'll come after you.'

'It'll be too late then.'

'You mean, you're really going to . . .?'

'Yes.'

Sandra gave a great shudder of admiration. 'Honestly, June, you're mad! You mean they'll have to let you get married?' June nodded. 'Wait till Miss Propert finds out – can't you just see her face!' She giggled but grew serious again. 'What've you come here for?'

'Will you lend me some money?'

'Hasn't he given you any?'

'I left it at home.'

'Can't you go back and get it?'

'No, they'd be onto me.'

'Well, I haven't got any.'

'It's only a loan. I'll send it to you the minute I get to London. It's just for the fare.'

'I don't see why you haven't got any.'

'Well, I haven't!' Exasperation lent her urgency. 'He's waiting for me. I've got to go now. Honestly, Sandra, I'd do it for you.'

'Yes?' Sandra was torn between cynicism and response to so romantic an appeal. 'How much do you want?'

'How much have you got?'

'You said it was just for the fare.'

'Yes, but I've got to have bus fares the other end.'

'Won't he meet you at the station?'

'No, he can't. The police may be looking for me by then and they might spot him. I'm going straight to his place.'

'It sounds funny to me.'

'It isn't, it's just ordinary plain common sense. Honestly, Sandra, we're just wasting time. I've got to get to the station.'

'Well – wait here then.'

In a little while she was back, creeping down the stairs so that her mother should not hear her. She carried some clothes rolled up against her chest.

'You'll need these. If the police are after you the first thing they'd spot would be your uniform.'

'Gosh, thanks, Sandra!' She jumped up and began to undo her dress. 'I'd never have thought of that.'

'And here's three pounds. It's what I had saved up for a tape-recorder.'

'Honestly, you're wonderful.'

'I've got to have it back, mind. My mother'll kill me if she finds out I've taken it. I'd better have an IOU.'

'Don't you trust me?'

'It's what I'd saved up,' Sandra repeated obstinately.

June dropped her dress on the floor and slipped on first the shirt, then the skirt Sandra had brought her. 'It's a bit big in the waist.'

'You're so skinny. It won't show under the blazer.'

'I can't wear the blazer – it'll give me away.'

'You'll freeze if you don't. You won't be there till late.'

'Gosh, you think of everything.' It was almost enjoyable, dressing up, conspiring, fooling Sandra, all in a vacuum against 'The Trial of Raymond Cavendish Banks' on the shelves of the Public Library, like a play. *Twelfth Night* or *What you Will* long ago in the real world of Jervis's. 'I'll put my hair up. Have you got a mirror?'

'Outside. Don't let Mum hear.' They crept into the dark passage and Sandra switched on the light. June had some kirby grips in the pocket of her blazer and was able to twist up her hair. 'Doesn't it make a difference!' whispered Sandra. 'You look quite fab.'

They crept back into the room as the record played itself to an end. Sandra hastily started it off again. 'Mum comes down if this isn't playing, she thinks I'm not doing my homework.'

'What about my uniform?'

'I'll hide it.' She picked up dress and beret and bundled them under a cushion. 'Perhaps I'll throw them in the river later, then they'll think you've drowned. You'd better take the satchel to put things in – besides, I can't hide that so easy.'

'Well – thanks a million.'

'Here, sign this first.' She scribbled an IOU on the page of an exercise-book and June signed it.

'Swear you won't tell?'

'Of course not. Honestly, I never thought you were this kind at all. I mean, you never let on, you were always so square about sex and that. Here, take the chocolate.' She took a half-eaten bar from the litter of schoolbooks on the table and thrust it at June.

'Thanks. I'll send you the money back, and the clothes.'

'I wonder if we'll ever meet again. Perhaps you'll be in the papers.'

Her stomach seemed to turn over. 'I must fly. I don't know when the train is.'

'What's he like?'

'Who?'

'Your Tony.'

'Oh – fair and blue eyes and a moustache – a big moustache, like flyers always have.'

Sandra giggled. 'Like Jimmy Edwards.'

'Well – something. But it's distinguished.'

'Does it tickle?'

'Tickle? Oh . . .' She turned away in embarrassment and picked up the satchel.

'Ceddy's beard tickles. It makes you feel ever so funny.'

'I must go. Thanks again, Sandra, ever so much. You've saved my life.'

She went quickly up the steps and away, back into the city, to Temple Meads Station.

SEVEN

IN THE TRAIN she had slept, secure in the compartment bearing her away from everything she could not face. It was dark when she awoke, no outside world, nothing but her own face reflected in the murky window until London began to stretch its lighted streets on either side.

As she stepped out into Paddington Station she began to shiver. The enormity of her solitude here caught and crashed on her like icy breakers and all she could do was inwardly gasp and strike out for shelter, any shelter. She found the Ladies Waiting room, washed her face, redid her hair; then she sat in a corner of the bleak vestibule, thinking what to do.

The story of her romance with Tony had been invented solely to get Sandra's help; only something with sex in it would do that, and it was as though God had put the right lies into June's mouth. She had made it up as she went along, but as she went along it had seemed as if it were true. Not that she was in love with him – she knew quite well she was not, even as she played with her fabrications – but that she could go to him. There was no one else. Never again Auntie Norah, traitress, liar. There was only Tony. Had he not said she ought to go to London? Had he not sided with her against Them? He was not Theirs but hers only, her private friend, worldly and brave. He would know what she should do, where she should go, although she would not (she drew breath sharply) would not tell him why she had run away, why it was impossible ever to see either of Them again, yes, even Her, for She not only endured him but loved him. ... June could make up some story for Tony as she had made up one for Sandra.

Now, sitting cold and close as a stray cat in a cellar, she thought of him again. She knew where he lived, Pevensey Terrace, Bayswater, for she had not forgotten anything he had ever said to her; if she altered it in any way, it was only for her own purposes. He had not told her the number of the house but had said there was a pillar box outside and that his name was on the bell. She could look, anyway. If not to him, where else could she go? It was late, perhaps the station closed, she did not know. She could sit here for a time but soon someone would notice her perhaps and ask questions, tell the police . . . She had heard of hostels where you could stay, but how to find them in the great wastes of London? She could ask nobody, for fear of their questions.

For an instant she longed for Auntie Norah, the flatlet neat as the inside of a First Aid box, and the brown photograph of Auntie Norah's mother in the lopsided silver frame, the brisk order, rational comfort. But that, of course, was impossible. Auntie Norah was unspeakably part of Them. She would never see any of them again.

What, then? Sit here till turned out or suspected? Gather herself together and step out into black London to walk all night or sleep on a bench (where?) or sit in a café (but did they close?) or go to Tony?

There was no question, really.

She rose and stepped cautiously out into the station. A long train from Wales was just drawing in on a far platform and she mingled with its passengers, finding herself presently in a narrow shiny street of closed shops and empty pavements, the other people hurrying, scattering away. In desperation she asked one of them, 'Please, which way to Pevensey Terrace?'

'Where?'

'Pevensey Terrace.'

'Never heard of it.' He made to move on.

'It's in Bayswater,' she cried.

'Number fifteen – along there.' He jerked his head towards a bus stop and hurried away.

On the bus she said, 'Bayswater, please.'

'Wrong way,' snapped the conductress and rang the bell crossly. The bus stopped with a shudder. 'The other side,' she called, waving June off with what seemed a menacing gesture.

Trembling, she crossed the black road. A car hooted at her irritably; some youths, roistering by, whistled and shouted remarks at her from the other side of the road; a bus snarled by without stopping. When one did stop she got in and sank down near the door. The brown conductor, round-headed, round-eyed, rattled his money-pouch absently.

'Pevensey Terrace – will you tell me, please?'

'OK.'

Presently he told her. She pulled her weak knees upright and stepped off. 'Right down there, love,' he called, his long fingers pointing.

The house was quite easy to find. The pillar box stood in front of two porticoed doors and the first one had his name in rain-splashed ink on a piece of card, with 'Second Floor' underneath. The front door stood ajar and she pushed it open onto a dark hall. After a moment she was able to see, in the light from the streetlamp, an electric switch near the staircase, which when lit showed two dark doors facing the hall, linoleum-covered stairs and a dark dado leading upward. There was a smell of curry. Her apprehension that one of the doors would open and someone come out to demand what she wanted was stronger than her nervousness, and without further time for thought she went upstairs, past the sound of a radio on the first floor to the oilcloth silence of the second. She had just read 'TOWNSEND' printed on another piece of card pinned to the door facing the stairs when the light went out.

She was so startled that she immediately knocked on the door more loudly than she had intended. The sudden darkness, the sharp rapping, seemed to trap her, and she stood with panic beginning to shake her limbs, impatient, ready to scream. From inside the room there was a sense rather than a sound of confused movement. He was there, she knew he was there, asleep perhaps but present, able to open the door and take her problems from her. The darkness and the silence began to suffocate her and she beat on the door again desperately, not caring who heard her.

Now there was a definite stirring and then his voice called sharply, 'Who is it?' At the sound tears pressed out of her eyes and a pain like a knife across her throat cut all sound in her. She managed a sort of croak, and knocked again at the adamant wood, but feebly this time, for the promise of rescue which his presence there, the other side of the door, held for her seemed to send the strength seeping away as though she was bleeding tears. There was more shuffling inside, the rattle of a curtain being drawn, his voice again saying, 'Just a minute,' and then the door opened a little way and he peered out, holding a dressing gown close to his throat. 'Who is it? What d'you want?' he asked irritably.

She thought she would faint and could only whisper, 'It's me.'

'Me? Who? It's bloody late, you know,' opening the door an inch or two wider so that the light from the room fell on her face. 'Good Christ!' he said, and his mouth gaped open.

'Can I see you?' The lame words were hardly audible.

'Well . . .' He glanced back into the room, clutching the dressing gown to his neck. 'You'd better come in.' He stood back and opened the door wide enough for her to enter. Beneath the robe his legs and feet were bare, his hair was ruffled, even his moustache seemed dishevelled. It was so wonderful to see him she could do nothing but stand just inside the door staring helplessly at him, the tears stiffening on her cheeks. 'What on earth's happened?' he asked. 'Why are you here?'

'I've run away.' As she spoke the nightmare terror lifted. She was safe. This was Tony, with his nice blue eyes and his bare legs a little ridiculous under the robe as if he'd been paddling, half friend, half father, shadow of the lover invented for Sandra. The memory swam into her mind of half a dozen films in which the heroine, wearing the hero's pyjamas far too large for her, slept in his bed while he had a comedy scene with pillows and blankets on the floor. It would be like that. They always fell in love and had breakfast together in a kitchen with frilly curtains. There were no frilly curtains here, only a printed cotton one across one corner, but the bed was there, a rumpled divan with the covers thrown back, and an armchair with his shirt thrown over it and his socks in little balls. There was a wardrobe with his suit on a hanger hanging outside, and a table by the window with bottles on it. The room was warm with the smell of cigarettes and – was it? – sleep.

All this June perceived in the moment as she stood passive inside the door, limp with the passing of her problems to Tony, for he would know what to do. Perhaps later she would act for herself again but for the present it was all his, he was haven and she had reached it. She looked round for somewhere to sit down, for suddenly she had begun to shake again.

'Here,' he said, and held out his hand to help her

to a chair; but at his touch she began to cry again, half-conscious of its effect, falling against him so that he supported her with his arms about her. She lay against him, surrendering to safety and release, her head in the hollow of his bare neck, soaking his flesh and the collar of the dressing gown with tears, smelling the warm, faintly oily smell of his body which her own told her was naked beneath the robe. She could feel it, smell it, smooth under the cloth, electric with hair and soft hanging things that, at the parting of the gown against which she rested, would peer out and be recognised, his thighs naked under the skimped cloth against her own, his buttocks taut under the sash, and his smell, welling from the hollows and creases of his body, smoky and hairy and full of bed.

She put her arms tight round his waist, sobbing and pressing against him as though she were a child, feeling a heat rise up and dissolve all her joints, her bones, her most secret pulses, trembling into him. Now to be dissolved and made anew, destroyed and begun again, relinquished and held fast ... She gasped as he put her from him and into a chair. She was suddenly terribly cold and sat shaking while he poured liquid from a square green bottle. Her teeth chattered and she could hardly take the glass.

'Here, drink this,' he said. 'It's only gin but it's better than nothing.' She drank some but it was disgusting and she pulled a face. 'I've no squash or anything,' he said distractedly, hitching the gown more closely around him, 'only tonic or bitters. Drink a bit more, there's a good girl, it'll pull you together.'

She took another sip, then put the glass away, pushing the hair from her forehead and looking up at him while he poured himself a drink. 'I've run away,' she said again.

'Why? What for?'

A flood of colour swept her face as the truth plunged into her. 'Don't ask me.'

'I must ask you. What the hell did you come here for if you didn't expect to be asked?' He took a long swallow and stared at her over his moustache. 'Don't they know where you are?'

'Of course not.'

'I shall have to get in touch.'

'If you do I'll kill myself.'

'Oh, don't talk cock!'

'I thought you'd help me.'

'How can I help you? The only thing to help you is to tell me what's happened.'

'I'd rather die.'

He made an effort at calmness and sat down on the arm of a chair, dragging the dressing-gown skirts primly across his knees. 'You must tell me.'

She looked away, her face shutting. 'I can't.'

'You have to. How can I tell you what to do if I don't know? Is it school? Have you done something you shouldn't?' She shook her head. 'Has someone been unkind to you?' She was still. 'Who? At school? What happened?'

'Not school.'

'Who then?'

'Him. My father.' She plunged further to hide the real horror. 'Only he's not my father.'

'He's not? I thought . . .'

'He's not, he's not! He couldn't be!'

He waited a moment. 'What happened then, June?' She shook her head violently. 'You must tell me if you want me to help.'

'I can't. It's too awful. He's done something awful.'

'Your – stepfather?' She nodded. 'To you?'

She nodded again, convulsively, twisting her hands in her lap, hanging her head so that he could not see her face for the hair falling lopsidedly over delicate cheek and nape.

He stared at her, appalled at the implications of her words. A stepfather – a teenage girl – something awful – flight. . . . He said weakly, 'But what will you do?'

'I don't know. I thought you'd help me.'

'How can I? You're a child.'

'I'm not.'

'In law you are. Oh Christ, what a mess!'

There was silence for a moment, then June said with dignity, 'I'm sorry I troubled you.'

'It's not that. At least – the whole thing's impossible.'

'I'll find somewhere to go in the morning.'

'In the morning!' He started up agitatedly, found and lit a cigarette. 'We must find somewhere now.'

'Now? It's the middle of the night.'

'I'm well aware of that.'

'Can't I stay here tonight? I could sleep in the chair.'

'No, you bloody well can't stay here!' He sat down on the bed, screwing up his eyes against the smoke from his cigarette, and began to put on his socks with shaking hands.

'But why not? I'd be ever so quiet.'

'Because you're not the only one involved.'

'But no one need know. I could creep out in the morning before anyone was awake . . .'

He reached for his shoes under the divan and slid his feet into them before straightening. His face looked pouched and he gazed at her with harassed weariness. 'My dear sweet clot,' he said, 'we are not alone.'

'Not alone?'

'No. I had a – a friend with me this evening.'

She looked round, bewildered. 'Where is he?'

'Behind the kitchen curtain, dear, and it's not a he.' He got to his feet. 'You'd better come out now, Jacky.'

'Just a sec.' To June's stupefaction a woman's voice came from behind the curtain, which shook with a sudden flurry of activity. Tony hitched his dressing gown about him and, going wearily to the armchair, picked out shirt and underclothes from a pile which June now saw also contained stockings and a dress.

'I'm sorry, June, but that's how it is. You caught us on the hop.'

June got slowly to her feet as the curtain was pushed back and Jacky came out. She was little and light, with a puffball of almost white hair, and her eyes inside their mascara rims were a dark starry hazel. She wore only a petticoat with a jumper of Tony's slung over her thin shoulders. Tony took her hand. Submissively they presented themselves, half-clothed, half-married. 'June, this is Jacky.'

Jacky took a step forward. 'You poor kid,' she said, 'would you like a cup of tea?'

'No. No thank you.' She retreated, clutching the blazer tightly across her chest.

'Tony, pop the kettle on, love.' She gave his hand a little shake while propelling him towards the curtain. 'Sit down, duckie, you look all in.'

'No.'

Behind the half-drawn curtain Tony was dressing. Jacky turned aside, as though by presenting her back she were for the moment invisible, and pulled the dress over her head and over her narrow hips, twisting to draw the zip up under her arm. Then she wriggled herself into shape and turned back to June, her eyes candid and her mouth, with its lipstick half kissed away, gentle. 'I'm sorry about this,' she said, 'but that's the way life is.'

She bent down for her shoes, which June now saw stood pintoed under the bedside shelf where they had been kicked off. And suddenly the tumbled bed seemed to writhe and heave, heat and the oily, hairy smell of Tony's body seemed to rise like a miasma from the squashed pillows, the wrinkled, moistened sheets. She felt a paroxysm in her guts, as though a vice clamped suddenly on the inmost vitals of her body, and she snatched up the satchel from the floor where she had first dropped it and fumbled for the door. Behind the bed, behind Jacky, Tony emerged from the alcove, a shirt almost covering his pants, his legs hairy above socks, his face hairy above open collar. They were both staring at her as she plunged from the room, both calling after her, 'June – don't go – June . . .' and Jacky, 'June, you can stay with me . . .' but, following her out onto the dark landing, softly, so as not to rouse the other lodgers, despairingly, as June ran down the stairs and out into the street and on, on towards darkness, knowing they could not follow her.

EIGHT

MRS PARSONS HAD NEVER been used to sleeping alone and when her husband was absent, which was fairly often, she was in the habit of bundling into her bed such of her children as were of convenient size; at this moment they were Dawn and Kevin, aged three and eighteen months, who made comfortable cushions with which to buttress Mrs Parsons' mounds and indentations. They had the advantage, too, of waking at first light, serving as alarm clocks when Mrs Parsons was on the early shift at the canteen of the office buildings where she worked, but being pacified by a drink of 7-Up and some potato crisps if she were not. Then they could all three go back to a kind of a sleep while the other children got themselves up and out, Garry first for his present job as van-boy started at 8 a.m., Sharon next to be at the hairdressers, to which she was apprenticed, at nine, then Colin and Digby hammering off to school, dressed anyhow, jam round their mouths, bawling and scuffling already. Then, if it were Mrs Parsons' late turn, she and the babies would rise frowsty and benign to tea and a big fry-up, for by then they were all hungry. Sometimes Kevin would not have been able to hold out, and the bed would smell of ammonia; but bless him, he couldn't help it.

This morning they all lay together, the two children on either side of her like tugs at the side of the *Queen Elizabeth*. Some crisps had got into the bedclothes, but not enough to notice, and drowsily she could hear Garry and Sharon getting their breakfast in the kitchen downstairs. The Parsonses occupied the ground and first floor of a house near Harrow Road. The rooms above were let separately to people who constantly varied, while in the basement lived an elderly couple who kept a haberdashery stall in a nearby street market. There was no bathroom and the lavatory was a dank cell in the yard, but Mrs Parsons and Sharon kept the front room windows of their section sprucely washed and curtained, whatever the rest of the house might be like. If she felt like it, she might wash the kitchen floor this morning, she wasn't on till the noon shift. She'd see how she felt. If it was a hot day, she wouldn't. She turned on her side and cuddled Kevin up against her belly. He was moist and smelt of crisps. At her back Dawn lay awake, sucking her thumb. Mrs Parsons let out a long, contented fart.

She heard the door open and Garry's voice asked, 'Mum?' Although she sank her head further into the pillows, he came to stand by the side of the bed. 'Mum?' he repeated, 'can you 'ear me, Mum?' She grunted. 'Mum, I got a girl downstairs. 'Er name's Janie.'

'Eh? What's that?' Mrs Parsons reared up on her elbow, the two children rolling into the cavity left by her body.

'I got a girl downstairs. 'Er name's Janie.'

'What's she there for?'

'She 'adn't got no place to go. I picked 'er up las' night inna caff.'

Now she was really awake, her mottled face ferocious beneath the tousle of yellow hair. "Ere, what you bin up to?'

'Take it easy, Mum. She's all right.' He stood lightly, as though poised to elude whatever might threaten, thin, tall, hollow-chested because of the mock-leather windcheater hanging open over his striped shirt.

'What's up with 'er, then? Why isn't she at 'ome?'

'Look, I gotta get to work. Sharon's give 'er a cup of splosh.'

'You get 'er out of my kitchen! I won't 'ave you bringing your tarts into my kitchen . . .'

'It's not what you think, Mum. You let 'er stay, see? I'll be 'ome soon's I get me wages.' He was gone.

Mrs Parsons lay back on the pillows again, pushing the children to either side of her. 'The nerve!' she muttered, and shut her eyes. Best let all the kids get off first and Miss Muck too, she wouldn't be surprised. She knew that sort, fly-by-nights, after what they could get, like stray cats, they were, sneaking round the boys. Let her clear off soon's she saw there wasn't nothing laying around . . . Curiosity was too strong, however. She got up, lit a cigarette, put an overall over her nightgown, outer clothing over the children's vests, in which they slept, and took them downstairs.

Colin and Digby were still at the table, pushing and sniggering in the direction of a washed-out-looking girl about Sharon's age, but seeming ten years younger. She was trying to ignore them by reading the newspaper which acted as tablecloth, a half full mug of tea by her hand. When Mrs Parsons appeared she looked up, scared.

'That's enough of that, you boys. Get out of it,' said Mrs Parsons. Hushed, the boys gulped their tea and clattered past her, Digby pausing to give Dawn a smacking kiss. 'You be'ave now!' Mrs Parsons called after them automatically, studying the girl meanwhile.

'Well,' she said belligerently, 'what're you up to?'

A wave of colour came into the girl's face and she stood up. 'Nothing. Garry said it would be all right.'

'What would?'

'For me to stay.'

''E did, did 'e?'

'Yes.'

''E says a lot, 'e does.' She advanced into the room and felt the teapot. 'Put some more 'ot water in, will you? Shut up grizzlin', lovie, your tea's just comin',' to Kevin, who was whining and pulling at her skirt. The girl lifted the encrusted kettle from the stove and filled the teapot, her hands shaking a little. 'That's right,' said Mrs Parsons, gave the pot a vigorous stir and poured out two mugs of tea, added milk and sugar from the packet, sat down and took Kevin on her lap. Dawn clambered onto a second chair and began to blow on her tea. 'What did you say your name was?'

'Janie,' said June.

''Ow old are you?'

'Eighteen.'

'Don't give me that, dear. You don't look no more than fourteen.'

'I am!'

'Only if you're under sixteen, dear, it makes trouble for all of us, see? I won't 'ave nothing to do with you if you're under sixteen.'

'I'm not – honestly.'

'I believe you, thousands wouldn't.' She held the mug for Kevin, who drank lustily. 'Pop the frying pan on, will you, dear? Where you from?'

'Birmingham.'

'Birmingham, eh? You on the trot?' The girl looked blank. 'Run away from somewhere?' The girl coloured again and turned away to light the gas, not answering. 'It's nothing to me what you done, dear,' said Mrs Parsons, rising and setting Kevin in her chair, 'only I don't want no trouble, see? If the coppers are after you, I can't 'ave you, see? There's fat in the pan, i'nt there?'

'Yes, but it looks very black.'

'That's all right, it'll fry up.' She took some slices of bread out of a packet and dropped them in the pan. Smoke and sizzling filled the kitchen, and they had to raise their voices. 'I can't 'ave no trouble, see, not in my position.'

'I haven't done anything, honestly. It was just – my train arrived late and I didn't know where to go and I met Garry in a café and he said I could come here.'

'Want a bit of bread, dear?'

'Yes, please.' At the thought of it the saliva ran in her mouth, for she had eaten nothing since the pie and coffee in the place where Garry and his friends had been. All legs and elbows, they had lounged into the café and filled it with their bravado, raucous, scuffling, putting coins in the jukebox, gulping minerals direct from bottles and belching loudly afterwards, eyeing her, needling her to each other. She had shrunk, shrunk behind her table, hoping the man behind the counter would call them off, but he appeared to notice nothing. After a while most of them got tired of it, but a couple came and sprawled at the table and started talking to her. They were not as frightening separately as in a mob, and she was able to reply. One of them was Garry and he brought her here. She had slept in the armchair by the fireplace, for he shared his bedroom with his schoolboy brothers. She could not quite remember what lies she had told him, but perhaps neither could he.

Mrs Parsons was stirring eggs in with the fried bread and the smell was delicious, despite the clouds of black smoke. 'So you 'aven't got nowhere to stay?'

'No. But I can easily find somewhere.'

Mrs Parsons grunted. 'Got any cash?'

'A little.'

'That won't get you far then.'

'I'll find a job. That's why I came to London. I couldn't find anything I liked in Birmingham.'

'You won't find it no different 'ere. It's this Bulge, see, what they never took no thought for. Kids leaving school like my Garry can't find nothing they fancy. 'E's tried all sorts but 'e don't stick at nothing. 'E can't find nothing to interest 'im, see? Course, it's different if you got all them passes. It's a cryin' shame, that is. I mean, it's not everyone wants to be bothered with all that stuff, is it? Course, you can always say you got 'em. I mean, 'oo's to know? Give us some plates, dear, will you?' She ladled the delicious mess onto the plates June held for her, and filled up the teapot again. They all began to eat.

Presently Mrs Parsons asked again, 'Where d'you say you come from?'

Where had she? Gulping, she remembered. 'Birmingham.'

''Ave you got a mum and dad?' She shook her head. 'Where d'you live, then?'

'With an aunt. Auntie Norah.'

'She know you've come down 'ere?'

'Of course. It was her idea. She has to go into hospital, you see, and there's no one to look after me so she said why didn't I come to London and see if I could find a job, and then when she's better I could go back. Or she could come here. Honestly.' She gazed at Mrs Parsons, stretching her eyes wide with candour.

Mrs Parsons stared back impassively. 'Only I don't want no trouble, see? You mind your business and I'll mind mine, only if you're on the trot from one of them approved schools or some'ing, then I can't 'ave you, see?'

'No, I'm not, honestly. It's like I said . . .'

'Yeah, well, I don't want to know no more. Only I don't want the law coming round after you, we seen enough of them – 'aven't we, you lovely bundle of love, you!' she suddenly cried exuberantly, snatching Kevin to her and giving him a kiss. He gave a yell of protest and struck out at her with his spoon.

'How old is he?'

''E's comin' on two. And Dawn's three.'

'She's sweet.'

'Yeah, she's all right. She will keep suckin' 'er thumb all the time, it gets on me nerves. Sometimes I think she's retarded.'

'Oh no!'

'Lady down at the Welfare says she's all right but look at 'er, suck, suck, suck all the time. It turns me up.' They regarded Dawn, who stared back at them gravely across the litter of the table, her mouth a small pump round her thumb. The sight was hypnotic and June gave a large yawn. Mrs Parsons glanced at her shrewdly. 'Why don't you go and 'ave a lay down on Sharon's bed? I'll give you a shout when I take the kids to the nursery.'

'Could I?' The food and the peace had suddenly filled her with overwhelming drowsiness, as though months of sleep denied were crowding in on her.

'Go on. Upstairs at the back. You 'ave a bit of a laydown, you'll feel better. You know where the toilet is, don't you?'

She went up the linoleumed stairs and into the back room. It was small and dark, looking out over the yard to replicas of itself, but tidy. Of the two beds one was obviously not in use and piled with children's clothes, the other nearly covered, the wall alongside stuck with pin-up pictures of pop singers. Ornaments and cosmetics were arranged on the narrow mantelpiece and chest of drawers, and from behind a half-drawn curtain in the corner protruded a meringue of stiffened petticoat and some pin-toed, pin-heeled shoes. It was not like June's own room but it was a girl's room, and she lay down on the bed thankfully, unable to hold on any longer to the shreds of consciousness that the last twenty-four hours had left her.

She awoke to a slant of sunlight on the far wall and Garry shaking her shoulder. With his flapping black jerkin and spindle legs, he looked like a huge hovering bird. She gave a gasp and shrank away to the wall.

'I brought you some char.' He held out a mug.

'Oh – thank you.' She sat up, feeling foolish, and took it from him. 'What time is it?'

''Arpars two.'

'Your mother said she'd call me.'

'She's gone to work. She left this.' He gave her a sheet of pink notepaper with silver deckled edges on which was written in pencil: 'Dear Janey. You can stay toonight if convenient Sharons room. Mrs Parsons.'

She looked up at Garry radiantly, 'She says I can stay!'

'Yeah, well, she reckoned you 'adn't got no place to go.'

'No, I haven't.' She took a sip of tea, then made a face.

'Whatsa matter?'

'It's so sweet.'

'Yeah, I put plenty in. I gotta sweet tooth.' He sat down on the bed and stared at her in a meaning way. Flustered, she drew her legs up under her and asked, 'Shouldn't you be at work?'

'No, I come off sick soon's I got me pay.' He reached out and took hold of her ankle. 'You're quite a doll,' he said, 'I could go for you.' She pulled away, retreating up onto the pillow. 'Aw, don't be like that! You like me, dontcha?'

'Yes but . . .'

'I bin good to you, 'aven't I? I took you in, di'nt I?'

'Yes . . .'

'Well, come on then.' He advanced up the bed and tried to put his arms round her. He smelt, not altogether unpleasantly, of cigarettes and sweat.

'Don't!'

'Aw, come on!'

'No – no!' She beat off his inept, wiry hands but he managed to plant a kiss on the side of her mouth, pushing her back against the wall with his face and sending his hands in new directions. She ducked sideways and with all her strength pushed his chest so that he fell back a little.

'Whatsa matter with you?' he asked astoundedly, and for answer she burst into tears.

She cried as though she were an elemental force, a tropical storm, the tears pouring down her face, her mouth open, gasping and howling like a lunatic, rocking to and fro. He stared at her and backed away a little. 'For Chrissake!' She howled and beat the pillow, washed away in the collapse of all the disciplines in which she had been brought up. The howls and the tears poured out of her, bearing away like flotsam the tensions and uncertainties of the months since life ended at Havenport, the cataclysmic shock of her father's past, the flight, abandonment, revulsion and ugliness all climaxed in the slobber of this boy's mouth, his hand foraging her still sleeping body. Gone, gone, everything gone in a great floodwater of release – manners, control, gentility, all Mum's training, the gentle sunniness of childhood . . .

He felt uneasily for a cigarette. 'Belt up, can'tcha?' he muttered, 'I get the message.'

Hiccupping and drenched, she drooped on the pillow, wiping her streaming nose on the back of her hand. Her hair was falling down and great wet splodges of tears soaked the front of her blouse. 'Christ,' he said again. 'What you carryin' on like that for? I di'nt do nothing, did I?'

'I'm sorry,' she blubbered.

'Yeah, well, you wanta keep a grip on yourself, dontcha?' He stood up, thin as a stork. 'D'ya want some'ing to eat?' She nodded from under her hair, still hiccupping and gasping. 'Come on, then.' Without a further glance he left the room.

He was eating bread and jam at the table, legs and elbows sprawled, when she came down. She had been unable to find anything to wash in so had wiped her face dry on her petticoat. The kirby grips had fallen out and were mostly lost, so she let her hair hang round her face in the old childish way. She was shivering, still catching her breath, but rinsed clear of hysteria.

'You wanta cook some'ing, you do it,' he said.

'No thank you.' She sat opposite him and he pushed the packeted loaf towards her.

''Elp yourself. You want some splosh?'

'No thank you.'

He shrugged and lit a cigarette.

She buttered a slice of bread and began to eat. Presently she asked humbly, 'When will Sharon be back?'

''Bout arpars five. She 'as to fetch the kids from the nursery.'

'Will she mind me being in her room, d'you think?'

'Nah! She 'as the kids in there with 'er when the ole man's 'ome.'

'Is he a sailor or something?'

He looked at her for the first time since the scene upstairs. His eyes were grey, with long lashes of great beauty, and when revealed like this and not defensively aside, of candid clearness. 'Nah,' he said, and smiled faintly. ''E's inna nick. You know what the nick is, dontcha?' She nodded, gaping. 'Cos you don' know much, do you? I mean, you're dead simple most of the time, arntcha?'

'I don't know about London,' she said.

'Yeah, well, I can see that. I mean, look at your 'air and your clothes. You look a proper nit, dontcha?'

Although his tone was kindly, she was piqued into asking sharply, 'What did your father do?'

'What 'e always done. Larceny. On'y this time they give 'im armed robbery too and 'e never done that. It was a frame-up, that's what it was. If 'e's not careful 'e'll end up with a PD. Mum'll do 'er nut then and no error.'

She asked faintly, 'Doesn't he ever work?'

Garry laughed. His teeth were surprisingly good. 'That is 'is work. 'E's a carpenter like in 'is spare time but 'e don't bother with that much. 'E reckons carpentry's a waste of time when you can buy stuff like that on the HP.' He jerked his head towards the black and white contemporary sideboard on which the television set stood. "E's a nut case, my old man.' He leaned back and began to pick his teeth with a fingernail. 'You goin' to stay 'ere?'

'I don't know.'

'I mean, it's nothin' to me, see. On'y if you 'aven't got no lolly and no job and no 'ome, seems like you 'aven't got much of anythin', 'ave you?' She shook her head meekly. 'It's nothin' to me,' he repeated, ''on'y if the law's lookin' for you, you'd better stay 'ere, see. Otherwise they'll 'ave you.'

She stared at him. 'Will they?'

'Yeah. I mean, you must've done some'ing, mustn't you, cos you're too dead simple to be loose on your own otherwise, arnt-cha?' She bowed her head. 'You take my tip. You lay up 'ere. Mum'll see you right. On'y don't let on they're after you, see, or she'll be dead chuffed, see? She don' like the law.' He got up and stretched himself. 'I'm goin' to 'ave a kip.'

'What shall I do?'

He gave her a sardonic look. 'You don't wanta bunkup, you better stay 'ere, 'adn't you?'

'Shall I tidy up?'

'Suit yourself.' He flipped the cigarette-butt into the sink and lounged out of the room. She sat staring at nothing for a little while, then rose and began to clear the table. As she moved about her gestures became more assured. She found an apron stuffed under the sink and put it on, filled the kettle with water and set it to boil, screwed up the empty wrappings of loaf and butter and dropped them in the rubbish pail. Apart from the gas stove, everything was clean except where stains or time had rubbed the surfaces through, but she had never been in a place of such confusion. The table, covered with newspaper, filled most of the room, leaving only a narrow belt between it and the blackened cooker, the sideboard covered with objects, a cupboard full of food and pots and pans, a refrigerator, and the window looking out onto the street. The armchair in which she had slept last night was in one corner, another smaller one with wooden arms pushed up against the table with a collection of upright chairs of various kinds. She had never seen so much crammed into so small a space and all in such a muddle, yet it gave a strange sense of security, as though nothing alien could possibly force its way in at you through the jungle of possessions.

She ripped the stained newspaper off the table and, when the kettle began to boil, settled to wash and scrub.

NINE

SOON AFTER EIGHT that morning the front doorbell of the Baxters' house in Hellebore Road sounded briefly, so briefly that Esther, lying fully clothed on top of the bed, did not hear it. She lay with her eyes shut but her mind racing behind the closed lids, her hand clenched on a handkerchief drying out now from the tears that had soaked it. Neither bed had been slept in but the covers of both were crumpled. The curtains were half-drawn, for Raymond had hoped she might sleep a little at last.

When he came in she opened her eyes quickly and half sat up.

'It's news, Ett,' he said. His voice shook.

'Is she safe?'

'She was. She's in London.'

'London?' She swung her feet to the floor and wiped her face over with the handkerchief, scrubbing it as though to scrub away bewilderment. He sat down beside her and put his arm round her shoulders.

'It was last night. Mr Townsend saw her. His mother's downstairs now.'

She got up hurriedly, slipped on some shoes, pushed her hair from her face. He followed more heavily down the stairs.

Mrs Townsend sat in the front living-room as though on springs, hands and knees bunched together, her big old wedding-ring standing up like an extra knuckle. Her hair was in its meticulous waves, her twinset hung in meticulous straightness above the worsted skirt, but her face was carelessly powdered, confirming the confusion seething within her, the astonishment both of being here against her dearest convictions and of the extraordinary news she bore, thrust on her by her son.

As Esther came in she lifted herself from the chair but then sank back again. 'Oh Mrs Baxter, good morning . . .'

'Ray says she's safe?'

'I presume so. It was last night. My son telephoned.'

'Last night?' The reproach in her eyes, reddened and swollen, stung.

'No, this morning, not half an hour ago.'

'It was the only thing he could think of, us not having a phone,' Ray said, 'and it was too late last night.'

'What time did he see her? Where was she?' Esther sat down, clasping her hands round the handkerchief.

'Well, it was most extraordinary. I'm afraid I didn't quite understand it all, what with the surprise of a telephone call so early and the pips kept going and Anthony was so disturbed he was hardly coherent at times. But I gather she called at his flat late last night, about midnight he said.'

'Was she all right?'

'Apparently. Apparently she told him she'd run away.' Curiosity gleamed naked in her eye for an instant.

'And then?'

'Well, apparently she wanted to stay with him.' Esther drew in her breath, and at the sound a dark blush rose over Mrs Townsend's sallow neck and face. 'Of course he said it was impossible.'

'Why?'

'Why?'

'Yes, why? Where else could she go?'

'He was going to suggest somewhere, some friend of his, but she ran away.'

'Ran away . . .' It was a whisper and Raymond came and put his hand on her shoulder.

'She ran off into the night and Anthony couldn't find her. It would be after midnight then.'

Esther looked up at her husband. He tightened his grip on her shoulder and asked, 'He didn't see where she went?'

'No. He's on the second floor, you see, and I presume it took him a moment or so to go after her, bolting off like that without warning.'

'Perhaps she went to Norah's,' Esther said.

'Norah'd have let us know. You can phone a wire any time. What did June say, Mrs Townsend?'

'Just that she'd run away. At least, that was all I could really gather from what my son said. It was such a shock. He never telephones me although he insisted I should have it just in case of emergencies, you know, as I live alone and he worries, poor boy. But he never uses it, always sends me a postcard when he wants to come down, and when the bell went this morning I couldn't think who it was. When I heard his voice I thought something dreadful had happened, and of course he was in a hurry, just on his way to business, you see, and very upset by the whole affair, I could tell. As indeed you must be.'

'Yes, it is a bit of an upset,' he answered and smiled unsuccessfully. 'She didn't come home last evening, you see, and we thought at first she'd gone round to a friend. But the time went on and we didn't know what to think.'

'Have you told the police?'

'No,' he said noncommittally, 'we haven't told the police.'

'Don't you think you should? After all, they have ways of tracing missing persons. She might come to some harm . . .'

'I shall have to go up,' said Esther.

'Now Ett . . .'

'I must.'

'She may come back.'

'She won't.' They looked at each other for a long moment, the silence between them full of statement and answer.

'I hope she's not in any trouble?' ventured Mrs Townsend.

Raymond shifted his gaze to her. For the first time she noticed how blue his eyes were, a little faded now in middle-age and puffy from worry and sleeplessness no doubt, but of a remarkable china blue just the same. 'No, she's in no trouble,' he said. 'Junie's a good kid, a sweet kid. It's just – one of those teenage upsets you read about.'

'Ah.' Mrs Townsend nodded knowingly. 'And of course girls are easily upset. I'm so thankful I never had any trouble of that sort with my Anthony, always the best of sons, so conscientious, and then, of course, he went straight from school into the RAF. He was a pilot-officer, you know.'

'Where does he live?' asked Esther.

'Anthony?'

'Yes. I must see him. Write it down, Ray.'

'You won't find him there till the evening. He's at business all day, at Fletcher's in Oxford Street, you know, and they don't close till half-past five.'

'I'll wait for him.'

'Well, it's 37 Pevensey Terrace, Bayswater.'

Esther nodded and took the paper from Ray, studying it as though the address would tell her something.

'He may not even be home this evening. He has a great many friends . . .'

'I'll wait till he comes.'

'Well . . .' She gathered herself together and stood up. Esther rose too, and her husband put his arm round her shoulders so that they stood as one unit in the middle of what Mrs Townsend had already noticed was a nicely furnished, nicely kept room. 'I don't think there's anything more I can tell you. I do hope all will be well.'

'Thank you,' they said.

'It was so quick of Anthony to think of sending the message through me, don't you agree? Knowing you hadn't a telephone.'

'It was ever so kind,' Esther said, and he, 'At least we've got something to go on now.'

'Yes. Well, I'm sure she can't have gone far.' They moved into the hall and Raymond opened the front door. The linoleum shone and the brass on the door was like gold. On impulse Mrs Townsend said, 'If there's anything I can do . . . If Mrs Baxter has to go away, perhaps supper – or I could get in some shopping . . .?'

'That's very kind of you,' he said. 'We appreciate it.'

'After all, neighbours, you know . . .' Mrs Townsend heard herself say. 'Or if you need any telephone messages, please don't hesitate . . .'

'We're ever so grateful.'

'Any time – any time . . .' she said and went off down the path on her thin, neat legs to her own neat other half of the house, where no disturbance had penetrated for years, since – since when? Since Stanley's death, and even then, hardly.

Raymond shut the front door and turned back to Esther. He went to her and took her in his arms, and they stood together in silence, her head against his cheek.

'Let me go up,' he said.

'She wouldn't come back for you.' After a moment she drew gently away and went into the kitchen. 'Besides, there's the shop.'

'Miss Turner can do the shop. My place is with you.'

'You can't help me find her.'

He wrung his hands. 'Why did she go to *him*? Why not to Norah?'

'Fancy him letting her go.' Running hot water into the sink, she automatically stacked the dishes left in disorder since last night's despair.

'Perhaps the old girl's right, Ett. Perhaps we should tell the police.'

'No.' The word was a stone.

He walked about the room. 'Why did she do it? What made her run off like that? I thought I'd got through to her. I thought she was beginning to – to come round to me a bit.'

'Where did she get the fare from? She only had her bus fare to school and back. And no proper clothes . . .' She bent her head over the washing-up.

'D'you think she found out, Ett?'

'How could she?'

'I don't know. These things never die out. You can pay and pay but you never get rid of it. You think you've buried it all in the past but there's someone knows somewhere, there's a record kept somewhere, nothing's ever wiped out.'

'She couldn't know, Ray.'

'By Christ, they should have hung me, Ett! They should have hung me, they should have hung me.' He fell into a chair and hid his face in his hands.

She whirled round on him, her voice high. 'And left me with that to remember?' Then she wiped her hands on a cloth and came to him, dropping to her knees at his side. 'Don't ever say that, Ray. Don't even think it. We've been together again, haven't we? We've had all these months given back to us, and the future. All that we mean to each other – everything – proved, like a blessing . . .'

He took her hands and kissed them, holding them against his crumpled face.

After a little while she said, 'I'll catch the 11.27. Norah'll put me up. When I find her, I'll send for you.'

When she reached Paddington she telephoned Norah at the hospital. Norah, calmly appalled at the news, was on duty till the evening but said she would arrange for the caretaker to let Esther into the flat. 'Go straight there,' she said, 'make some tea. I'll be thinking what to do meanwhile.'

Esther came out of the telephone-booth and walked, as June had done twelve hours before, up the ramp into Praed Street. 'Take an Inner Circle,' Norah had said, 'it takes you practically to the door,' but she could not shut herself underground and go like a mole to the place where June had not been. She had to come out into the air of London to cast about like a gun-dog searching for the scent, as though some instinct would respond to June's having been there, as though to be where June had been must mystically reveal to her where June was now. She stood on the pavement passively, waiting to receive some message. Nothing came, no revelation. But from here June must have gone direct to Mr Townsend, and Esther did so too. Somehow, following step by step, she would force out the secret of June's whereabouts.

It was over twelve years since she had lived in London but she had not forgotten any of it. Perhaps you never really lived anywhere but the place where you grew up and the place where you were most fully alive, being happy or suffering. The tranquil years at Havenport, tranquil because dead save for the passionate determination that June should grow up happy, had been nothing but a long sleep. It was here, in London, years ago, that she had been awake, had stirred from the quiet treadmill of her life with Gran, day after day the same, going to business, dependable Miss Wilson, the invoices and files of Winters' Stores, and home again to Gran and supper, the television and twice a week cinema. Into this non-life Raymond had come, late, when she was thirty, she and Gran given up hope of such a thing as marriage. With his blue eyes and his jokes, his jaunty courtliness that so skilfully found the chinks in Esther's shyness and the gaps in Gran's imperishable coquetry, Raymond had flooded her desert with blossom, had given her marriage, a child, fulfilment – himself. And with himself, the dark nightmare of the truth, the other side of the moon.

It was long ago now. But the memory came sometimes of the day the police had come for him; and the day she learned from his Counsel, Mr Haylett, that Raymond had killed women and must stand trial for one of them; and the day the jury filed out and the eternity of their absence, she sitting in the stone corridor of the Old Bailey with Norah, forbidden the court by Raymond, unable to stay away; and the day she saw him last before the slow routine of her monthly visit to Parkhurst was established – white, shrunken, his hands gripping the table between them, saying, 'Divorce me, Ett – go on, divorce me,' but both had known that was impossible for, dark uncharted moon or not, they were one flesh.

Those days had seemed to pass as one long soundless scream, echoing, limitless, without end. They were beyond endurance; but she had endured them. They had screamed by somehow, one after the other, with nothing to mark their passing save the somnambulistic routines of the house, making beds, washing up, cooking meals for baby June and Gran, nursing one forward and one back to childhood. Like a chrysalis that one day you find light and empty at last, Gran had died, and Esther had moved to Havenport with June in order to be near Parkhurst and the monthly visit and so had started the long, tranquil, trance-like lie that had brought them all to this . . .

She got off the bus at Westbourne Grove, as June had done, and walked as June had done to Tony's house. There was no sense in going in; he would not be there. But she went in, for the front door was left open, and walked up the stairs to the door with his name on it on a curled piece of card. The flat faces of the doors denied her. There was no sound in the whole sterile house, nor no echo of June coming to her though she stood where she must have stood so little a time before – her own child, her own blood and womb!

She took a breath, steadying herself. Then, putting down the holdall that contained her night clothes, she tore a leaf from the spare pages of her handbag diary and, leaning against the panels of the door, wrote: 'Dear Mr Townsend, I am staying at Flat 7, 120 Gayton Gardens near S. Kensington. Please will you phone as soon as possible re my June, Fre4746, it does not matter how late. Thank you. Esther Baxter.' She folded it and pushed it under the door, picked up the bag and quietly went downstairs. On the steps she paused, casting about for scent again, then walked slowly back towards the main road in the opposite direction in which June had gone last night.

She was tired when at last she got to Norah's flat, for she had walked about the streets of Bayswater and Westbourne Grove aimlessly yet with tenacity of purpose, willing herself to come upon June. She had drunk a cup of tea in a café and asked if they had seen a fair-haired girl of sixteen in school uniform, but they had not, for it was not the café where Garry had picked up June.

She made some tea and bread and butter and lay down on Norah's bed. She was at that stage of exhaustion when one is neither asleep nor awake, and although she closed her eyes and may have slept, there seemed no alteration in the sterile activity of her mind. The sound of the doorbell shook her to her feet. It was Tony.

They shook hands formally and he sat down while Esther carried her cup and saucer into the kitchen alcove. He refused her offer to make more tea; a mild scent of whisky came from him, for he had strengthened himself at a pub before coming here.

'I found your note when I got home. I thought there was no point in ringing you first.'

'Is it so late?' she asked absently.

'Going on half-past six.'

She must have slept, then. She sat down opposite him and for a moment they regarded one another, not knowing what to say. Then he asked, 'There's no news?' She shook her head. 'I'm terribly sorry about all this.'

'What did she say to you?'

'She simply said she'd run away. I think she'd come straight off the train. She asked if she could stay the night and find somewhere to go in the morning. When I said that wasn't possible, she just beat it.'

'Couldn't you have gone after her?'

'I wasn't ...' He hesitated and looked suddenly uncomfortable. 'I wasn't dressed. It was late. By the time I got down to the street she'd vanished.'

'Had she any money?'

'I haven't a clue. I suppose she must have had or how did she get to London? She wasn't wearing school clothes, only the blazer. She had on some kind of a skirt and blouse, and her hair was done up.'

'Didn't she say what her plans were, where she was going to go?'

'Not a word. As soon as she saw she couldn't stay at my place she was off and away like a bird.'

Esther rubbed her forehead as though somehow to clarify her thoughts. 'I don't understand,' she said. 'Why did she come to you, Mr Townsend, in the first place? I mean, she's only a child really, isn't she?'

'I suppose she felt we were friends.'

'But you're nearly old enough to be her father. What made her think she could come to you?'

'Good lord, I give you my word ... There was absolutely nothing ... We were friends.' As he protested he remembered her small buttocks and the look that had been like an intercourse that day in his mother's lounge, he hot with Jacky's adamance, she with what dreams and hungers? Both for an instant had acted out their fantasies, using the other not like real human beings but like machinery. He had known his own impulse, but what of hers? What had she needed from him, what had she been trying to ask or state in the conversations he had hardly listened to and now defended as friendship? He clasped his nicotine-stained fingers almost in supplication. 'We just talked, that was all. She was a sweet kid. We never met except when you knew about it.'

'She knew where you lived.'

'I may have told her. I must have, I suppose. But I never, for one moment – and nor, I'm sure, did she. We just chatted of this and that.'

'And yet, having felt she could come to you, she ran off again without a word.'

He looked away from her, pressing his hands between his knees, his face flushed and sagged behind the flamboyant moustache. 'I had a friend with me. It was all a bit of a shambles, actually.'

'Oh.' Now she understood, and the pain of June's shocked flight into the immensity of London silenced her. Even her thoughts seemed to stop. She could not guess what June might have done then, finding a woman there – and he had not been dressed . . .

'I never dreamed,' he was babbling. 'Let's face it, it was the last thing I was expecting. When the bell rang. . . . It was impossible, you see, but Jacky'd have taken her back to her place, given her a bed, looked after her. She's got a heart as big as a house, Jacky has, and that's what she wanted to do, but June just blew. We hadn't a clue what to do after that. Isn't there anyone else she might have run to?'

'No. Only here, and she hasn't been here.'

'Then I honestly think – don't you? – the police ought to be told.'

'No.'

'But Mrs Baxter – they have this sort of thing the whole time. It's their job. They must have hundreds of missing girls to find every year and they find them in a matter of days, hours even.'

'We don't want the police.'

'But how else will you find her?'

'I don't know. I don't know.' She suddenly hid her face in her hands, although without tears.

'Look, I know all this is hell. But let's face it, we haven't a clue how to set about finding her on our own.'

'Perhaps she'll come back.'

'Can you wait for that?'

She lowered her hands and looked at him. 'I don't want the police, Mr Townsend. I don't want the newspapers. Once you start that, there's no end . . .'

The telephone bell made them both jump. For a moment they stared, then Esther went to it quickly and snatched up the receiver.

'Ett, is that you?'

'Yes, yes – have you heard anything?'

'Nothing to go on, no. Have you?'

'No.'

'But I went round to see that school friend of hers, that Sandra she went to a party at, remember? And she'd been there. Ett, she'd been and borrowed some money and clothes and spun this girl a tale about running to London to shack up with that bastard.'

'Who? Who, Ray?'

'That Tony Townsend.' His voice was shaking with rage.

'But that's ridiculous. He's here with me now.'

'You ask him what he's been up to with our girl. You ask the bastard.'

'Ray, be quiet. It's not like that at all.'

'Of course he'd tell you that. You'd let anyone pull the wool over your eyes, Ett, you was always soft, I always told you you was soft. By God, if he's interfered with our girl I'll kill him, Ett, I'll kill him!'

'Raymond, listen to me. Listen to what I say. June went to Mr Townsend but he had a friend there with him, a young lady. Yes, a young lady. They're going to be married.' She looked at Tony over the receiver and he smiled wanly. 'There was nothing like that at all, Ray. She just felt Mr Townsend was someone she knew here, someone she could think of as a friend.'

'This girl Sandra said June told her she and this fellow'd been carrying on for months. She said she was going to live with him so's we'd have to agree to their getting married.'

'But that's silly, dear, it's just impossible. He's nearly your age and he's got a young lady already. It was just June spinning a story to get what she needed.'

'This Sandra believed it. Swore her to secrecy and all, borrowed three quid off her, left her school uniform there and told her they'd been carrying on for months.'

'June made it all up. She'll make things up when it suits her.'

'Terrible state this Sandra was in once I got the truth out of her. Sobbing and howling. Her parents didn't know what to make of it. I suddenly got to trying to think what friends she had, see, racking my brains here after you'd gone, and I remembered this girl and called round and taxed her with it. At first she made out she'd not seen her, didn't know anything. Then she began to get scared and came out with it all. You think it's all nonsense, then, her and this Townsend chap?'

'I'm sure it is.'

'But where is she, then? Can't he help?'

'He says we ought to tell the police.'

There was a pause, then he said slowly, 'He's right.'

'I don't want to, Ray. Think what it may mean.'

'June's more important than that. On our own we don't even know where to start.'

'I walked all round the streets looking and hoping. She can't just disappear.'

'He's right. You'd best go to them right away.'

'Ray . . .'

'Right away. God knows what can happen to young girls roaming about on their own. Right away, Ett? And Ett?'

'Yes?'

'I'm coming up. I'm shutting the shop and coming up.'

'There's not room for us both at Norah's.'

'I'll find somewhere. I'll be up first train tomorrow.'

'All right, dear.'

'Keep smiling, dear. You're sure he's telling the truth?'

'I'm sure.'

'Get off to the police as soon as you can, then. I'll see you tomorrow.'

It was after eight when they left the police station, where a sergeant had taken particulars with an indulgent air that comforted, and Tony took her to a nearby restaurant. It was her first proper meal for thirty-six hours and she was sorry she felt too sick to eat it all. On the pavement afterwards he took her hand. 'I'll keep in touch,' he said, 'and if you hear anything, ring me.'

She smiled faintly, her hand cool and passive in his. Exhaustion had given translucence to the middle-aged texture of her skin and had stretched the flesh over the bones as though in this short time she had lost all the cushioning of the years. Pared down like this, it was easy to see she was June's mother, although June had a lightness that Esther could never have possessed.

He felt a sudden terror for all of them, the same terror he had felt sometimes in the mess between sorties when, in relaxation, characters had somehow shown themselves vulnerable as at no other time. Then they had become people, trusting and candid without affectation, not attitudes of bravery or bravado. He too had been a person then, swelling with love, with an empathy that held him still in the dead world of those years, that had brought him Jennifer; Jennifer whom now he could hardly remember, save as a wound that had for ever after crippled him, held him transfixed in time like a moth on a pin – until now, a shop assistant of nearly forty, he had Jacky. A shop assistant of nearly forty – that was the truth, not Trigger Townsend; and this woman whose hand he held now was not the quiet, middle-aged neighbour he hardly knew but a woman tormented by anxiety and who knew what dramas hidden in the years behind her, to cause her child to bolt for it. If only he could remember what June had said as she chattered on to him, if only he had listened instead of using her only as an escape from boredom and his own obsessions. What had he idly said to June, how ignorantly encouraged her so that, yielding to pressures to which he had no clue, she had felt confident that he was the one to help her? And what in the name of God was he doing here, shaking this nice woman's hand and promising to keep in touch, involved up to his neck in matters he neither understood nor was concerned in?

He released her hand and said goodbye, turning away briskly towards the Underground, homing for the club where Jacky would be waiting. But even there June would impinge. Even if they redressed the interruptions of last night, their talk would be of June, Jacky would worry, blame him, blame herself. They were affected.

At the flat Norah was waiting. They kissed, cheek to cheek in the cool way of women's love.

'Is there any news?'

Esther shook her head. 'We've told the police.'

'That's sensible.' She took Esther's coat and hung it in the cupboard. 'Does Ray know?'

'It was him insisted. He rang up.' Norah said nothing but went into the kitchen and poured some milk into a saucepan. Esther sat down in one of the armchairs and laid her head back wearily. 'I wish I could make you understand.'

'So do I.'

'You've been such a friend. I don't know what I'd have done always if I hadn't had you.'

'You'd have managed. You're the sort people always put on and you always manage.'

'Nobody's put on me. You don't understand.'

Norah came back into the living room, a mug of milk clasped between her hands. She sat down opposite Esther, looking at her with unforgiving, loving eyes. 'You know it's him has been the cause of all this?'

'You shouldn't say that. Young girls get all sorts of troubles and fancies into their heads . . .'

'Don't be daft. You know very well she found out.'

'How could she?'

'How do I know? A dozen ways — someone recognised him or said something or she's read the case somewhere or she's been through your papers and found out her real name . . .'

'She wouldn't. June would never . . .'

'Of course she would. Girls will do anything when they're that age, any mortal thing, good or bad. Nothing matters to them at that age but their own selves, they haven't time for anything else. She found out and she's gone. She'll never come home again, even if you find her, not while he's there, and perhaps not even if he went.'

'Don't!' Esther's face contorted and she shut her eyes.

'It's no good saying Don't.' Straight-backed, she sat implacable. 'You've got to face this now, Esther me darling, like you should have faced it years ago when Raymond was sentenced. You should have left him then, for as sure as the sun rises you must have known that this day would come.'

Esther drew herself together, her voice desperate. 'You don't know what you're talking about. You never have, not about Raymond. All these years you've been saying Leave him, divorce him, cut him out of your life. How can I? He is my life. All the years he's been away I was half dead, like I was before I ever met him. We've talked and talked this over, Norah, you and me over all the years, off and on, and you'll never see how it is.'

'Don't you care what he did?'

'Of course I care! I care so much I thought I'd go mad thinking about it, trying to get it into my head that he'd killed people, women like me, deliberately, for their money. I'd say it over and over to myself, trying to make it real – but all that was real was that he was Raymond, my husband, who loved me and the baby like nothing was too good for us. Do you think I wouldn't have left him then if I could, with all the horror and shock and the future ahead with nothing but grief and shame in it, not only for me and Ray but for June, for the baby? Do you think I didn't give it a thought?' She broke off, clenching her hands on the arms of the chair, then went on more quietly, 'I did what was all I could do – I hung on. I hung on and went on loving him no matter what the truth was – in spite of the truth, for living was the truth too, though you won't believe it. You have to take the whole person to be whole yourself. You can go on if you have to with an arm or a leg cut off, but don't tell me you're still a whole person. Raymond's my arms and legs. He'll always be that.'

After a moment Norah said quietly, 'But you must have known this day would come.'

'I hoped it wouldn't.'

'Hoping's never enough. I warned you, long ago.'

'All right, all right! But what else could I have done? Should I have said to her when she was a little thing "Your daddy's in prison, darling, he'll be out in twelve or fourteen years if he earns his remission"? And when she asked what was he in for, should I have said "For murdering someone, darling, your daddy's a murderer and lucky not to be hung"? Wasn't it better to hide the truth and hope it'd never come out, with

Raymond and me breaking ourselves apart to see that it never did? You were with me, you helped me.'

'I was never easy in my mind.'

'Do you think I was? But I had to do what seemed best for us all.'

Norah said nothing. It was true that in the first years they had argued the future, and always she had managed to shut her lips on the thing she longed and dreaded most to say: that it would have been better if Raymond Banks had been hanged. But she had never said it and would not now. Her own withered history – the married man who had loved her but not quite enough, whom she had loved but only enough to relinquish – always lay at the back of their minds, an unused weapon for Esther, a shackle for Norah. For what did Norah know about love, who had not fought for it years ago?

She got up slowly and took the mug back into the kitchen. 'I'll have to go back,' she said, 'I only ran out for my off-duty break because I wanted to see you, I'm living in hospital just now.'

'Ray's coming up tomorrow. I said not, but he says he must come. He wants to be with me.'

'He can stay here with you then.'

'Do you mind?'

'Of course I don't mind.' Her whole skin crawled with distaste at the thought of Raymond sleeping in her sheets, washing in her bath, drinking from her cups. She came back, pressing Esther's shoulder lightly as she passed. 'Stay as long as you like, the pair of you. Now get to bed for I won't leave till you're tucked up.'

Esther rose slowly and went into the little bedroom. 'Do you think they'll find her, Norah?'

'Of course they'll find her. The police are marvellous fellows. You won't have to be staying here long.'

'You're a good friend.'

'Get away!' Absently she shook and hung up the dress Esther had just taken off. 'But you'll both have to think what to say to her when she comes back – and what to do with her, too. Or what she wants to do with herself.'

'How can she know? She's a child still . . .'

'For pity's sake, Esther, wake up! You've kept her a child and the shock of her growing up's nearly killed us all, now hasn't it, now she's faced with the ugly truth? A woman could face it – you faced it. But a spoilt child like you've kept June can only run away.'

'Oh Norah!'

'Oh Norah! Face facts, for pity's sake, woman. She's grown up now, the truth has grown her up in a night. She'll never come back to live with you and Raymond, and myself I don't blame her. You must offer her a different life now and pray God she'll accept it. She'd better come here and live with me. We'll get her a training – perhaps she'd like nursing, we'll see what she fancies. But it's her must decide, for she's out on her own two feet now and for evermore. She'll not trust any of us again.'

'Oh Norah, would you really have her here?'

'Would I offer if I didn't mean it?' The litter, the chatter, the self-absorption invading her own neat privacies like steam . . .! She cut such thoughts off firmly. 'Now hurry and get into that bed, for I'm on the edge of being late already.'

TEN

THE LIFE THE PARSONSES LIVED was so engulfing, the difference from everything June had ever known so extreme, that she sank and was utterly submerged in it from the moment she began to scrub the kitchen draining board, making herself part of the family through her service to it. It was as though June Baxter had never existed, Hellebore Road blanked out, Havenport the barely remembered dream of a child, a make-believe life compared with the raw reality of the Parsonses. Somewhere in between, like a half-forgotten nightmare, were the night streets she had wandered, the wolf-pack youths, Tony Townsend's hairy legs between shirt and socks, the woman's smudged mouth; but behind that, nothing. As she scrubbed, rinsed, tidied, she repudiated everything her mother stood for. Nothing of the past, no thought of her parents' anxiety, so much as brushed her mind as, absorbed in the strangeness, she worked through the afternoon until, with a clatter and crash, the Parsonses began to fill the rooms again.

First came the two schoolboys, shirts half out, smudged with dirt and smeared with orange lolly bought on their way home. They stared and giggled, shoving each other about the narrow space till they jogged the table crooked and she told them sharply to sit down. June would never had dared, but Janie did; and they had sat down, warily wolfed the tea she put in front of them, then rushed out into the street again to play.

Sharon came home next with the two babies. She received the news of June's presence quietly, perhaps even with some pleasure, for as she dumped the children on their chairs and poured them milk from the bottle, she glanced round the tidiness June had achieved and said, 'You've bin busy and no mistake.'

Then Garry appeared, yawning and stripped to a singlet from which his thin white arms hung like a puppet's limbs from the angular yoke of his shoulders. While the others sat at table eating, he washed himself meticulously at the sink, splashing and puffing above the television programme which Sharon had switched on.

When he had gone to dress, Mrs Parsons came home, moulded by her corset into a more spritely figure than the disordered matron of the morning. She filled the room with a spread of shopping-bags and bust, chatted, petted Kevin and slapped Dawn's thumb ineffectually from her mouth, sat down to a mug of tea. Garry returned, sharply dressed for the evening, his hair greased into an elaborate helmet, and Mrs Parsons opened a tin of salmon which the two of them shared. Sharon meanwhile washed nappies in the sink until Mrs Parsons claimed it for her own toilet. The two boys came stampeding back, seized more bread, lapsed into silence in front of the telly. Garry went out, Mrs Parsons dressed in different clothes and went out, the babies were settled together in a chair to watch a Western with the others, and then Sharon did June's hair.

As she worked she talked, an endless string of words spun out of her like the thread from a spider, sour and hard as her own fifteen-year-old face beneath its balloon of pink-rinsed hair. It was she who scrubbed and washed and tried to keep things nice, who fought her way against the family tide, who bathed the babies almost every evening in the plastic washing-up bowl, who put doilies on dressing tables and made jellies in little moulds like fish, and who tended her own appearance with fanaticism, for resentfully she knew it would be important for only a few years. Marriage, towards which all her energies were directed, would, she sensed, be the end, as it had been the end for Mum. 'I don't say she doesn't do herself up,' she conceded scornfully, whisking June's hair into a lather, 'but I mean, what can you expect when you've had kids? I mean, there's Mum, hair tinted, face done up, everything on bar the kitchen stove, but she's two stone overweight. I mean, once you're married you're finished.'

'I think she looks nice,' June said diffidently, for indeed the spectacle of Mrs Parsons dressed for an evening at the Club, hair sprayed, diamanté brooch, two-inch white heels, had been impressive.

'Oh, she don't wear too bad for her figure's a mess. I mean, it's dead loss, innit? It's sex, see. Every time Dad comes home they can't leave it alone. You'd think they invented it. I think it's disgusting. I mean, Dawn and Kevin coming along at her age, it makes you ashamed.' She whisked June upright out of the sink, rubbed her hair briskly, and began to comb it. 'I wish I didn't have to have kids when I marry. I mean, where does it get you? It's worry, worry all the time, seems to me, soon's you start sex. If you have it, you're caught, and if you don't have it, who wants to know you?'

June made some bemused sound but Sharon, twirling the hair round enormous rollers and spearing them with clips, continued, 'I mean, you can't always be careful, can you? I mean, I don't think that's very nice really. That's why I mean to keep myself till I marry. You just can't have sex with just anyone and keep your self-respect.'

'Have you got a boy?' June asked timidly.

'But natch. His name's Russell. We bin going together a year only I don't go out with him only at the weekend. I mean, he goes to evening classes, he's studying to be a radio engineer. We're saving up.'

'What for?'

'A place of our own, of course.' Sharon looked at her as though she were half-witted. 'You don't think we want to move in with this lot, do you?'

'Give *your* home the homely comfort of Fairydown,' murmured the television. 'Germ-free, strength-proved, perforated for easy tearing, caressingly soft for really tender skins. Give *your* home Fairydown.'

'I want a place where everything's nice,' said Sharon dreamily, 'Russell in a good job, me keeping on in business, a car, holidays on the continent, lovely clothes . . . Once I'm out of this place I never want to see it again.'

''Ere, Sharon, Kevin's wet 'isself!' shrieked Digby.

Kevin was asleep, his head hanging over the wooden arm of the chair in which he and Dawn were heaped like two puppies.

'He ought to be dry by now,' said Sharon disgustedly. 'He is at the nursery, asks to go like a little gentleman, but here there's no encouragement.'

She showed no curiosity about June. Beyond the bare question and answer of early morning, when Garry had shown her June dozing in a kitchen chair, she did not seem to want to know anything. She saw little to wonder at in a girl her own age loose in the city streets. People came and went on their own inscrutable purposes, as her father came and went or Garry or the boys, and because they never told you why you gave up interest in the reasons. Self was the only person you could be sure of.

She dried June's hair with a hand-dryer that made linked spots vibrate all over the television screen, then back-combed, swathed and lacquered it into an elongated tower. The result was startling; long and slender, a mysterious silvery gazelle stared back at June from the mirror over the draining-board. She could not speak, only stare and smile at the perfected reflection she had once, long ago, glimpsed in a mirror somewhere in another world. She let Sharon rim her eyes with green mascara and stared again at the strange woman she had become. Even Colin and Digby were impressed, rolling against each other in paroxysms of sniggers and exclaiming in mincing falsetto tones, 'Rub my arse with Bisto!', at which Sharon briskly cuffed them.

Mrs Parsons and Garry did not return till after the girls were asleep; and next morning, drinking his tea morosely by the kitchen table, he did no more than narrow his eyes consideringly at her new hair style. It had not worn very well in the night and beside the immaculate Sharon she knew she looked unkempt and juvenile. But he might at least speak to her. After all, it was he who had brought her here, and she had taken the trouble to get up to give him his breakfast. Perhaps, she realised with a sad new maturity, it was her childish behaviour in the bedroom which had made him lose interest in her. If that was it, he needn't trouble himself. Sharon was her friend, and she intended to make herself indispensable to the Parsonses so that they would forget she had not always been one of them. She would submerge herself in their yeasty atmosphere, take on their colours, forget even not to remember where she came from and the reasons for her coming.

She made herself responsible for the tasks Sharon had always done, and as she cleared the kitchen, made her own and Sharon's beds, she thought about Garry. When Mrs Parsons sagged downstairs later with the babies, hardly recognisable again with tousled hair and grubby overall, June cooked their breakfast and tried to pump her on the subject of her eldest son. But she did not get very much. Mrs Parsons seemed to regard her children rather as natural forces, interesting in a remote way but not susceptible to human influence.

"E's never bin no trouble, Garry 'asn't,' was as far as she would commit herself. 'Course, 'im and Mr Parsons don't see eye to eye. There's always a bit of a barney when Mr Parsons's 'ome, but I don't take no notice. It's natural reely.'

'Is it?'

'Well, you can't 'ave two cocks in the barnyard, can you? Specially with Mr Persons bein' away so much. I say to Garry, I say, Why don't you go in the Forces or some'ing, learn a trade or some'ing and shut up moanin', but 'e don't take no notice. Trouble with 'im is, 'e don't know what 'e wants. Oh well, it's no use me sittin' 'ere gassin' – got to get to work. Give the kids' faces a wipe, will you love, they don' like 'em in the nursery 'less they're washed over.'

June lifted Dawn from her chair and gently drew the sucked thumb from the child's mouth, curling the hand in her own. It was warm, like a little square animal. 'Shall I take them to the nursery for you, Mrs Parsons?'

"Ow, now that would be a convenience, dear. Then I can take me time gettin' to business. It's on'y just round the corner, you just 'and 'em in.'

June washed, brushed and polished the children, and Dawn began to talk a little. Kevin was rather slow and whiny, cross at not having his mother, but even that June enjoyed in the same way she used to enjoy getting round an awkward problem in maths in the old days at Jervis's, when she had still cared about solving problems. The children were like two large, unpredictable dolls, and impersonal female love for the young filled her as she curried and groomed them. She had never known any babies before and could not remember the emotions that had led her to play with dolls. She drew Dawn closely to her, resting her cheek on her head; the child was docile, warm, smelling faintly of crisps and soap. She would wash Dawn's hair tonight and see if it would curl.

When she returned from the nursery, walking nervously down the raucous streets so full of prams and coloured people in bright jumpers, Mrs Parsons had gone. The place was her own now and for the first time she went into the boys' room. Their beds were rickety, the linen not very clean, but she did not know where the sheets were kept or even if there were any to spare (she must ask Sharon). Garry's mattress was worn into a narrow trench into which his body must fit as into a sleeping-bag. Grey army blankets covered it; the wall beside it was plastered with pin-up girls of monstrous proportions and pictures of Stirling Moss and motorcyclists, gladiators in helmeted armour. A curiously pleasurable distaste spread from her fingertips to the hollow places of her body as she touched his bedclothes, vicariously taking his skin on hers, and piercingly she remembered the tumbled bed at Tony's and, further back yet, the smooth, lying beds at Hellebore Road. She slammed shut the door of her mind and tried to tidy the room. A dirty comb and a brush with few bristles, several pairs of ornate cufflinks, inside-out socks that smelled, a dirty black-and-white striped shirt, an ashtray full of butts were his spoor. Sweet-papers, lolly sticks and comics accounted for his brothers.

Mysterious Parsonses. Mysterious world of muddle and routine, warmth and indifference, bread eaten out of the wrapper, butter out of the paper, sugar poured copiously from the packet into boot-polish tea, hair and babies washed in the sink, each member apparently uninterested in the others yet living in hugger-mugger intimacy. Most mysterious of all, Garry. Before the mirror in Sharon's room she practised arranging her new hair, experimented with Sharon's cosmetics, Sharon's clothes. That evening she wore mauve slacks and an orange jumper, but Garry still remained impassive.

She washed and fed the babies again the next morning and took them to the nursery, but came straight back again to the safety of the burrow. Her instinct was to go to ground in this ramshackle world, for more than anything else she feared being lost in space again, to have to face without support the realities from which she had for so long been protected. So she busied herself in the Parsonses' four rooms as she had never busied herself at home, only for a few days of shadow life long ago at Auntie Norah's. As she scrubbed and washed and ironed she came to recognise the sounds of the other tenants passing on the stairs, the cat belonging to the basement, the cries of children and the rag-and-bone man, other people's wirelesses, quarrels, songs, smells. She washed the children's clothes, even the terrible socks of the three boys, and as the warm, solitary hours passed a calm and a comfort descended on her as though she were anaesthetised; and when the time came for her to go and fetch the babies back again she looked at her new self in the mirror, the slacks, the orange jumper, the hair, the green-rimmed eyes, and thought this is who I am, I am Janie. Soon I shall have forgotten who I was in the beginning, where I came from and why, and shall be Janie Parsons, with a job of some sort and money to spend, calling Mrs Parsons Mum as the others do, slapping Digby and Colin, cuddling Dawn, going steady as Sharon does with some boy I shall know better how to behave with if ever he tries again . . .

Garry worked only half-day on Saturdays, and after his usual sleep he came back into the kitchen at teatime where Mrs Parsons and June sat with the four younger children watching the television (Sharon was still at work, for Saturdays was the big day for hairdressing). As he sluiced and sleeked himself at the sink he said over his shoulder, 'Wanta come to the flicks?'

Mrs Parsons gave June a nudge. 'Garry's speakin' to you, dear.'

'Me?'

'Well, 'e's not askin' me or the boys,' said Mrs Parsons indulgently.

June stared at his bony back. Weakly she said, 'I don't know if I can.' She caught his impassive glance in the mirror over the draining board, and added hastily, 'All right then.'

'D'you want any tea, love?'

'Nah. Go down to the caff and 'ave a pie.'

'Can I come, Garry?' Digby shouted.

'Do me a favour,' Garry said scornfully.

'Why can' I come, Garry?'

'Cos I don' wantcha.'

'You and 'oo else?'

''Ow, get stuffed!'

'Me and my lot, we'll bust up your flippin' caff!'

'You do that and you'll get chivved, mate.'

'Garn, big mouth! I'm nearly's big as you . . .'

'You wait till you are, then.'

Digby suddenly lost his temper. 'You stinkin' bastard!' he yelled. He hit Garry as hard as he could with both fists and before Garry could recover his balance, crashed from the room. They heard him thundering down the stairs.

'What a villain!' exclaimed Mrs Parsons wonderingly. Colin got up and slid out of the room after his brother. 'Did 'e 'urt you, love?'

'Nah,' but he felt his ribs gingerly.

''E's gone off down the Buildings. Terrible rough lot of kids they are there. You wanta look out for yourself, Garry.'

'Yeah?' He sneered in the mirror, but drew breath carefully, for the fists had been like stones on the soft flesh of his belly. 'Well, you comin' or arntcha?'

'Yes.' June got up confusedly.

'Well, get on with it then. I'll give you five minutes.'

The pavements were crowded, Garry walked fast, and June was always half a pace behind him – perhaps the proper place for a woman in his society. He led her to the café where, centuries ago, he had first found her. At five o'clock it was almost empty and they sat at the same table behind which pale, childish June had cowered like the ghost of Janie. He bought pies and Cokes, but drank through a straw this time.

'That Digby,' he said at last, ''e'll be in trouble. 'E nearly bin on probation once. What can you expect?' She made an inadequate noise. 'I mean, Mum don' give a flippin' fag-end. All she's interested in is when the ole man's comin' out again. A proper 'ero 'e is then, Mum and the boys all over 'im, till 'e get restless and ends up inna nick again. It makes you sick. I mean, whatsa point of it? Mum all smiles one minute and doin' 'er nut the next, Dad doin' porridge for another two-three years and the chances are another dear little stranger on the way. I mean, where's it get you? It's dead irresponsible.' He stubbed out his cigarette morosely in the encrusted tin ashtray and lit another. 'I reckon Sharon's got the right idea all right – stash up and get out of it quick as you can. That Russell of 'ers – 'e's a nit but 'e's dead clever. But then, 'e's got a trade.'

'Couldn't you get a trade?'

'Nah, whatsa point? Go to work all day and then sweat your guts out all night studyin' night classes – whatsa sense in that? Anyway, it's all a rat-race. It's all clicks, see, all them stream As and Bs and grammar school lot. All 'em brains, win scholarships, get passes, and they're in, see? You don' get inna right stream, you're out, see?'

'I'm sure you're bright, Garry.'

'Yeah, well, I don' do it the right way, see? I mean, I'm not goin' to kill meself in some deadend job with no future like I'm in now. I like paintin', see, doors and window-frames and that, but it's all a closed shop. The small firms don' want you and the big firms can't 'ave you cos of the Unions, see?'

'Couldn't you do jobs on your own? You know, neighbours and friends and that?'

He laughed. 'With Dad inna nick for larceny? I'd be welcome!'

'You mustn't give up so easily,' she said indignantly.

'Give up? I ain't never started, mate.'

'But that's awful! Supposing everyone just gave up like that?'

'Go on. Supposin' they did?'

'Nothing would ever get done. They'd all be – sort of trapped.'

He nodded, blowing cigarette-smoke in two long plumes from his nostrils. 'That's right. So all you can do is live for kicks, innit?'

'I think it's awful,' she repeated stubbornly. 'I wouldn't just give up like that. I'd fight. I'd do something.'

He shot her one of those candid looks that so astonished. 'What you done, then? You bin in trouble?' She shook her head, uncertain again. 'What you on your own for then? I mean, a bird like you don't come on 'er own.'

She looked away, round the formica tables, the glass cases of buns and cheese rolls, the urns and great glass vat of orangeade. 'I left home.'

'Yeah, well, I can work that out on me tod. OK, you don' wanta tell me, I don' wanta know.' He stood up with a screech of chair legs, hoisting his trousers round his narrow hips. 'Let's get goin'.'

In the cinema he was transformed, as though in darkness he became an elemental creature like Dracula or some other carnivore. Arm round her shoulder to press her uncomfortably to him over the wooden armrest, his hands began slowly but presently increased their explorations above, behind, below. From time to time he turned her face to his and suffocated her with a long kiss which nearly dislocated her neck. Beating off his hands, breathless, she was hardly aware of the screen. Surely someone would notice what was going on and complain? Torches would be shone on them, they would be asked to leave. But nothing happened, save that the film ended, the lights went up, Garry released her with the speed of elastic and went into the aisle to buy ice-cream.

The ice cream seemed to cool him, and for the rest of the programme he sat quietly, doing no more than crane her to him, holding her hand. Slowly happiness began to fill her. The comfort of him to lean on (apart from the armrest pressing into her ribs), the sensual pleasure of his hand caressing hers, the smell of hair oil and flesh that came from him as she laid her head against his, filled her with peace. Without knowing it, she had missed the physical endearments she had accepted from her mother without thought throughout her life, the comfortable tenderness of goodnight kiss and affectionate hug, even the gestures that sometimes irritated, like the putting back of a strand of hair or the setting straight of a collar. For months now she had stood rigid against these gestures till Esther had become afraid to offer them; and so to this gentle Garry June yielded with increasing willingness. When he began to kiss her again she kissed him back, lovingly and then with a quick fever that was not tender or comforting but which made her blood sing. By the time the lights came on again she was a dazzled woman, not a child, and she followed him docilely out into a street where the lights were beginning to be stronger than the sky. The shops were shut but most of their windows were still lit up, and a late greengrocery blazed like a box of Christmas bonbons in garish orange and green. There was a lurid, hectic feeling, people loitering or pushing by, teenagers swaggering, grinning groups of coloured men in oddly angular hats, coloured women with big rumps and bony legs, old Cypriot women in coiffed dusty shawls, neat Indians, their women caramel soft in sari and ugly jackets, plump Italian women with thick curled hair, pushing prams four abreast in noisy conversation, and children of all colours and sizes, pulled, pushed, carried asleep or stolidly sucking lollies, flotsam floating on the tide of their elders.

Garry paused outside the cinema. 'Well – see ya,' he said.

Her mouth fell open. 'Aren't we . . .? Are you going?'

'Yeah. Meetin' the fellas.'

Disappointment made her angry. 'Are you just leaving me here?'

'Whatsa matter? We don' 'ave birds at the caff, on'y the sort 'at 'angs out there. You don' wanta be tanglin' with that lot.'

'But I'll be lost. I don't know where I am!'

''Ere.' He walked briskly to the corner of the street, June tagging behind. 'Go down there, see, and cross over by the zebra and round the corner past the Tottenham Arms and it's on the left. It's dead easy.' She still looked dismayed. A faint smile touched his face, so rare as to be like a caress. 'Go on,' he said gently, 'you're a big girl now. See you tomorrow,' and he swung away.

She dreamed that night, not of him but of Tony Townsend, a confused, pounding dream that was somehow shameful. Garry did not appear until noon, by which time she and Sharon had cooked a loin of pork and Mrs Parsons had made a treacle pudding. The companionship of women working in a kitchen, the babies under foot, the Sunday somnolence outside, the desultory gossip, the cups of tea, the rich smell from the oven, was an embracing comfort, wiping all memory from the mind, even the sting of Garry's indifference. When he appeared, in a clean white T-shirt, she could look at him calmly although her heart gave a great heave, whether of anger or excitement it would be hard to know. They all sat round the table, eating the flavoursome food almost in silence, and it was while spooning up the pudding that June saw, on the newspaper freshly spread over the table in honour of Sunday, the headline MISSING BLAZER GIRL.

Her throat seemed to close. She looked away, then back, furtively pushing her plate aside a little so that she could read. Yes, she was the girl.

It was only a small paragraph at the foot of an inside page, a sub-editor's fill-up, fruit of a police court reporter's hope that a missing teenager might end in rape or murder. Hardly anyone would notice it, but to June it seemed to scream up from the page, shattering the safety she had built up about her in the timeless days since he had joined the Parsonses.

She pushed her plate over it again, panic making her sweat.

In that family of prodigality and waste nobody seemed to notice that she did not finish her pudding or that she could not speak. Each was as usual intent on their own activities, the boys to get back to their gang at the Buildings, Sharon out with Russell, Mrs Parsons to a Bingo session. Bickering and bustling, they got themselves ready, leaving the house with a bang or the clip of high heels, shouts or cries of 'Cheerybye, you lot!'

They had all accepted that June stayed home to look after the babies, and as she mechanically cleared the table, stacked the crockery in the sink, she wondered drearily what to do with them if she ran away this afternoon, as she must. There was nothing else she could do now. She could not lie like a rabbit crouched in its burrow while the terriers close in. But run where? Now that she was publicly searched for, there was nowhere to which she could escape. Wherever she went outside, people would be looking for her. Despite the different clothes, the different person she had become, some pair of eyes would recognise her, carry her back to face that unspeakable truth before which, as it sprang out at her at last, here where she had been anonymous and safe, she writhed and shut her eyes. She could not bear it, she must kill herself.

She read the paragraph again, then quickly tore it from the newspaper and crumpled it into a ball. She must go, she must run, for there might be other paragraphs in other newspapers that the family would see, and then Mrs Parsons would turn her out anyway, for had she not said there must be no trouble? It might somehow damage Mr Parsons in prison if the police found his family was harbouring a runaway girl, and they would all hate her, the boys would jeer and throw things, Sharon would turn her back, Dawn would be snatched away just when her hair was beginning to shine from the brushing June was giving it . . .

She kneeled down and clutched Dawn from the game she was playing. The child wriggled a little but then stood patiently in June's embrace, watching Kevin crawling under the table pushing a plastic lorry. June began to cry against the child's soft hair.

'Whatsa matter?' asked Garry from the doorway.

She looked up with a gasp, for she had thought herself alone. 'Nothing.' She released Dawn and got up, turning back to the sink, furtively wiping her cheeks with the back of her hand.

He came into the room. 'I said, whatsa matter? Some'ing upset you 'alfway through dinner, dinnit? All of a sudden you was dead choked. So I reckon it must've bin some'ing you read inna paper, right?' He looked down at the table and with his finger traced the rough edge of newspaper where she had torn out the paragraph. She still said nothing. Dawn came to stand beside her, taking hold of the hem of her skirt. 'C'mon, Janie,' he said gently, 'let's 'ave it.'

'It's nothing.'

'Do me a favour! You tore some'ing out, dintcha? If it's trouble, I wanta know what.' As still she did not answer he sat down on the edge of the table and said, 'I can easy find out, can't I? I mean, I on'y gotta go out and buy another paper, 'aven't I? Then I'll know and you'll know, but I won't wanta 'elp you, will I?'

She bent and picked the ball of newspaper out of the pail where she had thrown it. He smoothed it out and read it.

'This you?' She nodded. 'What you done that for – run away and all?' She shook her head and the tears began to run again. 'Look,' he said, 'I reckon I gotta right to know. I mean, I broughtcha 'ere, din' I? If the law's lookin' for you, I gotta right to know why.'

'I ran away,' she whispered.

'Yeah, I know that, it says so 'ere.' He put the crumpled paper down. 'What I wanta know is why?'

'It was my – my father.'

'Yeah?'

'He's – I found out he'd done something.'

'So?'

'Something terrible, awful. I couldn't bear even to look at him again. And my mum had known all the time and kept it from me. She pretended he was an ordinary person, and all the time he was – he'd . . .'

She could not go on but bowed her face into her hands, crying unrestrainedly. Through the horror and misery ran a bright, thin thread of joy that at last she was saying it, sharing it. If they turned her out, if she floated in the river, at least the horror had been known by someone else. To share could not solve, but it could ease a little.

He got up from the table against which he had been lounging and put his arms round her and she leaned against him thankfully. Dawn still held her skirt, anxious but ignored. ''Ere,' he said, 'you don' wanta upset yourself. What's your dad done, then, been inna nick?' She nodded against his chest. 'So what about it? There's thousands of fellas bin inna nick, my ole man for a start.'

Muffled, she said, 'Yours is just – just ordinary.'

'Why, what's yours in for then, eh? 'E in't one of them sex maniacs, is 'e? Boy, if 'e was one of them you'd really be in trouble. I reckon there's nothin' you can do about one o' them, little kids and all. What's your dad done, then?' He was rocking her gently and her sobs had died down. 'Did 'e 'ave a bash at someone? Did 'e kill them?' Hardly perceptibly, she nodded. 'Well, you don' wanta worry about that. I mean, fellers is gettin' creased alla time.'

'It wasn't like that. It was – famous.'

'You mean 'e 'ad a big case and all? Like Hanratty and that? Cor!' He was silent for a moment. 'Why di'nt they 'ang 'im? She trembled in his arms and he held her steady. 'Take it easy, Janie. I spose it was noncapital, eh, no larceny nor nothing with it. Is 'e out?'

She nodded again. 'I couldn't bear it. When I found out, I just ran, I just – just came away.'

He stroked her back gently. 'Yeah, well, it's all inna past, innit? I mean, 'e's done 'is time, 'asn't 'e? Whatsa use keep rakin' it up?'

She raised her head and stared at him. 'But you don't understand. He's a murderer. He killed someone, deliberately, for their money. And Mum wanted him home. She destroyed our whole life together just so's he could come home.'

'Well, that's natural, innit? I mean, she's still married to 'im, in't she? She probably don' mind what 'e's done – I mean, take my ole lady. Don't matter 'ow long Dad's bin in for, every time 'e comes out there she is with bells on. That's sex, innit?'

'It's horrible! She lied and lied to me all my life, and Auntie Norah lied too . . .'

'What, din't you know then? Where d'you think your ole man was then?'

'They said he was ill, in Australia.'

He laughed heartily, showing his white teeth. 'An' you believed 'em? Honest, Janie, it's like I said – you're dead simple. You din' ought to be allowed out, you din't. So when 'e come out and you tumbled to where 'e'd bin, you lit out, is that it? Never left no note nor nothing?'

'Why should I? I hate them. I never want to see them again.'

'We gotta keep you safe then, 'aven't we?' He drew her close once more. But now it was different, as though a car had changed gear or a tune been transposed into another key. His voice was soft. 'The law catches up with you, they'll send you straight back to your mum and dad.'

Her arms slid round his waist. 'What can we do, Garry? I can't go back. I'll kill myself.'

'You don't wanta talk like that. I'll work some'ing out.' He began to kiss her, small delicate kisses along the line of her hair, mere brushings of his lips against the taut surface of her skin, questing with almost absent-minded purpose towards the hidden hollows of her neck and ear. She stood outwardly passive but within her blood began to throb with the thrusting power of engines within the smooth hull of a ship; and at that moment Dawn uttered a moan which rose steadily to a bellow, her fist still clenched on June's skirt, eyes tightly shut to squeeze out tears of uneasy jealousy.

'Shit!' said Garry as in a flurry June pulled away from him and knelt to the child. She gathered her up and lifted her, lavishing on her implacable woe the caresses she could not so quickly have loosened towards him, using the child provocatively as both protection and goad. As though consciously, Dawn responded, roaring her need for love, locking her arms round June's neck, so that the two female faces looked almost complacently at the exiled male from the security of their embrace. Kevin had fallen asleep under the table.

'They're tired,' said June solicitously.

'Put 'em to bed then.' Garry picked Kevin up and went to the door. 'I said, put 'em to bed then.'

'All right, I'm coming.' Cuddling Dawn, she brushed past him and went, not too quickly, upstairs. He followed close behind, Kevin's fat limbs jogging, into the Sunday silence of the bedrooms.

ELEVEN

ALTHOUGH THE POLICE had advised the Baxters to go back home, they could not do it. June was here, somewhere in London; round every corner, in every bus Esther might come on her; and she knew, too, that whatever else June might do, she would not go back to Hellebore Road. It was in London that June was to be found – if she were found. So Esther hung on, through days which seemed made up of a hundred years, rootless and unoccupied, deprived of the framework of domestic tasks on which women can hang their miseries, for Norah's flat was too small to need much care.

Raymond was even more rootless, and she urged him to go back and reopen the shop. But he would not. Obstinately he was determined that he must stay with her, that being with her now would make up to both of them for his absence during the other years. To put aside everything to be with her now was at once atonement for the past and support for the present.

But of course it was not. There could be no atonement, only expiation. His crime had been punished but could never be undone. Mewed up together in the ascetic smallness of Norah's flat, with nothing to occupy them but anxiety for their child, Esther felt as though she were in a padded cell and Raymond the straitjacket, confining, pliable yet totally binding. Looking at him as he sat in Norah's cold chair, skimming the newspaper or a magazine, she saw him diminished by guilt, shrunken by impotent remorse, helpless to help her because he was the cause of it all and nothing they did, nothing they felt, could alter it. She wished desperately that he would leave her and go back to Bristol, to the life she had recreated for them both, in which he fitted and had dignity; that he would leave her alone now to cope with the anguished problem of June as she had been forced to cope before. She loved him; her place would always be beside him; but his was not necessarily beside her, he had forfeited that to his penitence. She wished he would leave her now so that to the burden of anxiety for June need not be added the burden of his humility.

They got through the interminable days. Norah, who was living in hospital, came in from time to time, hiding her love for Esther and dislike of Raymond behind the starched friendliness of the professional nurse, but deceiving neither. Tony telephoned, and one evening he and Raymond went out for a drink together, but it was not a success. Fear that Tony might know the truth about his past, suspicion still as to Tony's real relationship with June, led Raymond into a stiff effusiveness which chilled even Tony's old-boy-Raff act. Every day Raymond telephoned the police station for no news. For the rest, Esther and he walked the streets together, took bus rides, visited the museums which satisfied Raymond's appetite for scattered knowledge; but they did not like to be away from the flat long in case there was news. When their glances met, they smiled quickly and were silent. Sometimes an unspoken bickering seemed to fill the air around them, like a cloud of midges, stinging yet hardly seen; an edge would creep into their voices, instantly controlled, over trivial things like milk boiled over or which bus to take. They were hardly ever natural together, too considerate, too aware of apportionment of blame, of vulnerability to hurt. Before, they could have quarrelled and done no harm; now they deferred to one another and the chill crept little by little nearer to the living core of their love. So far it was safe, but each hour it was endangered more.

At night a wall separated them, for Raymond had to sleep on the living-room couch. Once or twice he came to lie beside her but all passion was scoured from them and the comfort of each other's presence was hardly more than the comfort when they parted, each to lie stretched straight in their strange beds and end the day at last. It was as though June had neutered them, had achieved what Raymond's crimes and the long years in prison had been unable to do. She had defeated them at last, draining them of the passion, infrequent but powerful, which had excluded her. Raymond on his living-room couch wondered drearily if prison had sapped him, made him even in that useless to Esther; and Esther, before saying her prayer that June should be safe and found tomorrow, thought sadly that at middle age she was too old, had always been deficient, and that the two wild periods of their life together – when June was conceived and again when Raymond came back to her a year ago – had been glories not ever likely to recur. She slept, dreaming of trouble. But Raymond lay awake a long time, watching Norah's nylon net curtains sift the street lights, ranging in bitterness and fear over the prison years about which he never spoke, captive again of that barren world in which he was the only citizen.

So the days and nights passed. Not many really, for the police found June less than a week after her disappearance, picking her up on her way back from the nursery with Dawn and Kevin.

She had to be fetched, like a package at a Left Luggage office. Esther went alone. With hands that trembled she had pushed Raymond away when he tried to hold her, fumbling with coat and hat and handbag, blind to him but her voice high to the edge of truth at last. 'Wait here,' she repeated, buttoning, searching, setting straight, 'wait here, can't you see? I'll bring her back here but you're not to come. Wait here.'

Helpless, humbled, he watched her go. From the window he saw her half-running down the street, from this height a squat dark insect bumbling urgently on confusing business, and he was pierced with hatred that he loved her so, was bound to her by his own wish, and so must accept her rejection now because he could not live without her devotion. Raymond Banks of twenty years before had long ago been lost, blown away in the gales of terror and retribution, leaving only a husk to be filled by Esther, warmed by her blood, nourished by her gifts. Esther and June, his baby, his little girl – unreal and dreamed of, terrible in reality, killing with her cold eyes . . .

He rang up Norah. 'She's safe. She's at the police station.'

'Thank God!'

'Ett's gone to fetch her.'

'Did they say where she's been?'

'With some family. She had two little kids with her when they picked her up.'

'She's come to no harm then?'

'It seems so. We'll have to make sure.'

'Leave her alone, Raymond.'

'We've got to know . . .'

'Leave her alone – leave her, leave her!'

'But she's my girl.'

'That's true enough, God knows.' Her voice was bitter. 'Can't you see, Raymond, this is for Esther. You'll only do more harm. Go away, go back to Bristol. Esther and I'll work something out for June.'

'Esther needs me.'

'You mean it's you needs Esther.'

He did not speak for a moment. Then he said, 'Well, I thought you'd want to know as soon as we heard. Will you be 'round this evening?'

'No, I'm on duty. Tell Esther I'll come tomorrow morning and we'll arrange something.'

'Very well.'

She made an effort. 'I really am glad she's safe, Raymond.'

'Yes. And thanks for the loan of the flat.'

'Och, I was glad.'

'Well – cheerybye then.'

He stood by the telephone for a little without moving, his hands hanging by his sides. Then he went into the kitchen alcove, filled the kettle and put it on a low gas, set the teapot to warm and put three cups and saucers on a tray with some biscuits. He went into the bathroom, remembering to put the seat down again when he had finished, rinsed his hands. He stood looking at his reflection in the mirror over the basin. It was no one he knew. Slowly he began to put his toilet things into the spongebag until the bathroom was clear of his presence. He got the tartan holdall from the bedroom and put the spongebag in, together with his other few belongings. Then he stood the bag inside the bedroom door and went to the window to wait.

The taxi pulled up and he saw them get out, Esther first, then, slowly, June. She stood without moving while Esther paid the fare, then Esther took her arm and led her out of sight. He dropped the curtain and turned to face the door.

Esther came bustling in, face flushed, eyes glistening, babbling in a way he knew meant she was almost not in control. June stood just inside the door Esther had closed behind her, motionless, looking down at the floor. Save for the sullen droop of her head, the fragile planes of cheek and temple, he hardly knew her; her clothes, her piled hair belonged to a woman not a schoolgirl.

He spoke to Esther when she paused for breath, blundering about the room taking off gloves and coat. 'You found her all right then?'

'Yes, it was ever so simple really. I just went in and said who I was and there she was, with such a nice policewoman, wasn't she, Junie, really kind and sympathetic, you know, not a bit starchy like they always look, and we just talked a bit and they wanted particulars, and then we couldn't find a taxi for ever such a long time, could we, and I didn't want to take the bus. But then one came along all right and here we are.'

'You've not been long.'

'No, well, it was so simple really, I was surprised, and the police being so nice it made all the difference, really, didn't it, dearest, somehow not official at all.'

'Did they want to know why . . .?'

'No, not really, I mean nothing that wasn't immediate came up, it was just sort of general, you know? It was all just matter-of-fact, as if they were dealing with things like this all the time, and it isn't as if anything else was involved, you see, just a silly misunderstanding and so here we are.' Her words suddenly drowned in the silence that spread from the motionless girl, and she stood in the middle of the shiny little room as though she were lost.

He made a movement towards her, then checked. 'I put the kettle on,' he said. 'I expect we could all do with a cup of tea.' He went into the kitchen.

'June. Junie.' Esther went to her and took her in her arms, closely, as though she would press her back into her own body. 'Oh dearest, we've been so anxious!' She shut her eyes, smelling the warmth of hair and skin as she had smelled them a thousand times before, savouring the atavistic possession of light body and limbs restored to her once more – a body and limbs which, chillingly, she perceived stood in her embrace like a doll.

She drew apart, still holding June, to look at her. Beneath the piled hair the painted little mask was expressionless. 'Junie! Look at me.'

The mascaraed eyes that grudgingly met hers were hostile. Even her passivity between Esther's hands was hostile. She asked weakly, 'Have you been all right?' June shrugged, looking away. 'Really all right?'

'I told you.'

'Come and sit down.' She drew her to a chair and sat, holding June's hand, but the girl pulled away. As Raymond returned with the tray she turned her back, fiddling with the ornaments on the mantelpiece.

He poured the tea.

Esther said, 'Were they nice people, this family you were with – the Parsonses, wasn't it? She's been living with a family, right near Paddington Station somewhere, they seem to have been ever so kind. What sort of people were they, dearest? How did you meet them?'

'Inna caff.' Her accent was deliberately rough.

'In a café. When was this?'

'Wednesday.'

'We were so worried. When the time went on and on and you didn't come home . . . Where did you go to, Junie?'

'I was in a caff. Garry picked me up.'

'Picked you up?'

'That's right. Then he took me home.' She turned at last, leaning back against the mantelpiece, looking at her mother with eyes like glass.

Esther felt the strength seep out of her. 'Is Garry one of the Parsonses?'

'He's the eldest. Then there's Sharon, my friend, and Digby and Colin and then the babies.' Her hardness softened for an instant. 'Dawn cried when they took her home without me.' She added fiercely, 'She'll miss me. No one keeps her nice but me.'

'How old is she?' Esther asked weakly.

'Three. Her hair curls if it's brushed enough. She'll only let me.'

'Did they look after you?'

'I looked after myself. And the babies and the cleaning and some of the cooking.'

'They shouldn't have made you do all that.'

'They didn't make me. I wanted to. I wish I was back there.'

The hatred in her voice made Esther catch her breath. She had to clasp her cold hands together in her lap to have something to hold on to. After a moment she said, 'Why did you do it, Junie?'

'I . . .' She faltered, for an instant a child again in terror, and her eyes flicked towards Raymond.

'Didn't you know how we'd worry? Not to leave even a word . . . How could you do that?' No answer. 'And these people, the Parsonses? What happened to you, Junie? What sort of people? I didn't ask at the police station because all I wanted was to get it over and done with and come away home, get you safe home, but who were they? All these days you could have sent us a word, just that you were safe . . . How could you do that, Junie?' No answer.

Raymond put down his cup carefully on Norah's shiny table. 'This isn't getting us anywhere,' he said quietly. 'The plain fact is you found out, didn't you?' He raised his eyes and for the first time held her gaze, unwilling and loathing. 'I don't know how you found out and I suppose it doesn't much matter, though if it was someone told you perhaps we ought to know who, so as to save any awkwardness.'

'No one told me!' she flared at him. 'D'you think I'd let anyone know? It was in a book. It's famous. Anyone can read it.'

Esther said, 'But the name . . .?'

'I found out. I found the paper in your box.'

'My box is locked.'

'So what? I opened it. You was hiding things from me so I hid things from you. Then I went and read it all inna library. You don't think I'd stay in the same house with him after that?'

'You might have left your mother a note.'

'And have her come after me?'

'We have come after you.'

'Well, I'm not coming back!'

'Junie, don't . . .'

'D'you think I'd stay in the same house with him, knowing who he is? I feel sick just being here, I feel sick just thinking about him! How can you bear even to look at him, let alone have him touch you? You're as bad as him, you're wicked and dirty like him! You don't care what he's done, all you think about's covering up, all those stories about Australia and being ill and poor Daddy loves you, when all the time he's a dirty murderer and ought to be hung!'

Raymond rose quickly and took a step towards her and she screamed, the high exultant scream of hysteria. He slapped her, not hard but stingingly, and stood back as she collapsed sobbing into a chair. Esther had risen to go to her, but Raymond said, 'Leave her, Ett. She's got to work this out for herself.' He pushed her gently back, then plunged his hands into his pockets to hide their trembling. He had gone very white.

'You may be right, June, but you'll not speak like that to your mother. There's a lot of people would agree with you. I would myself. If I'd been hung things might have been a lot easier for your mother and for you too. She'd have got over it and you need never have known – like she hoped you'd never know anyway. But it's no good talking like that. I'm here and your mother wanted me back. God knows I wanted to come back. The only thing that kept me going was knowing she was waiting for me, no matter what. I couldn't believe it. Go on, I said, divorce me, I said. But she wouldn't. Knowing her, of course she wouldn't.'

He looked across at his wife and their glances were like light falling and being lost in the inexhaustible dark depths of a lake. He went on, 'I never liked it. I always felt the truth'd come out in the end and hurt worse – as it has done. But your mother felt it was best, and I didn't feel I had any right to say to her what she should or shouldn't do then. I'd forfeited that, see? So we did the best we could. And that's the truth.'

There was silence save for the catching of June's breath as she huddled into the meagre comfort of the chair.

'And while we're about it,' he said, 'you may as well have the whole truth. Because that's where we've all gone wrong, it seems to me, your mother as well. She should have told you the truth. She loved you so much she tried to keep everything ugly away from you. You grew up in your own snug little world like a bird in a nest and never gave a thought to what was happening to other people. But of course, you have to. What happens to other people can happen to you too. There's nothing special about any of us, no special law that says one person has it good all the time. I used to look at the chaps in prison sometimes and wonder what they was in for. And when I knew I used to wonder more often than not how they ever come to do it, and they wondered the same about me, I expect. We're all mysteries, that's what we are.'

He paused, then continued in a slightly louder voice. 'Now I don't suppose we'll ever talk like this again, so we may as well get it straight. I don't remember now why I did what I did. It's like a different person had done it, it just doesn't connect up. But before I met your mother I lived off women – silly women who wanted something I thought then was worthless – and I got money off them and sometimes I married them and three of them I . . .' He faltered, swallowed, clenched his hands. '. . . I killed. I didn't hurt them. I pushed them and they fell. And their money came to me. I couldn't hurt anyone. I never did that. Never.' He was sweating. 'This was before I met Etty. I met her and her gran and I saw the home they had together – nothing grand, just simple and homely. And we got married. And whatever I had been, whatever I had in my mind that had made me do the things I had done, got sort of melted away. It didn't seem real no more, didn't seem important. What was important was Ett and the baby and my home. I couldn't hardly remember how I'd lived before, she washed all the memory of it away. I forgot it, forgot the truth. When it caught up with me, I couldn't hardly believe it had happened.'

Esther sat with her head bent, withdrawn from them both.

'I was tried for the one,' he said, 'and sentenced to life – that's between twelve to fifteen years, you know, if you behave yourself. Your mother wanted to speak for me at the trial but I wouldn't have that. She'd got enough on her plate without that. And I said to her then, I said Get rid of me, Ett, in twelve years' time you could've married again, had the kind of life you deserve. But she wouldn't. She's a rare woman, your mother.'

June was quiet by now, her face hidden against the chairback. Raymond straightened his shoulders. 'So that's how it is. Wishing won't alter it. People do as they have to do and mostly they pay for it. You didn't ought to have been kept so much a child, the real world's too much of a shock to you, I see that. Well, you're not a child now and whatever you're going to do you've got to face up to the facts. Etty's your mother and she's poured her heart out to bring you up safe and happy. And I'm your father and I'd give my right arm to be different.'

Now the silence was very long. In it the sounds from outside seemed extraordinary, the revving of cars, a vacuum-cleaner in the flat above, the jingle of milk bottles as a late dairy float wheezed by, the music of ordinary actions in uneventful lives.

'So that's it,' he said. 'I'm going back home now. You and your mother and Norah must work out what's best to do – she'll be in tomorrow morning, Ett, she said to tell you. There's nothing of me that's any good to you, June, I see that, except that I love your mother. Remember that.'

He moved towards the bedroom for the holdall. Esther rose swiftly.

'Don't go, Ray!'

He paused and put his hands on her shoulders as though to hold her together within his grasp. 'You was always soft, Ett,' he said tenderly. 'Can't you see she'll be better when I'm not here?'

'Where are you going?'

'Home.'

'Promise me.'

'What do you think?' He smiled, and gently kissed her mouth. 'I'll get back and open the shop. Send me a line when you're ready to come back, and I'll be waiting.'

He released her, picked up the bag, took his hat from the peg by the door. 'Goodbye, Junie. We may not see each other again, I suppose. Take care of yourself.'

He looked at her for a moment, searchingly. She stared back, and between the shrunken middle-aged man with the faded blue eyes and the sharp-boned girl crouched in the chair there passed a look of recognition, of hardness and respect that, in a different time, might have been love.

He opened the door and went.

Esther turned back. 'I'm sorry, Junie,' she said. 'I'm sorry . . .'

The girl recoiled, clenching her hands on the arms of the chair. Her face was vivid, hard as a doll's. 'Sorry?' she cried, 'You're not sorry! You've got him, haven't you? You've always had him, hidden away behind my back. Have him, then! Have him like you've always done, I don't care! He's enough for you, I don't need you. I'll get along on my own like I've always been, only now I'll have got Garry. Me and Garry, we won't ever be like you. Never, d'you hear? Never – never. We won't ever be like you!'

DAUNT BOOKS

Founded in 2010, Daunt Books Publishing grew out of Daunt Books, independent booksellers with shops in London and the south of England. We publish the finest writing in English and in translation, from literary fiction – novels and short stories – to narrative non-fiction, including essays and memoirs. Our modern classics list revives authors whose work has unjustly fallen out of print. In 2020 we launched Daunt Books Originals, an imprint for bold and inventive new writing.

www.dauntbookspublishing.co.uk

We ensure all our products comply with GPSR, CE marking, and other applicable EU Directives. Our EU Responsible Person for GPSR product safety compliance is EU Compliance Partner.

EU Responsible Person (EU RP):

EU Compliance Partner

Postal address: Pärnu mnt. 139b – 14, 11317 Tallinn, Estonia

Contact Email: hello@eucompliancepartner.com

Website: www.eucompliancepartner.com

Phone: +33757690241